Whispers Through Time

Barry Homan

Bedside Books
An imprint of American Book Publishing
5442 So. 900 East, #146
Salt Lake City, UT 84117-7204
www.american-book.com
Printed in the United States of America on acid-free paper.

Whispers Through Time

Designed by Troy D. O'Brien, design@american-book.com

ISBN-13: 978-1-58982-654-0
ISBN-10: 1-58982-654-X

Homan, Barry, Whispers Through Time

Special Sales

These books are available at special discounts for bulk purchases. Special editions, including personalized covers, excerpts of existing books, and corporate imprints, can be created in large quantities for special needs. For more information e-mail info@american-book.com.

Whispers Through Time
By
Barry Homan

Dedication

To my wife Karen,
for her love, support,
and faith.

Chapter One

Jill Palmer couldn't believe that her best friend had tricked her like this. She was lying on a massage table, her face in the headrest, staring at the flickering shadows of a lemongrass candle that was burning in the corner of the room. "You want me to do what?" she said.

Lauren Masters had a wide grin on her face. The therapist was deftly moving her hands around Jill's lower back, finding one sore spot after another. "What are you so worried about?" she asked. "It's quite simple. You lie on a couch, get hypnotized, and wind up telling the doctor a wonderful story. What could be easier?"

It had all started the night before, when Lauren called Jill with a simple question. "Can you do something for me tomorrow after your appointment?" she had asked. "I have a client coming over right after you, and I can't do it myself."

Jill, thinking it was something routine like picking up dry cleaning, had quickly said, "Sure thing, no problem." Now she had just found out the true nature of Lauren's request.

"You can't honestly believe I'm going to do something like that?"

"Why not?" Lauren said. "You'll probably be surprised by how easy it is."

"A past-life regression?" Jill still couldn't believe what she was hearing. "No way."

Jill knew her closest friend since early childhood loved to investigate anything in the spiritual realm: ghosts, premonitions, talking to the dead. Lauren would explore them all, and often tried to get Jill involved. Jill invariably put her off, although she always wound up hearing about them anyway.

"Couldn't you just sign me up for a bridge club?" asked Jill. "You know I've never been interested in any of that new age stuff."

"You will love Simon Taylor," replied Lauren. "He's a very nice man, down to earth and easy to talk to."

Jill just groaned.

"Come on, Jill," argued Lauren. "You haven't done anything in the last two years. You need to start living again."

Jill stared at the floor. She knew Lauren was just trying to help. "You're right," she finally said. "I have been in a rut lately."

Lauren found another sore spot on Jill's side and noticed her wince. "A rut? Is that what you call it? You haven't had a single date since Tony left, have you?"

"You had to mention him, didn't you?"

Tony was Jill's former husband. They had met in high school and moved in the same circle of friends. Though they never dated, they did go to the senior prom together. A few years after graduation they met again, and this time they started dating immediately. They married just six months later and had two children in the next three years. Bret was fifteen now, and Mark was thirteen.

Tony worked at a manufacturing firm in their hometown of Willis, South Carolina. He had moved up the ladder quickly, and at thirty-four he became the youngest vice-president in company history. Jill had worked the first year and a half of their marriage, then became a stay-at-home mom once Bret arrived. Two years ago, their sixteen-year marriage came to a crashing halt when Tony had an affair with his twenty-five-year-old secretary. She became pregnant, and he chose the buxom brunette over his wife.

Jill had been stunned, yet soon realized he must have been cheating on her for a long time. There was his declining interest in sex, the tender caresses that were suddenly missing, the late nights at the office. The divorce became final three weeks after Susan Arnett, soon to be the new Mrs. Palmer, gave birth to a baby girl.

Lauren wasn't a person to mince words. "Tony's gone, Jill. He's been gone for a long time now, and he isn't coming back. You need to move on with your life. He sure has."

This wasn't the first time Jill had heard this message from Lauren. She'd never paid any attention before, but she knew Lauren was trying to help. She sighed deeply. "You're right," she said. "I know it's time, but a past-life regression? Lauren, I don't even believe in reincarnation."

"Well, maybe it's time you opened your eyes to the spiritual world around you. Besides, it's really interesting."

Jill was more than a little skeptical. "I doubt any past life of mine was that interesting. What's he going to tell me, that I was Cleopatra in another lifetime, just so I know how far I've fallen?"

Lauren put the finishing touches on Jill's massage and said, "Get up, girlfriend, you're good as new."

Jill arose and sat on the side of the table. She always had to take a few moments to get her equilibrium back after one of Lauren's massages. "I was feeling so much better until you mentioned Tony," she said. In truth, she always felt better after her massage, and thoughts of Tony had not changed that. However, she did sense a bit of unease creeping into her stomach as she considered the idea of a past-life regression.

Lauren ignored her remark. "Come into the kitchen when you're ready, and I will tell you all about my previous life." There was a twinkle in her eye as she spoke. She knew Jill would want to hear all about her adventure, even if she didn't believe it.

Jill sat on the table for a minute, legs dangling over the side, then slowly stood up. Standing naked, she looked into the full-length mirror on the back of the door. She had short auburn hair, hazel eyes, and a sprinkling of freckles on her cheeks. Her breasts were small but firm. She still had a nice figure, although keeping it was becoming harder as the years passed. "Not bad for forty," she muttered to the mirror. She took a deep breath, inhaling the lingering aroma of lemongrass, and began to dress. She hated to admit it, but Lauren was right. Her life was boring.

Lauren and Jill had been friends ever since Lauren's family had moved into the house across the street when she was two. It was evident early on that Lauren was a free spirit. She loved the outdoors and enjoyed roaming through the woods that were her backyard.

Jill was more reserved as a child, not wanting to take chances on unknown adventures or risk getting into trouble with her parents. When Lauren jumped in mud puddles, Jill walked around them. At times they simply exasperated each other and had to take a break, but it never lasted very long.

By the time they were in high school, Jill looked up to Lauren both literally and figuratively. At five-foot six, Lauren was three inches taller than Jill. What most people noticed when first meeting Lauren was her jet black hair, which she usually streaked with a variety of vibrant colors. She had crystal blue eyes, a well-endowed chest and long, shapely legs.

Lauren always seemed to know what she wanted and went after it, usually succeeding. Her only major failure had been in marriage. She had waited until she turned thirty to marry Henry Masters. They never made it to their second anniversary. Unlike Jill, she recovered quickly and moved on. She went to massage school and finished first in her class. She ran her business, which had become immensely successful, out of her home. Jill had a standing appointment, eight a.m. on the first Tuesday of every month.

Lauren was setting two cups of chamomile tea on the kitchen table as Jill entered. "Watch it," she said, "it's steaming hot."

Jill took a sip. She was still a coffee drinker at heart, but she did enjoy the flavored teas that Lauren always served. "Tastes nice," she said as Lauren, who had a bright streak of green running through her hair this morning, sat at the table. "So what is this story you have to tell me? Do you really believe in this past-life regression stuff?"

"Absolutely," Lauren beamed. "It's answered many questions about why I am the way I am. Besides, I've always believed in reincarnation."

Jill slowly shook her head. "I don't know. What's the point if we just keep coming back? Doesn't it ever end?"

"We have lessons to learn," replied Lauren. "Each time we come back, we hopefully learn more. Just let me tell you my story."

Jill took another sip of her tea. The full effects of the massage were settling in, and she felt more relaxed with each passing minute. "Okay," she said, "tell me this amazing tale of yours."

Lauren's face brightened. "Well, I first heard about Simon from my friend Bernie at the diner down on Broad Street. You know Bernie. Short guy, cheeks always flushed a bright purple, not much hair."

Jill nodded. "The short-order cook."

"Right. Anyway, Bernie went to see Simon twice and traveled back to a number of different lifetimes. He was so enthused about the experience, I just had to go and try it for myself."

For the next fifteen minutes Lauren recounted her tale about her previous life in Italy.

"The year was 1848," she began, "and I was a young mother. My name was Maria. My husband, Guiseppe, was a dock worker, loading and unloading cargo. He worked long, hard hours and was away from home a great deal, but he was a loving husband and we had a great marriage. We had a daughter named Sophia, who was six years old. She was a beautiful child with black hair down to her waist. We weren't rich, but we weren't poor either. I stayed home taking care of my daughter, and my home was spotless."

Jill gave a short laugh and started to say something, but Lauren cut her off.

"Don't say it." Picking up around her house was not one of Lauren's strong suits. "See, I already learned that lesson, I don't have to do it again," she laughed. "Guiseppe and I met when we were both seventeen and quickly fell in love. In three months we were married, and a year later Sophia was born."

Lauren arose to refill their tea cups.

"So you get your beautiful black hair from your daughter," joked Jill. "That's a switch."

Lauren sat back down and said, "Wait until you hear who Sophia is today," and when Jill tried to ask Lauren shook a finger at her and said, "Not now."

She continued with her story. "Simon brought me forward in time. It was fifteen years later."

Jill sipped her fresh cup of tea. She thought Lauren's story was interesting, but she didn't believe any of it.

"My husband had been in an accident on the pier. His right leg had been crushed, and he needed a crutch to walk. I doted on him, and he let me because it obviously pleased me so much. Sophia was no longer living at home, having been married some years previous. To our great delight, she was pregnant and would soon be presenting us with a grandchild."

Jill listened intently as Lauren gave more details, but wondered how Lauren could believe this was real. *I could think up a story like this without being hypnotized*, she thought.

"Eventually," continued Lauren, "Simon brought me to the end of my life. He said, 'Go to your final days. See how your life ends. Don't worry; there is no death as we know it. No harm will come to you as you watch your passing.' He was right. I was floating over my body, looking down on it. Sophia and her husband were there. They now had two children, who were playing in another room. Guiseppe had already died. I passed very peacefully, and with that," Lauren said, "Simon brought me back to the present."

Jill finished her second cup of tea. "So you weren't rich, or famous, or a land baron?"

"No, just happy. And while I didn't recognize my husband from that life, I can tell you that Sophia in that time is my sister Kate today."

"What!" Jill exclaimed. "Your daughter then is your sister now. Lauren, you can't believe that."

"But I do," said Lauren. "Simon told me we go through many lifetimes with the same people around us. Your mother now may have been your daughter before. Sometimes we change sex from one life to the next, so your mother may once have been your father ages ago."

"Just how many lives do you think I've had?" Jill finally asked.

Lauren shrugged. "Dozens, maybe hundreds. I really can't answer that one."

"Gee, God really does have a sense of humor, doesn't he?"

"Maybe he does," Lauren said as she glanced at the clock. "Perhaps he can help you find your soul mate."

"Was Guiseppe yours?"

"Oh, he had to be. We had a fantastic marriage."

"So where is he now?" asked Jill.

Lauren smiled wistfully. "I guess you can't always meet him at seventeen, as we both know. Now it's time for you to go. Your appointment is in twenty minutes."

"I don't know," Jill moaned.

"Come on, Jill. Just do it for a lark, if nothing else. It doesn't hurt. I told you about my past life, now I want to hear about yours. He's going to write a book on this someday. Maybe your story will be in it."

"No one would want to put my life in a book."

"Maybe not this one," agreed Lauren, "but who knows what exciting adventures you may have had in your past lives. You can't bail on me, Jill. I told him you would be there. I promised."

Knowing she wouldn't let her best friend down, even for something as outrageous as this, Jill said "I'm going to get you back for this someday."

"Oh, I'm sure you will," said Lauren, "but maybe someday you will thank me too. Now go."

Chapter Two

It was drizzling as Jill left for the doctor's office. The massage had left her feeling very relaxed, yet now she felt a sense of anticipation coursing through her. She could not believe she was going to go through with this crazy idea. She had never been hypnotized and wondered if she could be. The idea that she was a princess, maybe even a queen, made her smile. Still, she wouldn't believe it. No matter what type of thrilling escapade her subconscious mind recalled, to Jill it would only be a made-up story.

The doctor's office was less than three miles from Lauren's home. It was the first building you came upon as you entered downtown Willis from the west. Jill had lived here all her life. It was a clean, enchanting town with fifteen thousand residents. Originally a mill town in the 1950s, it had been transformed over the last twenty years. First, a large computer company had opened up a plant on the northern edge of town. Then a tractor company, which gutted one of the old mills, opened an assembly plant. Together they had created a boom for the small town, which was still going strong despite the economic downturn across the country.

Jill pulled into the parking lot and found a space near the front door. This was one of her favorite buildings in town—four stories high, made of brick, with large glass windows on each floor. Her lawyer's office was here on the fourth floor. While the divorce had been painful for Jill, her lawyer had done a number on Tony.

She spent a few minutes sitting in the car and wondered what her parents would think. They had never been a deeply religious family, usually going to church only at Easter and Christmas. Her folks were simply good, hard-working people who wanted to do right by their kids. Jill loved them both. She considered them to be straight arrows, like herself, and doubted they would think much of past-life regressions.

Perhaps her younger sister Rose would be interested. She was the artistic one in the family. Rose lived in Charleston with her husband and three children.

Jill suddenly remembered a time from her childhood. She was about eight years old and playing with a group of kids from the neighborhood. One of them, a boy named Eric, said that he was Jesse James in a prior life. Everyone laughed, and then they all chimed in, claiming to be someone famous from long ago. Except Jill. "I thought they were all nuts," she mumbled out loud, "and I still do."

Jill noticed it was almost ten. She really thought this was going to be a waste of time, but she knew Lauren would be extremely disappointed if she didn't try it at least once. Besides, she hadn't had any excitement in her life for a long time. Maybe this would be good for a laugh. Shaking her head at the idiocy of it all, she grabbed her pocketbook and headed for the door.

The sign in the foyer listed Doctor Taylor as being on the second floor. Jill skipped the elevator and took the stairs. His office was the second door on the right.

The receptionist looked up as Jill entered. "Hi," she said. "You must be Lauren's friend Jill. I'm Melinda."

"Nice to meet you," said Jill. "I'm not sure what Lauren has lured me into."

Melinda smiled brightly. "Don't be nervous. It really is quite fascinating. I've done it myself," she said. "Have a seat, and you can fill out a little questionnaire for us."

"Thank you," said Jill, easing herself into what was one of the most comfortable waiting room chairs she had ever encountered.

The room was spotless. Melinda's desk was neat, with an appointment book and phone on one side, and paperwork which she appeared to be transcribing into a computer on the other. The nameplate on the desk said Melinda Stenhouse. Music flowed from a stereo in the far corner. It was a sweet jazz tune. Miles Davis, thought Jill.

Melinda handed her a clipboard with the questionnaire attached and a pen dangling from the side. "The doctor should be with you in about five minutes," she said.

Jill was used to filling out long forms at doctors' offices, but soon realized that the questions on this form were quite a bit different. Some were downright puzzling "Where would I like to vacation?" she muttered to herself. The form asked for three places in the United States and three more overseas. Another question asked for three things she was afraid of. The next one wanted to know if she ever pretended to be someone from the past when she was a child. She put an emphatic *no* next to that one. She was just finishing as the door to the back room opened.

Simon Taylor walked into the waiting room and came right up to Jill with his hand outstretched. "Hello," he said, "you must be Jill Palmer. Lauren's told me a little bit about you."

He appeared to be about six-two, with short, light brown hair, and brown eyes that might be able to hypnotize someone all by themselves.

"Hello, doctor," she said. "I'm afraid Lauren just sprang this on me an hour ago. I should warn you, I'm a little more skeptical than she is."

"Please, call me Simon." He had a lovely, honest smile that produced a dimple on his left cheek. "It's good to be skeptical about things," he said, taking the questionnaire from her. "Come on in, and we'll see if we can change that skepticism of yours."

Simon led Jill back to his office. He showed her to a seat opposite his desk, which was identical to the desk in the outer office. Her chair was just as comfortable as the one in the waiting room. She was impressed.

"Did Lauren tell you much about the procedure?" he asked.

"Yes. She told me her story about being back in Italy."

"Your voice tells me you didn't believe her."

"Well, to be honest I've never believed in reincarnation," she said, "but maybe you can change my mind."

"I'll certainly try. Give me a minute to look this over," he said, holding up the clipboard.

While he did that, Jill glanced around the room. His diplomas hung on the wall behind his desk. To her left was a couch that looked as comfortable as the chairs. An end table at the foot of the couch held another stereo system. No music played from this one. To her right was a small bathroom, with a wall clock to the left of the door.

Beyond the room she sat in was another, slightly smaller room. This had a cabinet against the left wall. It was closed, with keys hanging from the lock. To the right a large shelving unit filled with patient folders went from floor to ceiling.

Simon looked up from the questionnaire and smiled. "Okay," he said, "are you ready to get started?"

Jill nodded, but said nothing. The nervousness was growing in the pit of her stomach.

"It says here that you have never been hypnotized," he said.

"No, never."

He explained the process to her in detail, and finished by saying "You will always be aware of what is happening. No one can make you do anything you do not wish to do. You would never do anything that is against your moral or ethical values."

Jill thought about all that he had said, then said, "Okay."

"Don't worry. When you are fully relaxed, you will think you are going to melt."

"I'm pretty relaxed already," said Jill. "I just came from Lauren's where I had a full body massage."

"Wonderful," he stated. "You should fall under quickly then."

"What will happen when I do?"

"It's quite simple," Simon replied. "Once you are completely relaxed, we will try to have you go back in time. First, I will take you back just a year or so, then to a time in your childhood, and following that, to the time you were in your mother's womb. You may be surprised to find out how aware you were when you were waiting to be born. It's really quite amazing."

"Well, we'll see," was all Jill could muster.

"Finally," he continued, "I'll ask you to go back to your last life on this earth and see what you come up with. All set?"

"Ready as I ever will be, I guess."

Simon arose, showed Jill to the couch, and asked her to take off her shoes, lie down, and get comfortable. As she did, he walked into the back room to the cabinet. He opened the door and took out a tape. Returning, he said, "I tape every session, so I can refer back when I need to. Someday I hope to write a book on past-life regressions. Maybe your story will be in it, with your approval, of course."

Jill didn't think that was likely.

As Simon watched Jill get settled on the couch, he wondered how the session would go. Jill did not seem overly happy to be here, and she had made it known that she didn't believe in past lives. He had performed regressions on a number of skeptical people. Most regressed just fine and gave some account of their past life, then didn't believe it when they were finished and never came back. He expected Jill would fit into this category.

Simon had been a practicing psychologist for eleven years and loved his work. It was what he had been born to do. His schedule was full. Monday through Friday he often worked ten-to-twelve hour days. Saturday was basically for emergency patients, and there were always plenty of them. At thirty-seven, he had been married for nine years to an emergency room nurse. They had no children and no plans for any. They barely had time to see each other. Both loved their careers and neither wished to change.

Five years ago Simon heard about a colleague who was using hypnosis to help patients quit smoking. Believing it would help him in certain instances, he learned the process for himself. It had worked well. Using it only in circumstances where all else had failed, he saw remarkable results. Rarely did it fail to have at least some success.

Two and a half years ago, the regressions took him to places he had never imagined. A young lady of twenty-two named Pamela came to see him about severe back pain. Doctors had found nothing wrong with her and were unable to help. More than one told her it was all in her head. She came to Simon to find out if that were true. This time, he turned to hypnosis almost immediately. Finding nothing having to do with her problem in her recent past, he attempted to take her back to her early childhood. Suddenly she started talking about being hit by a car. He thought he had found the answer, and asked when this had happened. She had answered, "When I was twenty-six." Knowing her true age, he thought he had misunderstood, so he asked again. What followed was the first past-life regression tale he had ever heard.

"I live in Cleveland," Pamela said. "There are many cars on the roads now, much more than when I was little. Sometimes they still scare me. The horns are so loud, and people drive so fast, much faster than they're supposed to. I wasn't watching where I was going, just began crossing the street. I heard a horn, and turned to see a car coming straight for me. I started to run, but my foot slipped on some loose stones. As I was stumbling, the car's bumper hit me square in the back."

Fascinated, Simon had questioned her further. He learned the year was 1919, and that Pamela had died within the hour. Simon told her she did not have to carry that back pain over into this lifetime. She could let it go. Upon awakening, Pamela had a hard time believing her story. However, a week later she called to say her back pain had completely disappeared.

Simon had always believed that reincarnation was plausible. Now he had some semblance of proof. He started coaxing friends and relatives to give it a try. Before long, he began to set aside Tuesday mornings every week to continue his study into the phenomenon. Now most of his volunteers came by word of mouth, as Jill had.

"Are you ready, Jill?" he asked.

She was nervous, and hoped it didn't show. "I'm ready."

He began by telling her to take some deep breaths and clear her mind of all thought. Next, he had her concentrate on relaxing different parts of her body, from toes to head. She seemed to be having no trouble so far.

"I'm going to start counting backwards from ten. As the numbers become lower, you will go deeper and deeper. At one you will be totally relaxed. Understand?"

"Yes," she said.

"Ten," Simon said. "Picture yourself descending a spiral staircase. Nine … eight. Going deeper and deeper down the stairway. Seven … six … five. Becoming totally relaxed now, yet completely aware. Four … three. Nearing the bottom of the staircase, your body completely at ease. Two … one. You're there, fully relaxed, alert to my voice. Are you totally relaxed now, Jill?"

"Yes," she heard herself say.

"I want you to go back in time, just a year or so. Find a day when you had a nice time with a friend. Can you do that for me, Jill?"

Jill's mind wandered back to a day she had gone to dinner with her mother. They had eaten at Amelio's, a great little Italian restaurant. Her mother was visiting for the weekend because her father was at a conference. She remembered what they both ate. Linguini with clam sauce for her, chicken Alfredo for mom. They had a bottle of Chardonnay with the meal. Her mom had picked up the check.

"Good, Jill," said Simon. "You're doing fine. Now we're going back farther, back to when you were a little girl. Can you find a time that stands out to you, Jill? Maybe you were six or seven. What do you see?"

After a short pause, Jill said, "The horses."

Simon smiled. So far she seemed to be doing well. He hoped it would continue. "Tell me about the horses, Jill."

She had turned eight a week earlier. Her father had taken her to a farm owned by a friend of his. She had seen a variety of animals, but she loved the horses the most. They were beautiful animals. The smallest one was only six months old, a pony named Montana. They put Jill on its back and led her around the corral, one man standing on each side of her to make sure she didn't fall off. Later she had helped to feed him, and the pony had licked her face. Jill warmed at the sudden memory. She hadn't thought about Montana for a long time.

"You're doing very well, Jill. Now I want to take you back even farther. All the way back to the time before you were born, back when you were in your mother's womb. Go back slowly. See yourself at age three; then go to the age of two. Remember when you were just a year old, Jill? Now go back to the womb. Picture yourself in the womb. Can you do that, Jill?"

"Yes, I am there." It was so easy she would have been stunned had she not been in such a relaxed state.

"Can you tell me what's going on, Jill?"

His voice sounded far away to her. The scene in her mind seemed much closer. "We are at my grandmother's house, in the kitchen."

"How does your mother feel, Jill?"

"She's happy. Today is a good day; her feet aren't bothering her."

"Are your parents excited to be having you?"

"Oh, yes." A wide smile came upon Jill's face.

Simon was pleased with the way the regression was going, but he didn't want to linger at this point. Jill seemed to be an excellent subject, but the big leap was about to come. "Jill, I want to go back farther now. Back before you were born in this lifetime, before the womb. I want you to return to your lifetime before this one. Can you do that for me, Jill?"

Simon noticed a brief crease appear on her brow, as if she were thinking hard about a difficult problem. He waited ten seconds, then ten more. Suddenly, he saw her relax.

"Yes," was all she said.

"Can you tell where you are, what country you're in?"

"Hmm," she mumbled. The crease returned to her forehead.

"You're back in your last lifetime, Jill. What do you see?" Her response time had slowed considerably. For the first time in the regression Simon wondered if she would be able to do this.

Jill mumbled more words so quietly he couldn't understand. Finally, she said "Not the last. Before that. Long ago."

Simon realized she must have gone back more than one lifetime. That was not uncommon in regressions. He felt a renewed sense of anticipation. "Where are you, Jill? Can you tell?"

"There's a church," she said. Then, after a small pause, "I'm near water."

"Excellent, Jill. You are doing a wonderful job. Can you tell me anything more about your surroundings?" Simon watched as her eyes fluttered back and forth. "How are you dressed?"

"I'm wearing black," said Jill. "A coat of some kind. It's cold."

"Are other people with you?"

"Yes."

"Jill, can you tell what country you are in?"

It took her a while, but then a wonderful smile came over her face. "I remember," she said.

Simon smiled too. "That's terrific, Jill. Tell me where you are."

"I'm in Ireland."

"Can you tell me what your name is and what you are doing?"

There was another pause, as if Jill were trying to catch the name out of thin air. Then, slowly, her face brightened, but was quickly followed by a frown.

"My name is Sarah. There's a funeral."

Chapter Three

IRELAND, 1594

Nearly half the town was at Mary Whalen's funeral. Sarah had expected the men who used to fish with Mary's husband John, but the number of regular folk who came out surprised her. Mary had been her best friend and neighbor since Sarah and her family first moved here. Life would be different without having her to talk with every day.

As the coffin was lowered into the ground, Sarah tossed a single clover onto the box. She said a quick prayer for Mary as the grave-diggers threw the first shovels full of dirt into the hole, and then she turned and began the short walk to the cart.

She saw Mary's daughter Nuala walking a few feet away. Sarah looked at the child and sighed. She was such a pretty, happy girl with eyes wide as saucers. *Ah, but life has given you a sad little turn, now hasn't it*, thought Sarah. The day was dark and cold. No doubt it would be raining before long. Sarah shivered, as much for the girl as for the weather.

She turned to see her husband still standing at the grave. He looked handsome in his long black cloak and soft leather boots. "Come, Niall," she called to him. She watched as he stared down at Mary's coffin a moment longer, lost in his thoughts. John and Mary had been fine neighbors. Now, not two years after her husband had drowned at sea, she was gone as well. Mary had caught cold during the long winter and couldn't seem to shake it. The damp climate of Ireland's northwest coast didn't help. Last week, she took a sudden turn for the worse and never recovered.

"I'm coming, my love," Niall finally said. He turned and began walking towards his wife.

"Nuala," Sarah called, looking for the girl.

Nuala was standing behind her. She pulled on Sarah's hand and giggled. Sarah bent down and gave the girl a big hug. "Were you hiding on me?"

Nuala just laughed.

"It's time to go. From now on you get to stay with us." She took the girl's hand in hers; such a small hand. *Now*, she thought, *I have a little girl.*

Nuala, the Whalens' only child, had just turned five. Now an orphan, she would stay with Niall and Sarah and their three boys.

"I've spoken with Father Kearney," Niall said as he approached her. "There will be no trouble adopting her. Mary made her wishes plain enough to him before she passed. We will raise her as an O'Donnell."

"She already is," Sarah replied. She loved the girl, and Nuala and Sean, her four-year-old, were nearly inseparable. "She's spent most of her days at our place anyway these last two years, so it's almost like nothing has changed. I'll miss her mother, though. Such a sweet lady."

Niall nodded his agreement. "They never had much luck, those two. Let's hope the devil doesn't follow Nuala to our door."

That night the three other families who lived near the Whalens arrived at the O'Donnell home. Niall handed out silver bowls and filled each one with ale, and then they toasted their departed friend.

"To Mary," said Niall, raising his bowl, "a fine woman if ever there was one, and a loving mother. May her journey to the heavens be a quick one, and may she look down upon us when she arrives and send us a bountiful harvest."

"Here, here," the gathering said in unison.

They spent the night reminiscing about John and Mary. John had been a fisherman from the day he was born, it was said. He was sixteen when he first saw Mary. It was love at first sight for him, but she needed a little convincing. A year later they were married. As time went on it appeared they would remain childless. Try as they might, Mary seemed unable to become pregnant. Then, after fourteen years of marriage, Nuala suddenly arrived. For three years their lives were an absolute joy, and then John was tragically lost. A sudden storm caught him and his crew by surprise. It was appropriate that he died at sea, yet it had come as a shock.

Mary had carried on without him, but the sparkle in her eyes was missing. Not even Nuala could brighten her days. The child with so much joy could not transfer it to her mother.

The party ended when the first drops of rain, which had held off all day, began falling. All were in a rush to get home. Mary was safely in heaven now, but tomorrow was another day for the rest of them.

Bicksby was a small town of about four hundred souls nestled on the coast. The downtown area was barely forty yards from the shoreline. Leading out of town on the southern edge the road forked. One way hugged the seaside; the other turned into an S-curve that climbed steeply into the highland. The mountain overlooking the town was nearly eight hundred feet higher than the town itself.

The O'Donnell home sat on the edge of the mountain. It was a large stone house with earthen floors and a thatched roof. To the right of the house as you looked from town was a gigantic, round boulder, nearly seven feet high. No one knew where the huge rock had come from, or even how long it had been there.

From the backyard, the view of the town and the bay beyond was breathtaking. Niall owned three hundred acres of land here, much of it hard scrabble, rocky terrain suitable only for grazing sheep and cattle. He spent most of his time in the fields, growing cabbage, carrots, and peas. Across the road was a barn, home to two oxen, a dairy cow, and two horses.

Most of Sarah's days were spent cooking and cleaning, sewing, and watching over the children. The boys were growing faster than weeds, and she spent many hours making clothes for them.

The oldest boy, Kevin, was twelve. He was most like his father, both in looks and attitude. Kevin had helped Niall a great deal in the fields the past few years, but now he was going to become a fisherman. James Meehan, who owned three fishing boats in Bicksby, had talked Niall into letting Kevin come work for him. That meant Myles, who had just turned nine, would take over Kevin's duties at home. Sarah was leery about how that would work. Myles was a wonderful, happy-go-lucky child, but work was not something he had ever been attracted to. Sarah could see him and Niall butting heads more than once in the summer to come. Sean, the youngest, liked to help Sarah around the house. Mostly, though, he wanted to be with Nuala. They spent their days together laughing and running around as they invented new games to play.

Sarah didn't think life could get any better.

Simon listened intently as Jill spoke. He was delighted with the information she was communicating. Very few of the clients he had ever regressed started out this well, and he could only hope it would continue. He did not like to ask too many questions if he could help it, yet many people needed constant coaxing. He had done little of that with Jill since she first started talking about the funeral. It was as though she were actually reliving this time in Ireland.

For her part, Jill was aware that she was in his office, and knew he was sitting by her side. Yet … when he had asked her to find out where she was, who she was, it was as though a movie screen had suddenly dropped down in front of her and began playing the feature film. She saw the events perfectly, heard the voices of the other people involved, recognized the sense of loss one feels when losing a close friend. She realized how much she loved her husband. If Simon had asked if she wanted to end the regression now, she would have said no.

Simon had no intention of stopping at this point. They were only twenty minutes into the session. As Jill spoke, her voice was beginning to have an Irish inflection to it, as if she were becoming Sarah. He was aware from past regressions he had performed that many people take on the idiosyncrasies of their former self while under hypnosis. On rare occasions he'd heard people speak a foreign language which they did not know.

It was obvious to Simon that Niall was important to Sarah. Many people who came to him did so in search of their soul mate. Simon believed in the idea of a soul mate, because his research had shown him that people continually return to the earth plane with the same people around them. Now he wanted to steer Jill in a new direction, and her husband was the obvious choice.

"Jill, tell me about Niall. How did you meet?"

Her smile lit up her face. "Oh my," she said. "I was so shy. I didn't think he noticed me."

Chapter Four

It was the county fair of 1575 where Sarah had first seen Niall. She was only twelve. The fair was being held in his hometown of Kilmacrenan. The O'Donnells ruled over that part of Ireland, along with the O'Neill clan. Niall was fifteen, yet at five-foot ten he was the tallest member of his family, well built and good looking. He had long red hair flowing down past his shoulders, muscular arms, and strong legs. Sarah had fantasies of him carrying her across the moors and bogs, saving her from danger, and loving her forever.

She was a shy girl at twelve. Although she followed him around for much of the fair, she was too intimidated to walk up and speak to him. He was constantly surrounded by older girls who had no such problem. When the fair ended, she headed home with her family, assuming she would never see him again.

Yet three years later she did. Niall was passing through her hometown with his father. They were planning to sail to England the next day, but an Atlantic storm forced them to remain in port for three extra days. She saw Niall that first afternoon. He was six feet tall now, and a muscular 180 pounds. His red hair had been trimmed, but still brushed his shoulders.

This time Sarah made sure to make his acquaintance by literally bumping into him. "Excuse me, sir. So clumsy of me," she said.

"Not to worry, miss," Niall replied. He glanced quickly up and down her small, yet well-proportioned frame. "It's quite crowded around here this time of year. Happens all the time."

It really wasn't crowded at all. Sarah slowly turned her head in both directions as if looking for all the people, then said, "Oh yes, it certainly is." She hoped it hadn't been obvious she had bumped into him on purpose, but supposed it was. She noticed his eyes, a shimmering green with touches of gold that she had never seen before. "I saw you a few years ago at the fair," she said.

"You're quite kind, m'lady. I noticed you also."

"What?" Sarah, taken aback, shot him a look. "What do you mean, you noticed me? You couldn't have."

He heard the shock in her voice, but remained silent.

"I was only twelve, and you had dozens of girls around you," she continued.

Niall gave a small laugh. "Aye, but a pretty girl in a lovely green dress following me around for a week is hard to miss."

She was sure he was making it up. Her dress had been a simple one, nothing fancy about it at all. He could not possibly have picked her out of the crowd at the fair or remembered her after all this time. Yet her dress had been green.

"I did not," she started to object, but his smile stopped her. She looked at the ground. "Okay," she mumbled, "I did follow you, but how can you remember me after all this time?"

"You are a beautiful young lady," he said. "How could I forget?"

Sarah thought her knees would buckle, and knew she was blushing. "I should get back to my father," she said. "He will be looking for me."

"As well he should. A lady as lovely as you should not be wandering around aimlessly." He smiled again and winked. "Perhaps you would allow me to escort you."

Sarah wanted that, and he knew it, yet now the shyness of three years ago overtook her again, and she declined his offer. "No thank you. I must be off."

He pretended to tip a cap he wasn't wearing. "Perhaps next time I will run into you."

She giggled, then turned and ran.

Her father had been mentioning for a year now that it was about time she found a husband. Sarah had said no to every one of his suggestions. Soon he would choose a mate for her and not take no for an answer, so that night she brought it up.

"Father, I know you wish me to marry soon, and I thank you for the tolerance you have shown up to now."

Her father simply nodded, wondering where this was headed.

"Today," continued Sarah, "I met a man I believe I could say yes to. Perhaps you would do some inquiring about him, and see if he is available and suitable to you."

She saw the surprised look on his face. "What is his name?" he asked.

"Niall O'Donnell."

Surprise turned to incredulity as her father's mouth dropped open. "Glory, girl," he said, "you sure know how to pick 'em."

Unsure what he meant, Sarah explained the story of her running into him, leaving out the fact that it was on purpose, and how Niall had remembered her from years ago. Her father's smile widened as she spoke. By the time she finished, he was bursting at the seams.

"Do you know how many young ladies would love to be married to that boy? Why, half the married women in town would probably leave their husbands to be with him, including your mother."

"What!" Sarah exclaimed.

Her mother, sitting on the opposite side of the room, simply smiled, then said, "Perhaps if the offer were good enough."

"Mother!" Sarah cried out again, and then turning back to her father said, "I didn't know."

Her father gazed into space for a while as he thought. "Still," he finally said, "it sounds as though he showed some interest in you. Let me see what I can find out."

It took all three days that the O'Donnells stayed in town. Long days to Sarah's way of thinking. Her father did not mention it once, except to say, "patience, child," but she knew he was asking around. Her mother confirmed that he had spoken with Niall's father.

As Sarah absent-mindedly stirred a soup pot for her mother, her father entered their home. "Come," he said.

"I have spoken to his father," he continued when she caught up. "It seems Niall had already talked to him about you. He knew your name, which he apparently had asked about three years ago when he first saw you. He was captivated by your fascination with him then, and you made an even bigger impression on him the other day."

Sarah could swear her heart skipped three beats as her father spoke.

"So when I talked to him about you, he immediately said, 'I think the good fairies are doing their work here today'. He did some investigating about our family, and now he wishes to meet the young lass whom his son could not stop talking about."

Sarah was beyond words. So much was going through her head that she couldn't think straight. "My word father, do you think it possible?"

"Sarah," he said, stopping to give her a hug, "I will miss you. But I believe that when the O'Donnells return from England, you will be traveling with them to your new home in Kilmacrenan."

Five weeks later Niall and Sarah were married. They lived in Niall's hometown for six years. Kevin was born there the day after their third anniversary. Much of Niall's family lived in the area and their home was often crowded with people. However, Sarah longed to return to the coast. Willing to do anything for the wife he adored, Niall found the farm in Bicksby. It was farther north than her previous home, but brought her closer to her parents. She was pregnant with Myles when they moved, and he arrived two months later. Sean was born five years after Myles.

Now they had Nuala. She had moments of sadness at the loss of her mother, but for the most part she remained happy and carefree. She and Sean became closer, if that were possible, and Myles and Kevin became her protectors.

They settled into their daily routine. Kevin began his time on the water. Mister Meehan seemed pleased, saying Kevin was a hard worker for a lad of twelve. On the other hand, Sarah's fears about Myles proved to be well founded. He had little interest in working the crops or helping with the sheep. Niall was constantly scolding him for wasting valuable work time. Sarah was happy to get back to her chores, trying to keep her mind off the friend she was missing, but Nuala made that impossible.

One day, about a month after Mary's passing, Niall came home after spending the day in town. "I have news," he said, "some good, some bad."

"Bad news we don't need," Sarah said, "but you may as well get it out of the way first. I think I'd rather end the day with the good news."

"There is talk of war," Niall said. "The English are making plans to take over the country. It seems the O'Donnells and the O'Neills are joining forces in an attempt to stop them."

"Perhaps it is just a rumor," Sarah said hopefully.

"Perhaps."

"So tell me the good news."

"Ah yes, the good news." A wide grin lit up Niall's face. "I have something for you, my beautiful wife."

Usually when he said such a thing it was a fine cut of meat from the butchers, or a new pair of gloves for her gardening. Sarah couldn't imagine what had been on sale in town this time.

Niall took a pouch from his coat pocket. He opened the strings and reached inside. "Close your eyes, woman."

He was teasing her, and she played along. But what could be in the pouch?

"Now look," he said.

Sarah opened her eyes and gasped. It was the most beautiful thing she had ever seen—a necklace with emeralds and rubies on a golden chain! For a moment Sarah felt faint. Then she managed to say, "It's gorgeous, but how?"

"Never mind how," he said. "I bought it for you because I knew you would love it, and because I love you with all my heart."

He opened the clasp and motioned her forward. As he put the necklace on her, he planted soft kisses on her neck.

Sarah knew it would be the finest thing she ever owned.

Chapter Five

Simon was enthralled by the story Jill was telling. He wanted to continue on, but Melinda had signaled five minutes ago that his next client had arrived, so Simon gently brought her back to the present.

Jill slowly opened her eyes and saw Simon looking at her.

"Welcome back," he said. "That was quite a voyage you took."

Jill slowly rose and sat on the side of the couch. In her mind a part of her was still in Ireland four hundred years ago. She waited a moment for her thoughts to clear, then suddenly blurted out, "That couldn't have been real!"

Simon had heard this response before from skeptical clients. "I must say, Jill, that I have performed a great many regressions over the past few years, and rarely do they go any better. That was an excellent beginning."

"But I was just making that stuff up," Jill said. "I had to be."

"Is that what you truly think?"

Jill looked stumped. She was certain her overactive imagination had simply tossed out a good story for Simon to hear; yet it had seemed so real. "How could I have known such things?"

"If you believe in reincarnation, Jill, then you were simply remembering events from your past. They are still in your memory banks and always will be. Of course," he said, "if you don't believe, then I'm not sure what the answer is for you. I certainly believed your story."

Jill was fully back in the present now. "It was interesting, I'll admit, but I'm not ready to say it had anything to do with reality. It will give me something to tell Lauren anyway." She looked at Simon warily. "You must have been leading me on quite a bit."

"Actually," he said, "I did very little. Less than usual, in fact. You went back to a particular time that was obviously important to you; Mary's funeral. I suggested you go back to the point where you first met Niall. You explained that in great detail, and had the most marvelous smile on your face as you did so. Then, without any prodding from me, you brought the story back to where you had started and moved it forward a few weeks. Basically, I just sat here spellbound."

"Then I just stopped, because I couldn't make up anything more. Right?"

Simon was disappointed yet impressed by her unwillingness to believe. "No, Jill. You had been under quite a long time, so I brought you back."

"A long time?" She glanced at the wall clock and gasped. "It's been nearly an hour," she said, obviously surprised. She would have sworn the regression wasn't half that long.

"I should have brought you back sooner," Simon said. "I have another client waiting, but your story was so compelling, I found it difficult to stop. Tell me, did you recognize anyone?"

"Yes," she said. "Another reason I'm sure I was just making it up."

"Perhaps," he said. "Who did you recognize?"

"The children."

"The children in your past life are people you know now?"

"My kids," she said in a soft voice. "My kids in that life are my kids now. That can't be right. See, there's my proof right there."

"Proof of what, Jill?"

"That I had to be making it all up. I simply took my children from this life and inserted them into that one. That has to be it."

"A skeptic might certainly believe that."

"That has to be it," she said again. "How could my children then be my children now?"

"Actually," he said, "it's quite common. It seems we have a core group of people who stay with us from lifetime to lifetime. Not always in the same role, or even the same sex, yet always in our circle of friends or relatives."

"Lauren told me that," said Jill, "but it's hard to believe." In fact, Jill didn't believe it. Not for a second.

"So who was who?"

"What?" she asked, momentarily puzzled. Then she understood. "Oh, my oldest boy Bret was Myles, and my other son Mark was Kevin."

He glanced at the sheet she had filled out, and then said "So they have switched places?" Seeing the puzzled look on her face, Simon continued. "Your oldest child now was the second then, and vice-versa."

Comprehending now, Jill said, "Yes."

"What about Niall. Did you recognize him?"

Jill became pensive. "No." Then after a short pause, she added "But I sure would like to. Those two really loved each other. Lauren said she didn't recognize her true love from Italy either."

Simon shrugged his shoulders. "I suspect both of you will be meeting up with them sooner or later. If you believe in soul mates, Niall certainly could be yours. Anyone else you recall? Sean, perhaps."

"No, I didn't recognize Sean, or Nuala, but my father in Ireland is my grandfather here."

"Excellent. And your mother?"

"No," Jill said, "although my grandmother died before I was born. That's on my mother's side. My dad's parents are just the opposite. His dad died last year, but his mother is still alive."

"You didn't see either of them in the regression?"

"No."

"Jill, it is obvious to me that you are having a hard time believing that this story you have just conveyed to me is true. I want to reiterate that rarely have I been a part of a regression that has proceeded so well." Simon rose, and Jill did the same. "I hope you will come back again. I would love to continue your story and see what happens."

Jill gave him a smirk. "I don't know. It was a fascinating tale and all, but I really don't believe it ever actually happened."

"Jill, you are an excellent subject. Many people, like your friend Lauren, give details of an entire life in one sitting. Some go through multiple lives. Yet in all the time you were under, we only heard the beginning of your story. It would be wonderful to have you come back again and finish it."

Jill wanted to say no. She wanted to walk out the door and never come back. *This couldn't be real*, she thought. It had to be just a figment of her imagination.

As they moved into the waiting room Simon was silently praying Jill would agree to return. Her regression was the finest first session he had ever had. He honestly believed this was the person he had been waiting for.

She turned to him, intending to say goodbye, but before she could, he spoke again.

"I would greatly appreciate it if you would consider returning."

She heard the sincerity in his voice and wondered why it was so important to him. He must have plenty of other clients to choose from. Suddenly, the thought of Sarah and Niall came into her head, and it gave her a bit of a tingle. Much as she hated to admit it, their story intrigued her. True or not, a part of her did want to see where it would lead. "Okay," she suddenly said.

"Excellent." Simon's face lit up in a big smile, and Jill could see how happy he was. "Melinda," he said to his secretary, "take care of her, please."

Simon led his next client into the back room as Jill turned to Melinda.

"You seem a bit perplexed," Melinda said. "Can't quite figure it out, I take it."

"I don't know. It was interesting and all, but …"

Melinda just looked at her, eyebrows raised.

"… I don't really believe it."

"Give it time," said Melinda. "I have an opening at nine o'clock next Tuesday. That okay for you?"

"Sure." Jill took the appointment card Melinda handed her and left.

Chapter Six

Jill called Lauren as soon as she reached her car and left a message on her answering machine. Lauren never answered the phone when she was with a patient. When Lauren did call back twenty minutes later, it was simply to say she was booked solid and didn't know when she would be able to talk. Jill started to mention her regression, but Lauren interrupted.

"Don't tell me," she said. "I want to hear all about it, but not over the phone. Let's do brunch Friday morning. I'll pick you up at ten."

Jill tried to put the whole story out of her mind. She didn't believe any of it had actually happened, and nothing Lauren could say was going to convince her otherwise. Yet Sarah and Niall kept creeping back into her thoughts as she went through her day. Even the boys noticed as they ate supper that night.

"Mom, why are you looking at us like that?" Bret wanted to know. "I don't have any homework, honest."

"Sorry, honey," said Jill. "I was just daydreaming."

"You're staring at us, but it's like you don't see us. It's kind of freaky."

She smiled at him and apologized again.

"If something's wrong, he did it, not me," Bret continued, pointing at his brother.

Mark had been busy eating the homemade pizza she had baked for supper. Now he chimed in too. "No way, Mom. I didn't do anything wrong."

"I know, sweetie," she said. "I didn't realize I was staring. Eat your pizza, okay?"

After dinner, Jill took Bret to the bookstore to pick up his next reading assignment for English. As they were walking to the registers to pay, she saw a display of maps. Jill found a map of Ireland and decided to buy it.

"Planning to take us on a trip?" Bret asked hopefully.

"No such luck," she replied. "I'm going to do some homework of my own." Bret just gave her a quizzical look.

That night, after the boys were asleep, Jill lay relaxing on her bed with a cup of tea. She saw the map on her nightstand and picked it up. "Not that I'm going to find anything," she mumbled to herself.

Although her ancestors were Irish, Jill had never been to Ireland and neither had her parents. Her knowledge of her heritage was extremely limited. Embarrassingly so, she thought. She knew a few of the major cities: Dublin, of course, and Galway, Belfast, and Londonderry. She owned some Waterford crystal, but wasn't sure if there was actually a town called Waterford. She recalled that Ireland had two airports, one in Dublin, and Shannon Airport, although she wasn't sure where that one was.

She opened the map, folded it in half and began looking for familiar names. She searched the northwest coastline for Bicksby, but found nothing. Then she remembered the map would have an index of cities and towns. Finding it, she looked up Bicksby. It wasn't listed. "I knew it," she nearly shouted, now certain she had just made up the whole story. She thought for a moment, trying to recall anyplace else she may have mentioned in the regression. She had never named the hometown of her childhood, so that was out.

She did say where Niall was from, though. What was it? Sort of a long name, she thought. It came to her slowly: Kilmacrenan.

She knew that it was inland, so she turned her gaze back to the map. She searched for a minute, then another. "This is crazy," she said. She realized she had no idea how far inland it might be, or even if it was in the northwest part of Ireland. She was about to go back to the index when she saw a landmark on the map named Doon's Rock. She laughed to herself. "They put a rock on a map," she said to the empty room. Then her laughter was suddenly cut short. Next to Doon's Rock she saw another name.

Kilmacrenan.

Jill lay on the bed, staring at the map. Her first thought was that she must have heard the name as a child, and her subconscious remembered it. She dismissed that idea right away.

Jill refolded the map and stuck it in her nightstand. "Lucky guess," she said. She was not going to believe her story could possibly be true based on the name of one simple town. The cornerstone of her story had been Bicksby, and that was nowhere to be found. She couldn't explain Kilmacrenan, but if there was no Bicksby, then her story must be a fabrication.

She shut off her light and tried to sleep, but was still awake an hour later. Thoughts of where she could possibly have heard of Kilmacrenan gradually gave way to musing about a man named Niall. *If only he were real*, she thought. *Why can't I meet a man like that?* She relaxed as her mind lingered on her Irish husband of four-hundred years ago, and she finally drifted off to sleep.

Jill spent the next two days catching up on work. She was a medical transcriber for five local doctors, working from home on her computer. After high school she had waitressed for a few years before deciding she wanted something more. She had begun taking nursing classes at the local community college, but after meeting Tony and becoming pregnant with Bret she had let her studies slide. However, once the boys hit junior high school she took an online course for medical transcription. It paid well, and she could make her own hours. She supplemented that income with a weekend job as a hostess at The Ravenwood, a nice restaurant downtown.

Friday morning Lauren arrived at Jill's house as planned. She usually worked full days Monday through Thursday and then took Fridays off. Saturday was always busy with people who couldn't come during the week. "Sorry we couldn't meet sooner," she said to Jill, "but it's been a crazy week."

"Work is still picking up, I take it."

"Business is just booming," said Lauren, who had a streak of deep purple running through her hair. "Seems the word of mouth has been getting around and everybody is calling all at once. I don't know how much longer I can take Friday's off at this rate."

"Maybe you should hire a helper," offered Jill.

Lauren winced. "I don't want to do that. Too much hassle with the paperwork and all. I'll just have to draw the line somewhere. Hey, what smells so good?"

"Come into the kitchen," Jill said. "I decided we could eat brunch here rather than go out. Not sure I want to be telling you my story in public." She poured Lauren a cup of coffee, then made two omelets with ham, cheese, onions, and red peppers. Pancakes and sausage, already made and warming in the oven, completed the meal.

Fifteen minutes later, Lauren said "I won't have to eat the rest of the day." They had refrained from talking about Jill's regression while they ate, but now Lauren was ready to hear the tale. "Pour me another cup, and tell me how it went. Don't leave anything out. I want to hear it all."

Jill did. The story seemed as fresh in her mind as when she first told it on Tuesday. For the most part, Lauren stayed quiet and let the story unfold. Occasionally she would utter an "ooh" or an "ah", and when Jill said she recognized her children now as her children then, Lauren said "fantastic" and slapped her hand on the table. Finally, Jill told her about buying the map.

"There is no Bicksby in Ireland," she said, "although there is a Kilmacrenan."

"No way, really!" Lauren exclaimed. "That's way too cool."

Jill just gave her a non-committal stare, and Lauren jumped all over her.

"Come on, you have to believe it now. That is a great story. You pulled a lot more out of your regression than I did mine."

"I don't need to believe anything," Jill said. "There is no Bicksby. Sure I told a wonderful story, but that's all it was. My imagination is obviously as good as yours."

"You're really trying to tell me you made up that whole incredible story?" Lauren asked. "I find that hard to believe."

Jill sat stone-faced, refusing to budge from her position.

Finally, to break the sudden tension that was in the air, Lauren said, "It sounds like Niall may be your soul mate. Hopefully you can find him in this life."

Jill, still feeling defensive, said, "And where is your soul mate from Italy, your Guiseppe? Haven't found him yet, have you?"

"Actually," said Lauren, fluttering her eyes and smiling brightly, "I may have."

"What?" cried Jill.

"I didn't tell you because I haven't had many dates with him yet. Of course, I don't know if he is my Italian lover or not."

"Why not?"

"Funny thing about regressing. It seems we can recognize people back then who are with us now, but in this life we don't recognize people we knew back then, at least not consciously. You really do have to trust your instincts."

"But didn't you recognize him during your regression?"

"No, I actually met him a few days after my appointment with Simon."

"So go have another regression and see if it's him."

"To tell you the truth I don't want to influence the relationship that way. What do I do if it's not him, dump him? I like him."

"I can't believe you have had multiple dates with him and you never told me. What's his name? Is he a client?"

Lauren reached for her coffee and took a long sip. "No, he is not a client," she began. "Not yet anyway. I met him through a client, however. She thought we would hit it off, so she set up a double-date with her and her husband. We've gone out about five times, I guess. I can't tell you if it is Guiseppe, of course, but it feels right. It's hard to explain why. It's like the subconscious part of me knows it is him even though my conscious mind doesn't."

"So it's still a guessing game."

"Yes," said Lauren, "I suppose it is. I could go back for another session with the doctor, but something tells me to just go with the flow, and you know me, I always follow my instincts."

"So, have you told this guy about your regression? What's his name? What does—"

"Whoa, slow down," said Lauren. "His name is Bill. He has a photography studio over in Claremont, and no, I haven't told him anything about my regression."

Jill nodded her head. "I guess it would be hard to bring it up. 'Um, by the way, Bill, did you know you may have been married to me in a past life in Italy?'" Jill chuckled, and Lauren joined in. "So what does your gut tell you, Lauren? Is Bill Guiseppe?"

"I have to be honest with you, Jill. No one has ever made me feel this good. In so many ways, it is like we have known each other forever. It's weird. I don't know if Bill is Guiseppe or not, but I sure am excited to see where it leads. So, when are you going back?"

"Tuesday, nine o'clock."

"I'm looking forward to hearing more of your story with Niall. Hope you pick the same lifetime."

Although she still didn't believe it was true, Jill said, "Me too."

It was nearly one o'clock when Lauren left, and Jill began to get ready for her weekend. She worked at The Ravenwood from five to eleven on Friday night and five to midnight on Saturday. Tony took the boys almost every weekend, picking them up on Friday and bringing them home around six on Sunday night. The money she made at The Ravenwood helped buy extras for the boys and treat them to a night out on occasion. Tony was good about paying his child support, and covered all the insurance and doctor's bills. As much as she despised him, Jill was thankful for that. She couldn't count the number of times she had heard from her friends about ex-husbands being constantly late on support payments or paying nothing at all.

As Tuesday morning approached, Jill thought she might dread going back to see Simon, but instead felt a sense of anticipation. She still thought the idea of reincarnation was crazy. She did wish sometimes that she was as open-minded as Lauren, who believed in everything. Perhaps today would change her mind.

Melinda greeted her with a big smile as she entered. "What a great day. Almost makes me wish I had called in sick."

"Morning, Melinda," said Jill. "Don't let Simon hear you say that."

Melinda waved a hand at her. "Oh, he would know I was only kidding. I never call in sick on regression day. It's my favorite day of the week."

"Why is that?" Jill asked.

"Well," Melinda replied, "the rest of the week we have patients who need psychological counseling, some in the most desperate way. But Tuesday mornings, we have the fun people in, like you. Our regular patients are trying to find themselves in this lifetime. You're trying to find yourself in a completely different lifetime."

Jill had to smile at that.

"You should be in right away," Melinda continued. "His eight o'clock chickened out."

Jill was happy to hear she wasn't the only one who had doubts. She wondered if she would return to the same place she had left, or start somewhere else. Might it even be a different lifetime? She definitely wanted to learn more about Niall. It was truly the only reason she returned.

The door to Simon's office opened and he motioned for her to come in. "Good morning," he said. "I'm happy to see you."

"Believe me," said Jill, "I've been going back and forth all week about it." She asked him about the things she had been thinking about in the waiting room.

"I will attempt to take you back to the Irish lifetime," said Simon. "You have probably been thinking about Niall all week, unless I miss my guess, so your subconscious should return you there pretty easily, although chances are you will not pick up where you left off. The mind is a funny thing. It will choose a particular event that was important to you, and start from there."

"I understand," she said.

Moments later, Jill was lying on the couch, ready to go back in time once again.

Chapter Seven

IRELAND, 1602

Sarah stood on the edge of the cliff and looked out over the bay. The view from her backyard never ceased to amaze her even after all these years. The huge boulder, nearly two feet taller than Sarah, was off to her left. The day was cold and windy, but she saw sunlight out over the ocean and knew it would turn bright soon.

Bicksby looked quiet from her vantage point, as it often did these days. Many of the men were gone; off to fight in a war they now had little chance of winning. Sarah hated the war. It had taken Niall away from her for the better part of eight years now. He had been home a number of times in that period, but usually just for a month or so. She missed him so much, missed his touch, missed their lovemaking.

Her thoughts brought her back to the start of the war. It was 1594, shortly after her best friend Mary had died. She vividly remembered the day Rory O'Donnell had ridden into Bicksby. Niall was in the fields, harvesting what was going to be a huge crop. Sarah had gone into town with Kevin and planned on buying sewing materials and some new cloth.

Rory road into town just minutes after they did. Word quickly spread about an emergency meeting at the church. Kevin went home to summon his father, while Sarah did her shopping and headed for St. Brigid's, wondering why Rory was here.

Niall seemed to know when he arrived. "It must be war," he told her. "I don't think they would send Rory for anything less."

Rory entered the church and went directly to the pulpit to speak. "The O'Donnells and the O'Neills have banded together to strike a blow against our English oppressors." A rumbling went throughout the crowd. "We will need as many able-bodied men as we can muster to help with our cause."

Niall turned to look at her. He did not need to say anything. He was an O'Donnell. He had to fight. The look on her face told him how unhappy she was.

Rory spoke for half an hour, but Sarah was thinking of how much she would miss her husband, how she would have to run the farm without him, and how she would pray he wouldn't be killed. By the time Rory finished, the whole town was in fervor. As they mingled with their fellow townsfolk afterwards, many of the men said they would be joining up to fight. The only dissenting voice Sarah heard was that of Charles Dumont, the town doctor.

"It's madness to fight the English," he said.

Within a week the town had shrunk in population by nearly a quarter. As an O'Donnell, Niall was the acknowledged leader of the men leaving Bicksby. On that Sunday, the group went to the church for blessings of safety and then headed out to join forces inland.

With Niall gone, Kevin had to stay home most days and help work the fields. Whenever possible, he would go fishing with Mister Meehan. With so many men in town gone, Meehan's fleet had been cut from three boats to one. He welcomed Kevin's help whenever he could get it. Meehan had not gone off to fight like so many others. The town would need his fish now more than ever.

The war had started amazingly well for the Irish, but it seemed every time Niall came home the news was a little worse. Now, eight years later, defeat seemed imminent.

A sudden gust of wind brought Sarah back to the present. She heard a voice calling.

"Mother! Mother!"

It was Kevin, just returning from a trip into town.

"Mother," he cried again as he reached her, "father is coming home. For good."

Sarah felt her knees buckle. "What do you mean? Is the war over?"

"Thomas Cleary arrived back home this morning. He said father would be home in about two days. Apparently he has been injured, though Mister Cleary believed it was not bad. A leg wound, he said."

Fear coursed through Sarah's body. Then joy overtook her. Niall was coming home.

Three days later Sarah sat in her kitchen knitting. A mist hung over the morning like a grey blanket, the sky thick with clouds. Summer had been delightful and the fields had yielded a bumper crop, but autumn had been miserable, and the wait for Niall to return these last few days had seemed to take forever.

She went to the doorway and looked out. Sean was standing at the top of the road, keeping watch for his father.

As if on cue, Sean started jumping up and down, waving his hands and shouting. In the wind Sarah couldn't hear what he was saying, but it could only mean one thing. A minute later, two riders appeared. Sarah watched as Sean greeted his father by jumping up behind him and giving him a great big hug. As they rode closer, she saw that Paedar Dowling, who lived two houses up, was with him. Paedar's wife Deidre came out of their home and fell to her knees, crying tears of joy. Niall shook Paedar's hand and then headed home.

He brought his stead to a gallop as Sarah ran out to meet him. Sean jumped off when they arrived, and then Niall climbed down, taking care not to land hard on his right leg.

Sarah could not help but notice. After giving him a long, hard kiss, she asked, "How badly are you hurt?"

"I'll be alright. It needs some time to heal, I'm afraid."

She smiled at him. "You will have the finest nurse you could ask for, and," she cautioned, wagging a finger at him, "you had better obey her orders." By now all the children were surrounding their father.

"Papa, what happened to your leg?" asked Nuala.

"Let's go inside," he replied, "and I'll tell you all about it."

They listened intently as he spoke about hand-to-hand combat and how a knife had pierced his knee. "I imagine I will be walking with a noticeable limp for a while," he said. "I was no use on the battlefield anymore, so they insisted I go home. Not that I'm going to miss much."

"What do you mean?" asked Kevin. "Won't you miss the fighting?"

Niall stared at his son. "Fighting is no way to solve your problems, Kevin. Maybe someday people will learn that. What I meant was this war will not last much longer. Some are already saying that a peace treaty will be signed by the end of the year."

Sarah hoped that were true, although she was afraid of the consequences.

As the days passed, Niall slowly returned to his duties around the house. The crops were all in so he spent his time doing necessary repairs to the equipment they had. Occasionally new war reports would come in and he would update the townsfolk after the Sunday service.

Sarah remembered one such update about six weeks after his return.

"Good morning," he had said as he looked out over the crowd. "May God's biggest blessings be upon you."

"You too, Niall," someone called out. "Now what's the news?"

"Not much good news, I'm afraid. It seems many of our own Irish fighters who have lost their leaders have gone over to the other side and are now fighting against us."

The crowd moaned, and shouts of "treason" and "cowards" could be heard.

Niall continued on. "I am sad to say that Rory has lost his castle, and it appears that we will be receiving no more help from the Spanish government."

"Is there no hope?" he heard a woman in the front row ask.

"We are in a church, m'lady, so there is always the possibility of a miracle," Niall replied. "Barring that, I would say there is little left we can do to win this war."

As November arrived, the family fell back into their familiar ways. Kevin worked for Mister Meehan whenever the weather allowed. Sean and Nuala were still inseparable. Niall also spent a good deal of his free time with Nuala. They had little time to really get to know each other before Niall had gone off to fight. Now he fawned over her, giving her all sorts of trinkets he found in town to please her. It was obvious to Sarah he had always wanted a daughter.

Yet it was Myles who had changed the most in his father's absence. Sarah had noticed it over the years, and now it was obvious to Niall as well. Myles had been working in the fields with his mother the past few years. His change in attitude about work had been apparent. Now seeing his father's injury changed him even more. He worked incredibly hard to impress Niall. Every day he wanted to know what he could do to help out, often telling his father to rest while he did the job himself. Sarah could tell how very proud Niall was of Myles.

One night Kevin asked to talk to his parents.

"Good news, we hope," Niall said as he looked at Sarah and winked. For months now Kevin had been courting Catherine Boyle. Her father was a glove maker in Bicksby who owned a home adjacent to the church.

"Yes, father."

They both noticed the quiver in Kevin's voice as he spoke.

"I have asked Catherine to marry me. Her parents have agreed to it, and I hope you will too."

Niall answered, "Kevin, you know we love Catherine. You two make a lovely couple. Of course you have our blessing. So when is the date of this glorious wedding?"

Kevin was genuinely happy to hear his father's words. "New Year's Eve," he said. "At the church, of course, and then a party at the Boyle's home."

Sarah was delighted. "We are proud of you, Kevin. You have worked hard for this family. Who knows, soon you may have a family of your own."

"Hear, hear," said Niall. "Let's have a toast."

"You stay there," Sarah said to him. She went to the cupboard, brought out the mead, and poured small bowls for them all.

Niall raised his bowl and Sarah did the same. "To Catherine and Kevin. May they be married for a lifetime and live out their dreams." They all drank. After a few more rounds Kevin stumbled off to bed. Sarah took Niall's hand and led him outside. The air was surprisingly warm for November. They walked to the back of the house and sat on a bench Niall had made at Sarah's suggestion. They watched the light of the moon reflect off the gently lapping waves in the bay.

Sarah turned and looked into the eyes of her husband. "I love you, you know."

He smiled a warm, loving smile she never grew tired of. "I know, my love, and I love you too."

They sat there, holding hands, saying nothing more.

Chapter Eight

Jill hurried out of the doctor's office and headed home. Once again she was amazed by the story she told about Niall and Sarah. Was it true? How could it be? She knew by his reaction that Simon was thrilled with her, and she had agreed to go back yet again. Why?

She was trying to make a mental checklist of all the events she had mentioned during her regression. She had been surprised after her first visit to find Kilmacrenan on the map. She was still certain she had never heard of the place. She was also certain she had never heard names like Niall and Nuala. Did she make them up, or was she remembering people and places from four-hundred years ago?

Now, from this visit, she had recalled more names. Then there was the war. Jill did not know Irish history before the twentieth century. Was there a war with the English around 1600? She needed answers, and decided that she would spend her free time trying to verify the information she had recalled.

Jill heard her phone ringing as she walked into the house. Surprisingly, it was Lauren.

"Hey, I'm free until 1:15. How about meeting me at Grove Street for lunch? Let's say 11:30."

"Sounds good," said Jill, realizing she was hungry. "I have more to tell you from my meeting with Simon this morning. Might as well tell you over lunch."

"My thinking exactly," said Lauren.

The Grove Street Café was one of those nice little places that's overlooked by outsiders but well known to the locals. Nothing fancy, but great food at decent prices. Jill arrived first and grabbed a table. Lauren came in a few minutes later.

After the usual greetings, Lauren said, "So bring me up to date. Was today's visit as amazing as the first one?"

Jill nodded her head yes. "It is quite a story, I must admit. We've just gone through a war."

"Really? Can't say I'm up on my history enough to know which war that might be."

"Me either," said Jill.

The waiter came and took their lunch order, and then Jill told Lauren all she could remember from her regression. When she finished, she said, "I'm going to delve into Irish history this week and see if I can corroborate any of this. Somehow I doubt it."

"Still playing the role of doubting Thomas, are we?" said Lauren. "What is it going to take to convince you this is definitely a prior life of yours?"

Jill gave her a quizzical look. "Even if I do find that some of this stuff really happened, it doesn't mean that it was me living it. Perhaps the good doctor simply knows how to draw history out of people."

Lauren rolled her eyes in frustration. "Jill, you never took Irish history in your life. You know you never heard any of this before. Why can't you believe you are recalling this because you *lived* it?" she asked emphatically.

"I don't know," said Jill. "It all sounds so crazy to me."

"Someday you need to come to church with me," said Lauren.

Jill was surprised by the sudden change of subject. "You're going to church now? When did this happen?"

"It's a spiritual church. It's not like the normal religious churches. In fact, we don't even have our own building. We rent that old department store on West Street that went out of business about five years ago. Sunday mornings we have services, and on Thursday nights we run classes and have special gatherings."

Jill noticed how happy Lauren seemed as she talked about this. "If it's not a regular church, then what do you do?"

"Some of it is the same, but we have healing circles and receive messages."

"Messages from whom?" Jill asked.

"From whichever psychic is teaching that day."

"Psychic!" Jill cried, and noticed a few heads turn in her direction. She lowered her voice and said, "You have to be kidding me."

"You should come sometime. You wouldn't believe the people who go there, Jill."

"I don't believe what I'm hearing. Lauren, have you totally flipped out? Is that what led you to this past-life stuff?"

"It led me there and to a great many other interesting things. You need to keep an open mind, Jill. The world is full of amazing people who have some pretty stunning talents."

Jill didn't know what to say so she changed the subject and asked Lauren how her relationship with Bill was going.

"We are doing great, thank you," said Lauren. "It's one of the nicer relationships I have had in a long time."

"Like you've known him forever, right?" Jill said a little too caustically.

"You can make fun of me if you want, Jill, but yes, it does feel something like that."

"Lauren, you know I'm happy for you. I'm just not sure it has anything to do with knowing him from other lifetimes. I have a hard time believing that."

"You'll get there," Lauren said.

"Will I?" asked Jill. Somehow she didn't think so.

When the bill came, Lauren said, "Let me get this," and paid the waiter before Jill could argue.

"Thanks," Jill said. "Next time it's my treat."

Lauren grabbed her pocketbook and stood up. "I have to run. Let me know how you make out with your history study. I'll bet you find out a good deal of what you remembered is true."

"Maybe," said Jill. In truth, part of her hoped she wouldn't. Then, thinking of Niall, she realized part of her hoped she would.

Tuesday night after dinner Bret went right to the computer, telling his mother he was going to be on it for quite a while. It seemed he had waited until the last minute to start his history project. Mark took the opportunity to remind his mother he needed new sneakers, so Jill took him shopping.

"Can we get ice cream after we buy my sneakers?" Mark asked when they arrived.

"If I have any money left," said Jill. The boys always wanted the most expensive sneakers, and Jill had to fight tooth and nail to talk them into a more affordable pair. "Remember, you are going to outgrow them in six months anyway, so we are not going to spend a fortune on them."

Mark begrudgingly agreed.

Forty minutes later, he carried the box with his new sneakers in one hand and a strawberry ice cream cone in the other. Leaving the store they caught the last rays of a gorgeous sunset.

"Look at that sky," said Mark. It was a colorful display of reddish clouds with wisps of purple melted in. "Those clouds are beautiful."

It was a remark Bret never would have made. He tended to be the analytical child. Mark, on the other hand, was more of the artistic type.

The cloud remark made Jill remember a time years ago when Mark was three. They had been walking down the street to a nearby donut shop. Jill had pointed out a large cloud that was shaped like a poodle.

"I used to live there," Mark had said.

Jill had thought at first he was just making believe, so she played along. "You used to live there? Was it fun?"

Mark had just shrugged his shoulders the way three year olds do. "I don't know," he had replied. "I used to live there. Now I live here."

Jill hadn't made anything of it at the time, and seconds later Mark had been talking about something else. Yet Jill had never forgotten the conversation, and now she brought it up to him. "Mark, do you remember that time you said you used to live in the cloud?"

"Sure. We were walking to the donut shop. I used to love those walks, just you and me. We did it every Sunday morning."

That was right, she thought. I let Tony watch Bret for a few minutes so I could walk with Mark to the store. She had forgotten it was always a Sunday they did that. "Do you still think you used to live in a cloud?" she asked.

They had arrived back at the car in the parking lot. Once they were all buckled in, Mark said, "Well Mom, I know I didn't come from that particular cloud, or any cloud for that matter. That's pretty silly. I believe what I meant but couldn't say at that age was that I came from that side. You know, from heaven."

"So you think you were alive on that side before you were born on this side?"

"Sure," he said matter-of-factly.

"And do you think you have lived on this side before, honey?"

She was surprised when he answered so quickly. "Of course. Why not?"

"You believe you have lived before?" she asked again, the sound of amazement in her voice.

"It's called reincarnation, Mom," he said somewhat sarcastically, as if she were now the three year old, "and yes, I believe it."

Jill discovered that her little boy had believed in reincarnation since he first heard about the concept years ago. They discussed it for the entire ride home. To Mark, it simply seemed like something that was obvious.

"So tell me," she finally asked him, "who do you think you were in these other lives of yours?"

He became animated as he said, "Captain Kidd, or some swashbuckling pirate. And a pharaoh in Egypt, maybe that young one whose grave they found years ago."

"You mean King Tut?"

"Yeah, that's the one. Maybe that was me they dug up. That would be so cool."

In bed that night Jill shook her head in wonder at the simple believing of her child.

It wasn't until Sunday that Jill found any time to sit at her computer and begin her history search. The boys had taken turns tying up the machine every night, and Jill's job had kept her busy while they were in school. Even Sunday morning, after a long night at the restaurant, she really didn't feel like staring at a computer screen. However, her Tuesday appointment was fast approaching, so after lunch she decided to give it a try. She started by looking for Sarah and Niall O'Donnell. She searched through multiple websites, but none of the entries she found for those names pointed toward the early 1600s. After a bit more searching, she did find a site specifically dealing with Irish history in the sixteenth and seventeenth centuries. She decided to look for wars in that time period.

What came up caused a tingle to go through her body. A war did start in 1594 called the Nine Year's War, ending in 1603. "I'll be," she muttered. As she read, she realized the war had gone pretty much as she had remembered in her regression. Another chill rumbled through her when she spotted the name Rory O'Donnell. "You were real," she said to the computer. A moment later she saw that Rory had lost his castle in Ballyshannon during the war.

Jill sat back and stared at the screen for a moment. She was convinced she had never heard or studied any of this information before. Yet she had recalled it almost exactly as it had happened. "How can this be?" she asked herself. For the first time an inkling of doubt entered her mind. Had she been naïve all these years? Was Lauren right?

Suddenly Jill didn't feel tired at all. As she returned her attention to the computer, a plan began to formulate in her mind. She hadn't known any Irish history to speak of. Now she was going to learn all she could about the history that occurred after 1602. By the time Tony dropped the boys off shortly after six o'clock, Jill knew exactly how she wanted her next session to go.

Tuesday morning couldn't come fast enough. Jill had studied Irish history as if cramming for an exam. She worried, however, if she had done the right thing. Would she just say under hypnosis what she had learned, thus making the regression questionable? She hoped not.

She arrived at Simon's office fifteen minutes early, only to find the door locked and the room dark. *What's going on?* she wondered. She was about to go back to her car when she saw Melinda getting off the elevator. "There you are," she cried.

"Someone in a hurry today?" asked Melinda.

"For a moment I thought you were closed today, and I didn't get the message." Jill hoped the panic she felt wasn't showing on her face.

Melinda unlocked the door and opened it. "Come on in, Jill. The doctor should be here shortly."

As anxious as Jill was to get started, she decided a small wait was much easier to handle than a locked door. "Why are you just opening now?" she asked.

"Typical story," said Melinda. "We had a new person coming in at eight, but she changed her mind last night. It's not always easy to get people to do this. So rather than come in and shuffle papers for an hour, the doctor told me to sleep in."

Jill remembered how she had almost not come in that first time. "That was nice of him."

Melinda smiled. "He's a great guy to work for."

A few minutes later, Simon arrived just as Melinda was handing Jill a cup of tea. "I thought you might need this," she said. "You look a little tense today."

"Excited to get started, are we?" asked Simon.

"Very much so," Jill replied.

He looked at Melinda. "I'll take a cup of that too, if you don't mind." Then, turning to Jill, he said, "Give me a few minutes to settle in, and then we'll get started."

"I take it something happened to get you this wound up?" said Melinda.

"It shows, huh?" Jill wasn't surprised. "I did some checking on the things I said last week. Seems nearly all of it was true. I couldn't believe it."

"And now?" asked Melinda.

"Now I'm just really confused."

Melinda nodded. "Just try to stay open-minded, honey. We have had a great many people come in for regressions over the past few years, and those who come more than once almost always believe by the time they are finished."

"Really?" Jill wondered if that were true.

"Yes. The one-timers you never know about. Some have an open mind, some think we're nuts. When I saw the look on your face today, I figured you had started to believe."

"Not quite, but who knows, maybe today's the day."

The door to the back room opened and Simon stuck his head out. "Ready when you are," he said.

Jill felt a surge of excitement go through her as she stood up and went in. She told him about looking up her story from the last visit and finding out most of it was true.

He was impressed. "You seem to have excellent recall, Jill. I assume you want to continue on with the same lifetime?"

The idea of switching to a different life had never entered her mind. She simply said, "Yes."

"We may well reach the end of your Irish life today," Simon said. "I will take you farther along in your story, skipping ahead as I feel the need. We may reach the point of your death. Don't worry, it's not painful," he said. "The spirit tends to leave the body in the moments before the actual death. All of the people who have done this have said their deaths were quite easy. They were simply floating above their body when it expired. So, are you ready?"

"Ready," she said, "but I do have a request."

"Oh, and what would that be?"

"I want to try to resume my regression on a specific date, if we could."

"I've never tried that before," he said. "Of course, there are no guarantees."

"I understand," Jill said, "but I really hope we can pull it off."

He nodded agreeably. Grabbing a pen, he asked, "What date do you have in mind?"

"Friday, September 14, 1607."

"Can you give me a hint what you think you will be doing on that date?"

Jill gave Simon a huge smile. "I think I'm going sailing."

Chapter Nine

IRELAND, September 1, 1607

It was noon when Sarah saw the rider approaching the O'Donnell farm. Niall had just come in from the field and was sitting down to eat. She turned to him from the doorway. "Someone's coming. I don't recognize him, but he's moving fast."

Niall stood up and walked to the door. He gazed at the rider for only a second, then said, "That's Padraig." He watched a moment longer, then turned to Sarah and noticed the confused look on her face. "Sorry," he said, "I forgot you wouldn't know him. Padraig O'Donnell. Very distant relative of mine from Antrim County. I fought with him during the war."

"What could he be doing so far from home?" Sarah asked.

"No idea. Guess we'll find out soon enough."

They went out to greet him as Padraig rode up to the house and dismounted. Niall introduced Sarah and there were hugs all around.

"You look like a man on a mission, Padraig," said Niall.

"That's very true," Padraig answered. "I will tell you all about it, but first could I have some water for my horse? It's been a long ride."

Niall asked Sean to take care of Padraig's horse. "Come in and relax. Sean will do right by your steed."

Niall and Padraig sat at the table. Sarah gave their guest some ale and then served up bowls of the lamb stew she had made.

"As you know," began Padraig, "after the war Rory was appointed sheriff by James the First."

They both nodded. This was common knowledge.

"Well, God bless him, Rory still couldn't stand having the English army scattered all over Ulster, and they didn't much like him either. Word is he was planning to storm Dublin Castle and start an uprising."

"Oh dear," said Sarah, "not another war?"

"No, sweet lady. Rory denies he ever made such plans. Truth is we think it was a rumor the English started. In any event, the O'Neills and the O'Donnells are in grave danger, so they have decided to get out."

Puzzled, Niall asked, "What do you mean, get out?"

"Out of the country."

"What!" Niall was stunned. "They're fleeing?"

"In two weeks," said Padraig. "Any male family member who had anything to do with the war. You are to gather whatever things you can easily bring and meet in Rathmullen harbor. A ship will be taking us to the continent, either France or Spain."

"Preposterous!" Niall's anger had risen so quickly Sarah was taken aback. "Who exactly is leaving?"

Padraig stared at Niall for several seconds, measuring his response. Finally, he just said, "Everyone who fought in the war." He watched Niall for a moment longer as the words sank in. "The English will be coming after us, and soon. We must flee as quickly as we can."

"And the families?" asked Niall.

"The women and children who can be ready that soon will leave then also. The rest will travel at a later date. The English are not going to bother with them. It's the men that have to get out right quick."

"And Rory ordered this?"

"Hard to tell if it was Rory or Hugh O'Neill. They probably decided on it together, particularly once the plan, or rumor, became common knowledge."

"But it will leave Ulster defenseless. Who will protect the people left behind?"

Padraig had no answer for that. "Niall, change is coming, and fast. The English have no use for us, you know that. Soon they will be taking our lands from us, kicking us off as they did years ago. It's best to move on and start a new life somewhere else."

Sarah couldn't believe what she was hearing. She loved Bicksby. In her mind leaving Ireland was out of the question, and she was sure Niall felt the same way.

"You must come," Padraig continued. "It would be suicide to stay. Surely you know the English will take vengeance on any O'Donnell who remains behind."

"I know no such thing," replied Niall. "The war has been over for almost four years. We live an ordinary life here. The English need not bother us, nor will they."

They debated, sometimes argued, for another hour before Padraig left.

For the rest of the day Niall and Sarah talked about what to do. Neither one wanted to leave Bicksby. Ireland was their home and always would be. That night before supper they sent Myles into town to ask Kevin and Catherine to come to the house. They wanted to discuss everything with the family.

Kevin and his wife arrived just as the sun was setting over the water. Myles had obviously tipped them off as to what was happening. They listened as Niall told them the situation and explained why they were not leaving. Myles, Sean, and Nuala all shook their heads in agreement. Kevin, however, shocked his father by saying "We know leaving Ireland will be hard, but Catherine and I wish to go."

"What?" Niall said, taken by surprise for the second time that day. "I didn't ask you here to tell you we're leaving. We're not."

"We are," Kevin calmly stated.

"How could you make such a decision so quickly? Kevin, you're not thinking clearly about this."

Yet Kevin and Catherine had been thinking about such a move for a long time. They had always wanted to see more of the world and were excited about sailing to the continent and starting a new life.

The following days were hard for Sarah. Niall was in a foul mood most of the time. Sarah, too, was despondent, but she understood her son's desire to travel.

On the eve of Kevin's departure Sarah and Niall were lying in bed. "Do you think the English army will come here?" she asked him.

He tried to offer her a smile but it was a poor attempt. "I don't believe so, my love. I think we will be safe in Bicksby. From all I have heard, they seem to be concentrating on making changes on the east coast, not here. That's a long way from us."

Sarah hoped he was right.

IRELAND, 1614

Sarah walked into the doctor's house and looked for Marie Boyle. Catherine's mother had been assisting Doctor Dumont for nearly seven years now, starting soon after her daughter had left with Kevin. Her job in the office changed from day to day. Today she was screening patients as they entered.

Marie smiled when she saw Sarah. "Good morning, Sarah, how nice to see you. You're not sick, are you?"

"No," replied Sarah, "nothing wrong with me except a few old bones that seem to want to ache all the time. How are you, Marie?"

"Oh, okay I guess. The days seem to fade one into the other lately, but it's quiet here today, which is nice." There was a sense of melancholy in her voice, and Sarah knew Marie's life just wasn't the same without her only child. *Thank goodness I had other children to look after once Kevin left*, she thought.

"Have you heard from Catherine lately?" This was the reason for Sarah's visit. Marie heard from her daughter much more often than Sarah heard from Kevin. Traders from Europe would come through a number of times a month to visit John Boyle's glove making business. Many carried word from the couple as to how they were doing. In seven years only four people had ever stopped by Sarah's home with word from Kevin. Fortunately, Marie was good at sharing news and letters with her.

"Oh yes," Marie's eyes widened and her smile lit up when she spoke, "just the other day a man came by. He brought a letter from Catherine. I'm sorry I don't have it on me."

"How are they?" Sarah asked.

"They seem well. They like their new home in Italy."

Sarah was pleased to hear the news.

After telling Sarah all she could about the letter, Marie asked, "How are your other children doing?"

"Well, let's see. Myles and his wife are doing well." Myles had married five years ago and moved to Dublin to work on the farm that his father-in-law had given to them as a wedding gift. "Sean is still with us, of course, and seems content. He knows how much we rely on him, since Niall's leg has become worse."

"Still no lady in his life?" asked Marie. "How is that possible for such a handsome young man?"

Sarah simply shrugged.

"And Nuala, do you ever hear from her?"

"She sends word occasionally. You know how close she was with Sean. Nothing lately." Nuala had left the house three years ago—for London, of all places. She had dropped the O'Donnell name, fearing it would cause her nothing but trouble in England, and taken back her original name of Whalen. She never told what she did in London, but she seemed extremely happy.

"Perhaps the reason Sean is not married is that no one can replace Nuala in his eyes," said Marie.

"I think you're right. In fact I'm a bit surprised he has never gone after her."

Marie smiled. "I imagine he still thinks of her as a sister."

Sarah finished her visit with Marie and headed back towards the buggy. Sean had been doing some shopping and should be finished by now. She had to wait about ten minutes, and then saw him running towards her. Oddly, he wasn't carrying any supplies at all. Sarah wondered what he had been up to all this time.

"Mother," he called as he approached her, nearly out of breath, "they are coming."

"Who's coming, Sean?" she asked, hearing the excitement in his voice.

"The English Army, with the new settlers. Mother, they're coming to take our land."

They raced home to tell Niall.

Sean had been right. Soldiers of the English Army moved into Bicksby just two days later. Within hours they had taken control of the town and everyone in it. Niall kept Sarah and Sean home, avoiding the town. However, Nicholas Fleming, a neighbor who had gone into town to buy some fish, told them what was happening.

"They patrol the streets, groups of eight to ten soldiers everywhere," said Fleming. "They've closed some shops for now, others are still open. They have poor Mister Boyle working double time in his shop, but his wife has been forced out of the doctor's house.

That seems to be their headquarters. Most people are staying home as much as possible."

Niall noticed the empty wagon. "I don't see your fish."

"Aye, they told me I wouldn't need any fish today. It's not like I was going to argue with them."

After Fleming left, Niall turned to Sarah. "We need to hide the valuables," he said. "They may not let us take anything, and if they do they will probably search us first."

"Where will we go?" Sarah asked.

"From what I've heard, they're driving people towards the moors and bogs, hoping to starve them to death. Don't worry, we will think of something."

Around midnight that evening, Niall and Sarah went outside and sat on the bench. He carried a large metal box which had a smaller box inside. "I waterproofed it as best I could," he said. "I'm going to bury this under the boulder. Four, maybe five feet deep if I can. Keep your eyes open. I don't want anyone to see me."

He worked quickly. The ground beneath the rock was damp from the spring rains, but full of stones. He was able to bury the box about four feet down. "It will have to do," he said. He quickly chiseled a small line on the boulder, signaling where the box lay. "I'll show Sean where it is buried tomorrow, and we will have to get word to Myles and Kevin. Hopefully one of us will be able to return someday and dig it up."

"All our years together," Sarah declared, "and our valuables fit into a box so small." She gave him a forlorn smile, knowing he was the only valuable she cared about, and knowing he felt the same about her. Yet she felt a sense of sadness also. She knew her emerald and ruby necklace was in that box.

Two days later they sat on the same bench and watched as three ships pulled into the bay. They carried the foreigners, some English but mostly Scottish, who would be given their homes and lands.

Niall turned to Sarah as they watched. "I'm sorry," he said. "It looks like Padraig was right all those years ago. I never thought they would bother with a small town like Bicksby. We should have left when we had the chance."

She would not let him take all the blame. "Not your fault, my love. We made the decision together, and I would make the same choice again. We have had seven more wonderful years here."

The next morning Niall, Sarah, and Sean stood in their front yard and watched as a large group rode up the winding road to their home. Two dozen soldiers were escorting five wagons that held four to eight people each. They stopped when they reached the O'Donnell home.

"What do you want?" Niall demanded, although everyone knew.

The officer in charge was quick to reply. "Be quiet. This land is no longer yours. You have two minutes to gather your things and get out."

They knew it was foolish to argue, but it was not in Niall's nature to resist peacefully. "This land has been ..." he started to say, but was cut off.

"Silence! Your time is running." The Scots on the nearest wagon were already beginning to unload their belongings. Sean ran into the house to gather the bags they had already packed, knowing what was coming.

"I understand an O'Donnell lives up here," the officer said. "Would that be you?"

"My name is Niall O'Donnell." Sarah watched with admiration as her husband proudly spoke.

"Take him!" the officer shouted to his troops. Immediately, two horsemen rode up to Niall, dismounted and grabbed him. They dragged him to the wagon the Scots had just vacated and began tying him up.

Sarah was stunned. "What are you doing?" she screamed, as a soldier held her back.

"Shut up, woman, or you may join him."

Sarah would have gladly joined him, but Sean, rushing back outside at the sound of the commotion, took hold of her and wouldn't let go.

"Your time is up," the officer said. With that, the troops moved forward and began forcing them up the road towards their neighbors, who would soon share a similar fate.

Sarah fell to the ground, tears streaming down her face, inconsolable at the thought of losing Niall.

"Move!" yelled one of the soldiers, holding a sword to her breast.

Sean lifted her up and they began walking, but her eyes never left Niall. She called his name over and over in a plaintive wail, but soon the wagon carrying him headed back towards town. She watched as he fell out of sight.

She never saw him again.

They wandered for days, pushed inland, their numbers increasing by the hour. Sean, nearly twenty-four years old now, became one of their leaders. Sarah walked in a daze, haunted by the loss of her husband and fearing what the English would do to him. They were herded to an uninhabitable piece of land and told to stay there. Sean knew it would be the death of them if they did, so one night he and Sarah, along with Nicholas Fleming and his wife Davilla, escaped. They traveled south towards Sligo, hoping they could settle there and begin again.

Sarah had no desire to do anything without Niall. She cried every night for weeks. If not for Sean, she would have gone insane. She wasn't sure she could make it to Sligo. She was fifty-one years old now. Her legs ached from the constant pounding they took. The pace was slow, Davilla being in no better shape than Sarah was, yet they walked most of the daylight hours. It took them nearly a month, but they finally arrived in late May. Sarah had lost thirty pounds, and went from a strong, healthy woman to a thin, weak one who had trouble standing. She would not have lasted much longer had they not arrived when they did.

Sarah lived for six more years. She slowly regained her strength and eventually found work in a butcher shop, but in October of 1620, she caught cold. Soon her sniffles turned into a hacking cough, then a chest thumping rattle. Fever set in, and Sarah knew the end was near. It did not bother her. Life in Sligo was satisfactory, but it was not Bicksby. She missed Niall. He had been the love of her life, and always would be. She wondered if he was already on the other side, waiting to greet her. She knew Sean would miss her, but he was a strong man, and he would survive.

One morning, with death close at hand, she asked him what he would do when she was gone.

His answer was simple. "I will try to find father."

The answer pleased her, although she saw the danger in it. "He would be so proud of you, Sean."

He smiled, though tears welled up in his eyes.

She smiled back at him, her hand brushing his cheek. Then she closed her eyes, never to open them again.

Chapter Ten

Jill sat up on the couch. She felt a sense of sadness she had not felt in years. The regressions seemed so real. She had watched her death, and it resonated within her. Had she once been Sarah O'Donnell? She was beginning to wonder if it were all true.

Simon gazed at her with knowing eyes. Witnessing your death in a prior life had different effects on people. He had been through it many times. One lady, after viewing her passing, immediately had said, "Wow, that was so neat." Most, like Jill, sat reflectively for a few moments gathering their thoughts. "How are you?" he asked.

She looked up slowly, stared at his face for a moment, and then looked back down.

Finally, she said, "I feel heartbroken."

"You had a peaceful passing," Simon said.

"What?" She looked up again, then attempted a smile. "Oh no, not that. That was fine." Her voice was slow, measured. "It was just like you said it would be. I was floating above my body, just watching. There was no pain at all."

"That's excellent, Jill. So you feel heartbroken over Niall?"

"They just took him away." Her voice grew louder as she spoke. "I never saw him again."

"Yes, you were very agitated at that point. I almost brought you back. Fortunately, your story moved on rather quickly and you settled down." He poured her a glass of water. "Here, this will help you get back to the present." He walked behind his desk and sat down. "When you are ready, come and take a seat, if you would."

She took a long drink, finishing half the glass, and then went and sat in the chair opposite him, curious. After the other sessions, she had simply left. She assumed their sessions were over now, and he just wanted to say goodbye. "What's up?" she asked.

"Jill, you have done remarkably well in your regressions. Better, quite frankly, than anyone who has ever come to see me."

"Really?" She could see that he was pleased. "Thank you. It has been an extraordinary experience. Astonishing, actually."

"I wonder if you would like to carry on with the regressions?"

Jill hadn't thought about that. "You mean go to another lifetime?"

"Yes, I do. Tell me, has your belief in the validity of reincarnation changed at all since you have been coming here?"

"I ..." she stammered, and turned her eyes away. "I'm not sure."

"You said something interesting in your regression. I wonder if you recall what it was."

She looked puzzled. "What was that?"

"You said you wondered if Niall was waiting for you on the other side."

She lifted her head slightly and looked into Simon's eyes. "I remember that."

"So it seems that Sarah believed in life after death, if not reincarnation."

"Hmm," Jill said. If she had been Sarah, that meant she had once believed in the very thing she was so dead set against now. How could that happen? She thought about it a moment longer, then looked at Simon and said, "Yes, I would like to come back again."

"Wonderful. I was hoping you would agree. You do realize we are finished with your Irish lifetime?"

"We couldn't try to find out what happened to Niall, could we?"

"Sarah obviously doesn't know," he said, and Jill realized the truth of that. "I want to ask you about the date you gave me. You evidently read up on Irish history and thought that date was important."

"I did. I originally wanted to know about the war. As I read ahead I saw the part about the O'Donnell's fleeing. It was called The Flight of the Earls. I assumed we had sailed to France with everyone else."

"So now you are surprised to find that you didn't."

"Yes." She paused for a moment to finish her water, and then said, "Do you think I will show up in Ireland again?"

Simon gave her a bemused look. *She still wants to find Niall,* he thought. "Impossible to say. Some return to the same country in their next life, but most seem to move around. In the future, however, I would ask that you not look up anything in advance of your regression. We don't want to taint it in any way."

"I was worried about that. Sorry. Wherever I come back, I hope I'm fighting the English army somewhere. Right now I feel this real desire for revenge."

He nodded, but did not smile. "Karma can be an interesting thing, Jill. Eventually the cycle of revenge must be broken, or you may find yourself playing that game forever."

"Maybe," she said, "but right now I'd like to find that officer who arrested Niall and string him up."

"Perhaps in your next life you did."

Simon stood up to shake her hand and said, "Have Melinda make an appointment for you for three weeks from today."

"Three weeks!" she exclaimed.

He looked at her, mildly amused. "Vacation," he said. "The office will be closed for two weeks." *Two weeks ago you didn't want to be here*, he thought, *and now you can't wait to come back.*

Jill was thinking the exact same thing. She wondered what she would do for the next three weeks. One thing was certain. She would try again to find Niall.

Simon was humming to himself as he removed Jill's tape from the stereo. He hadn't been sure she would want to come back and was happy that she'd agreed to do so. She was the finest regression client he had ever worked with, and he would have been deeply disappointed had she decided not to return. Some people were barely able to recall anything about their past lives. Others flitted from one lifetime to another, not stopping long enough to get any worthwhile information out. Still others stayed in one life, but extracting any data from them was like pulling teeth. Then there were the successes—people who gave a strong accounting of their previous lives and made it all worthwhile. Jill was one of those.

After locking her tape in the cabinet, Simon sat at his desk and pulled Jill's questionnaire out of her folder. He was surprised that she was still unsure about the validity of her experience. What was it going to take? Of course, most folks who came into his office for a regression were believers to begin with. Many were New Agers, as Jill called them. She was different. Jill was certainly not a believer. Very few people came into his office that were as skeptical as she was. He'd been surprised when she came back a second time, but now she seemed almost excited about returning. Was she ready to accept her past life as true? Her grief at losing Niall and her desire for revenge made him wonder. Perhaps she did believe and simply couldn't admit it to herself.

As he scanned Jill's answers on the sheet, one popped out at him right away. To the question, *Which foreign countries would you most like to visit?* Jill's first answer had been Ireland. Of course, she was of Irish heritage, so that may only be logical. Still, it was interesting.

His phone buzzed, and Melinda told him his wife was on line one. They had two weeks off starting Sunday. The first week they were vacationing in Hawaii, their first real getaway in five years. The second week he would catch up on his backlog of paperwork. He picked up the phone and said, "Hi, honey."

What am I going to do for three weeks? Jill pondered the question as she drove home, then laughed to herself. Work, laundry, feed the kids; same as always. She was somewhat dumbfounded by her apparent turnaround. Two weeks ago she considered her visit to Simon a waste of time. A small part of her still felt that way, yet now her mind was being tugged at by an idea that wouldn't let go. What if the regressions were true, and what if all the other things Lauren had been telling her about were also true? Had she really been a close-minded person all these years?

She discovered she had no answers to her questions.

She called Lauren that evening and caught her just as Lauren was leaving for a yoga class. "Can we get together soon?" asked Jill.

"I'm not sure when," said Lauren. "Business is still booming, and Bill and I are going away for the day Friday. Actually we won't be back until late Saturday."

"Aren't you working Saturday?"

"No, I cleared my calendar for the day, so Bill and I could spend some time together. Let's go out Sunday night?"

"Not till then, huh?" Disappointed, Jill said, "Okay. I'll let Tony keep the boys until ten Sunday. That should give us enough time."

After talking to Lauren, Jill decided to start looking for Niall again. Surprisingly, the computer was free. The boys were watching a Harry Potter movie on television that she knew they had seen at least a half-dozen times. She searched for two hours, using old and new websites, but had no luck. None of the Niall O'Donnell's she found were hers, although she discovered Niall was a fairly common name in Ireland. Apparently her Niall had not been enough of an historical figure to make the history books. She also tried to find any mention of her Irish children, but again came up empty. She still could not verify anything about herself or her family, and of course there was no Bicksby in Ireland. She still wasn't sure what to believe.

Chapter Eleven

Jill woke up Sunday morning anxious to see Lauren, so when the phone rang at nine-thirty and the caller ID. told her who it was, Jill was instantly worried. Instead of hello, she answered by saying, "Don't you dare tell me you are canceling our date."

Lauren giggled into the phone. "No such luck," she replied. "In fact, I'm expanding it."

"What do you mean?"

"Well, you haven't met Bill yet, so I thought I'd bring him along."

"Oh." Jill really wanted the chance to talk to Lauren alone, but said, "That's okay, I guess."

"And he has a friend."

"Oh no!" Jill yelled into the phone. "You are not setting me up on a blind date."

"Hey, it's how I met Bill," Lauren said. "Maybe his friend will turn out to be your Niall."

It took some coaxing from Lauren, but Jill finally agreed. She had no illusions that finding the person who once was Niall would be this easy, but if she was ever going to find him, she had to get out there and try. Two years without a date was long enough.

That evening Jill heard a car pull into her driveway just as she finished getting ready. Lauren came to the front door to get her. As Jill came out she saw two men standing by the car.

"Are you ready?" asked Lauren. "He is kind of cute."

Jill couldn't believe how nervous she was. She had forgotten how difficult dating could be. "Ready as I ever will be," she said.

They walked out to the car and Lauren made the introductions. Her boyfriend Bill was a handsome man with a smile that could light up a room.

"And this," Lauren said, "is Dusty."

Dusty? What sort of name was that? Jill shook his hand. He was on the short side, maybe five-foot eight, with brown hair and eyes, and he didn't look like he weighed much more than Jill. Lauren thought he was cute?

"What's your real name, Dusty?" was all she could think to say. It turned out that was his real name.

The night was a total disaster.

Lauren called first thing Monday morning. "Sorry about that," she said. "You had a horrible time, didn't you?"

"It showed, I take it?" Jill was on her second cup of coffee, yet still felt half asleep.

"I guess Dusty wasn't the one."

"Not even close. Dating has to be better than that," Jill said. "All I wanted was to talk to you about my regression, and some other things that you are into now."

Lauren apologized about five more times and agreed to come over the house that night.

She arrived just after seven. Jill had a glass of wine waiting for her, and after chatting with Mark and Bret for a few minutes, they went up to Jill's bedroom so they could talk in private.

"I'm not ready to tell my kids this isn't the first time I have been their mother," laughed Jill. "So tell me, was that guy really a friend of Bill's? Because Bill seemed like a great guy, and Dusty didn't appear to be anyone Bill would really associate with."

"I'm sorry, Jill. Dusty is a customer at Bill's photo studio and has been bugging him to help him find a date, so Bill just took the opportunity. Don't worry, I told him never to do that again with one of my friends."

"Thank you," said Jill. "Apology accepted, and no more double dates."

Jill spent the next half hour catching Lauren up on all that had been revealed in her regression. She was surprised to find herself still getting choked up when she told about Niall's arrest and never seeing him again. She even noticed Lauren wiping an eye.

"You did a great job remembering all that. Simon must really be pleased. So are you going back again?"

"I am. We're going to try to find another lifetime."

"Aha. It sounds to me like someone is hooked." Lauren had an I-told-you-so look on her face.

Jill raised her eyes to the ceiling, then turned to Lauren and said, "Okay, you might be right. It all seems so real when I'm seeing it. It's like I'm there, and I can hear the people talking. It's subtle, almost like whispers."

"Whispers through time," said Lauren.

"I may, let me stress *may*, be coming around to seeing things your way. I must admit, it is fun to fantasize about. Are you ever going back?"

Lauren gave a small shrug. "I don't know. I liked what I found out. I'm not sure I want to ruin it by going back again to find out I was some kind of ax murderer or something."

Jill was surprised. "Come on. I'm sure you were never an ax murderer, or anything close to it."

"Jill, if we have lived one other life, we have probably lived dozens, perhaps hundreds of lives. I guarantee you we were not good in all of them, or even half of them."

Jill suddenly remembered what Simon had said about karma, and decided to ask Lauren about it. "Doesn't karma mean what goes around comes around? So if I'm mean to the boys tonight some kid will be mean to me sooner or later?"

"In its simplest form, yes." Lauren thought for a second, then continued, "Karma has to do with all your lifetimes. Maybe in a previous life Niall had been a sheriff, and had arrested that officer. Now in Ireland the officer returns the favor. I kill you in this life; you kill me in the next. It's a vicious circle, and it goes on until someone finally grows in spirit enough to break the cycle. They say we come here to learn lessons, and that would certainly be one of them."

Jill thought she understood.

"It also goes beyond the physical," Lauren continued. "The spiritual, mental, and emotional parts of your makeup are included as well. Positive thoughts produce positive results. Negative thoughts produce negative results. Good conduct produces good karma, and bad conduct …"

"… produces bad karma."

"Yes. Whether in this lifetime, or another one down the road. Before you get too caught up in all of this, though, understand what is most important is to live the life you are living now. Even the Buddha cautioned that thinking too much about past lives could make you stray from what you are doing in your current life."

"I think I get it," said Jill.

They talked a while longer before Bret interrupted them. He wanted to use the computer, and Mark had been on it all night. Jill knew the feeling. By the time she sorted out that problem, Lauren was ready to leave.

"Listen Jill, Thursday night at the church we are having a channeling session. Why don't you come and see what it's like?"

"Channeling? Is that where the ghost of someone's dead great-grandfather speaks to you?"

"Actually, the lady who does the channeling brings through the spirit of Saint Martin de Porres. She has been channeling him for nearly thirty years. She's good. Believe me, I've seen fakes, and she is not one of them. Just come and see for yourself."

Jill agreed. If she was going to open herself up to new and different ideas, she figured she might as well begin now.

Lauren said, "Just try to think of two or three questions you want to ask."

"About what?"

"It can be anything you want an answer to. You need to be specific. A general question will get you a general answer."

"What do you normally ask about?" Jill wanted to know.

"Oh, different things." Lauren thought about it for a moment. "I've asked about my business. Sometimes I ask about family members who may be sick or in trouble. Once I lost a ring and asked him to find it for me."

"No kidding. Did he?"

"It was the craziest thing," said Lauren. "Martin said he would return it to me. I thought 'great' but I didn't know what to expect. I went home and forgot about it. Three days later I found it on my kitchen counter. I had cleaned that spot a dozen times and it hadn't been there, and then all of a sudden there it was. It was weird."

"That is kind of freaky," Jill said.

"I thought so too at first, but the other side is there to help us. Believe me; I put a lot more stock into what Martin said to me after that."

With that, Lauren was off, and Jill had more to ponder.

Chapter Twelve

Jill was reading the new James Patterson novel when Lauren arrived just before six-thirty Thursday night. She still wasn't sure what she wanted to ask at the channeling. "What do most people want to know?" she asked Lauren as they made their way to the church.

"Many people just ask for a message. Some people want to know who their spirit guides are."

"Spirit guides?"

"Sure. When you decide to come over to this side, you choose spirit guides to help you accomplish what you came here to do. You also have a guardian angel who tries to protect you. You know, those accidents you don't know how you avoided but did. That's your guardian angel watching out for you."

"How would knowing who my spirit guides are help me?" Jill asked.

Lauren was pleased. Rather than dismiss the idea of spirit guides, Jill had asked a very good question. "They help mostly in meditation. You can talk to them any time of day, but if you are meditating you're much more likely to receive an answer. Some people may actually hear them, but most of us will get a feeling, an impression, or maybe a sudden idea."

"So you know your spirit guide, then?" asked Jill.

"I'm aware of three. We have many guides."

"So who are these three guides of yours?"

"First," said Lauren, "I have an old Native American guide who goes by the name of Red Feather. He was the first one I discovered, back when I was about twelve. His answers come in the form of images, and I almost always receive them soon after asking my question. Then I have a young Scandinavian woman named Naomi, who is particularly good with money questions. Last month I learned of a third guide named Sam, who has apparently entered my realm to help me with the studies I'm beginning on healing. You see, some guides are with you your entire life, while others come in to help with a specific matter, then leave when you have completed whatever it was."

The drive to West Street only took fifteen minutes. When they arrived Jill still had no idea what questions she would ask.

Much of the empty department store was still just open space. However, Jill could see where the services were held. The church had taken up one section by the front and turned it into a cozy little place of worship. A long folding table centered in the front acted as an altar, with a chair on either side. There were benches and folding chairs for the congregation to sit on. Jill noticed the altar had a number of different items on it, including a picture of Jesus, a Buddha statue, what looked like some American Indian artifacts, and a variety of crystals.

The department store had included a small food court which made it very convenient for the church to have a coffee hour after services. The booths that Jill remembered being there had been torn out and replaced with round tables and chairs so people could mingle easily. It was here that the channeling would take place.

"Follow me," said Lauren. "I want to introduce you to Reverend Doran." They walked up to a short, rotund woman and Lauren made the introductions. Reverend Doran seemed to be a jovial lady who was pleased to see a new face.

"Welcome," she said. "Please call me Brenda."

Brenda was barely five feet tall, with curly brown hair that was just starting to turn grey. Her eyes were a shimmering greenish-yellow. Jill guessed her age to be near sixty. She was wearing a long flowing white dress with a floral design on the bottom. This was someone Jill instantly thought she could trust, and she realized she hadn't thought that about anyone in a long time.

Five minutes later Brenda invited everyone to take a seat. Lauren guided Jill over to the left-hand side of the area. Brenda and another woman sat in front, facing them.

"That's her best friend Kathy," Lauren said. "Kathy will direct the questioning. She usually starts on this side. That's why I sat here. I hope you have your questions ready, because she is probably going to start with you."

"What?" Jill quietly said. "Thanks a lot. I was hoping to see how this works first."

Lauren smiled brightly. "Just jump in with both feet."

"I see we have some new people here," said Brenda. "How many of you have never been to a channeling?"

Jill looked around the room and counted fifteen people. Two people besides Jill raised their hands.

"Wonderful," said Brenda. "I will give you a little overview of what will happen. I channel an entity who in his last lifetime on earth was known as Saint Martin de Porres. He lived from 1569 to 1639. His story is fascinating, though I won't go into it tonight, other than to say he was well known for such things as bi-location, levitation, and miraculous healing. The church canonized him back in 1962. However, he prefers that you just call him Martin. A saint is not how he thinks about himself, as we are all equal in the eyes of God."

Jill found herself listening intently to Brenda. She was nervous about what she would ask, yet happy that she had come. She thought this might be extremely interesting.

Brenda surveyed the room. "When he first comes through," she said, "Martin will give a short message which he believes is important for us to hear. Many times it is about current world events. Other times it is a lesson he wishes to teach. When he is finished, he will ask for questions." She motioned to Kathy. "Kathy will direct the questioning. You may each ask two questions the first time around, and if we have time we will go around again, one question each, until Martin decides it is time to go. Any questions?"

A young man in the middle of the room asked "What happens to you? Does Martin take over your body?"

"Good question. My spirit steps aside when Martin comes in. That's the best way I can explain it to you. He will speak to you using my vocal chords, which he will control. Because his spirit vibrates at a higher rate than mine, he will become uncomfortable after a while and will have to leave. It will still be my voice," Brenda continued, "but you will notice a slight change to it when he talks. We tape each session, and the distinction shows up clearly on the tape. I need the tapes to find out what went on in the session, because I have no idea until I hear it."

There were no more queries from the audience. Brenda said goodbye and slipped into a meditative state. Less than two minutes later, a voice came through her.

"Good evening. This is Martin."

The audience said "Good evening" back to him.

Jill sat listening intently as Martin spoke through Brenda. The voice was hers, yet it wasn't. It was deeper and less forceful than her voice had been. She tried to keep track of the message Martin was giving about charity and being a servant, but her mind was racing. Is this real? What was she going to ask him?

She told herself to pay attention, but try as she might, Jill had a hard time focusing on his words. She attempted to calm herself

92

with a few deep breaths, taken as quietly as she could. Finally, feeling a bit more composed, she told herself once again to listen to the message that was being given.

"… please be kind to one another. The fortunes of your world depend upon it." Martin paused for a few seconds, and then said, "I will take questions."

What? Did he say questions? Jill was overtaken with alarm as Kathy turned to look at her. She nodded at Jill, who found herself tongue-tied.

"Say hello and tell him your name," whispered Lauren.

"Umm, yes, uh Martin," she stammered, "my name is Jill." Get a grip, she told herself.

"Yes, good evening," said Martin. His voice was calm, steady. "You are a new one, I believe."

"What?"

Lauren leaned over. "He means you are a first-timer."

"Oh, yes."

"Relax, my child. We are all friends here. What would you like to ask me?"

Jill took a deep breath. Finally, a thought came to her. "Martin, have I had many past lives? Is there such a thing?"

He spoke softly. "Yes, there is such a thing as past lives. We have the opportunity to live many lives, and you have done so. You have had dozens of lives. Do you understand?"

"Yes, thank you." Jill realized her question had been too general in nature. Now she knew what she wanted to ask next. "I have been told that I lived in Ireland around the year 1600. Can you verify that and tell me something about that life, if it is true?"

"I see this has been on your mind a great deal lately. You recalled your life in Ireland on your own. No one told you. From what I can see your recall has been quite accurate." Martin paused, as if he were reviewing Jill's previous life. "That was a good lifetime for you. You were honest, hard-working, and loyal. You loved your family very much, and they loved you. There was a great bond between you and your husband. You have carried many of those qualities over into this life. Do you understand?"

She wanted to ask more, but remembering the two question rule she just said, "Yes, thank you Martin."

Lauren was up next. She just asked for a message from Martin.

"Ah yes, my friend Lauren. I see that work is still busy. It will become more so." Lauren groaned. "You are about to reach a point where you will have to make a decision. How large do you want your business to grow? I would urge you to remember to take time for yourself. You understand what I am saying, yes?"

"Oh yes," laughed Lauren. "Tell me, Martin, have I met my soul mate?"

Jill sat up, anxious to hear the answer.

"The true meaning of a soul mate is much deeper, much broader than the way it is used on your planet. Perhaps someday I shall speak on the subject and try to clear up your misconceptions. However, I understand the question the way you mean it. You have met someone new, yes?"

"Yes I have," said Lauren.

"And you want to know if he is *the one*." The audience, all listening intently, gave a chuckle. "I understand. I am, however, loath to answer that question directly. We on this side are not allowed to interfere with your free will. Let me say your soul mate could be a sibling, a child, anyone in your circle of family or friends. I would ask you to follow your heart, and perhaps someday you will tell me the answer."

"I understand, Martin," said a disappointed Lauren. "Thank you."

The questioning went around the room. A friend of Lauren's named Sandy came in late and sat down behind them. Jill was hoping she would be allowed to ask another question. Suddenly she had a hundred questions, but when her turn did come again only one seemed important. "Martin, I was separated from my husband in that Irish lifetime we spoke about earlier. Can you tell me what happened to him after he was taken away?"

"Still living in the past, I see," Martin said as the audience again chuckled. He was quiet for a moment as he searched for the answer. Finally, he said "Yes, I have it here. Your husband was taken by ship to London and put in prison. It was a hard time for him. He missed you greatly, yet it was the thought of you which kept him going." He stopped again. Everyone in the room now sat spellbound by the story of Jill's past. Suddenly, Martin let out a quiet "ah," then continued.

"There was a young lady in London who was close to your husband. She helped him attempt to escape. Unfortunately, they were both caught. They had harsh penalties back in those times, I am afraid, and both of their lives came to an end."

"They were hung?" Jill had no idea where that thought had come from, but she asked it as though she knew.

"Yes."

Jill sat stunned. Nuala! He had to be talking about Nuala. In her heart she knew what Martin said was true, yet hearing it made her shudder.

"You are very much caught up in this Irish lifetime of yours," said Martin. "That is all well and good as far as it goes. We can learn from our past lives, yet it is important to concentrate on the life that you live now. I particularly want to stress to you," he paused, then went on, "you need to be aware of your surroundings. This is very important."

"I will," Jill said, not sure what he was talking about.

Ten minutes later, the session ended. Martin gave the group a blessing and said goodbye.

Brenda's eyes fluttered open. They had been closed the entire time Martin was speaking. "What did I miss?" she asked.

"Karen's going to have a boy," Kathy told her. A young black girl, Karen had recently found out she was pregnant, and had asked Martin if it would be a boy or a girl. Other members of the group gathered around Brenda and told her what Martin had said to them.

Jill and Lauren chatted with Sandy as they waited to say good-bye to Brenda. When they reached her, Brenda said, "Sandy, where did you come from?"

"I snuck in late," Sandy said, and Jill realized Brenda really did not know Sandy had come in.

Brenda asked Jill how she enjoyed her first channeling.

"It was fascinating," Jill replied. "I received confirmation of something that I had been doing recently."

"That's nice to hear. I'll be interested to find out what it is when I listen to the tape."

"You really don't know anything that was said here tonight?" Jill asked.

"Not a word." Brenda gave them all a hug, and Jill and Lauren headed for the door.

"You're coming around," Lauren said to her as they arrived at the car. "I'll have you believing in ghosts in no time."

Perhaps you will, thought Jill.

Chapter Thirteen

Jill awoke early on the morning of her appointment with Simon. She had spent the past few days debating the merits of the channeling session. Was it real? She had never believed in psychics, tarot cards, or anything else of that nature. Yet she did believe in Brenda, who seemed to be a warm, caring lady. Most of all Jill believed because Brenda had told her about things she could not possibly have known.

She quietly walked to the kitchen so as not to wake the boys and made herself a pot of coffee. She was not surprised she couldn't sleep. Her three-week wait was finally over. She was anxious to find where the next installment would take her and whether she would find Niall again. True or not, Jill was hooked, and she was starting to believe that maybe the regressions were true.

The last week had passed ever so slowly. She had concentrated on spending more quality time with Bret and Mark. They had gone to the movies on a school night, which they never did. She had taken them bowling. Last night they even went out for pizza rather than making it at home. The boys seemed to appreciate the extra attention. Mark had cleaned his room one day without being asked, and Bret had given her a goodnight hug three nights in a row.

Jill had been unable to hook up with Lauren except for the day of her massage a week ago, when they had talked about the channeling session. Lauren swore again that Brenda was on the up-and-up, and Jill decided to accept that the session was real.

She thought of Niall and smiled. Her sadness at how he had been torn away from her had passed. Now she remembered the love and joy they had shared, and laughed when thinking about how they had met. It was as though they knew they were meant to be together. We recognize each other on some subconscious level, she thought; spirit to spirit. How many times, she asked herself, have I met someone and instantly felt a rapport with them. Simon had said your circle of friends stay with you from lifetime to lifetime. Were these friends from the past she was running into?

Jill noticed a pamphlet lying on the counter as she poured a second cup of coffee. It was from a place called The Inner Peace Sanctuary. Lauren had given it to her last week, asking her to look it over to see if anything interested her. The pamphlet listed classes for yoga, chakra therapy, acupuncture, and Reiki healing. There was a book review section covering new releases for children and adults. More classes on shaman training, auras, drumming and crystals. She even noticed classes on channeling and regressions. Jill realized there were many subjects that she knew nothing about. Finally she saw a class on meditation which met every Wednesday night. Lauren had told her she should start with meditation. Maybe this was the answer. She checked out the address and the hours the sanctuary was open and decided to go over after her regression.

Jill arrived at the doctor's office at quarter till nine, and was happy to find the lights on and the door open.

Melinda was sitting at her desk when Jill walked in. "Hey Jill," she said. Melinda was beaming.

"Hi there," said Jill. "You seem happy. I take it vacation was good for you."

Melinda's face lit up even more. "Oh, it was fabulous. I went to Aruba with three of my girlfriends. One of them owns a condo down there, so all I had to do was pay airfare. We had a great time."

"Wow, that sounds nice. I'm jealous."

"It was fantastic. I didn't want to come back. Then last week I just chilled out, put in a few hours here, and now I'm good to go for another six months." Melinda looked at Jill and asked, "So, did you miss us?"

"You wouldn't believe," Jill said, shaking her head. "I didn't think this day would ever come." She saw the door to the back room was closed and asked, "Someone in there?"

Melinda nodded yes. "New client. Seems like a nice young girl. Relax, you'll be on time."

Jill looked at the magazines on the table but decided to pass. Instead, she closed her eyes and did some breathing exercises. When the door to Simon's office opened, the girl came out. No more than twenty, thought Jill. Imagine what I might know if I had started at that age.

The girl smiled at her, then turned to Melinda. "I'm going to come back," she said. "This was very exciting. I can't wait to find out more." The girl made her appointment and left.

Five minutes later Simon came out. "Ah, Jill," he said, "how have you been?"

"I think she missed us," said Melinda. "You'd better take care of her right away."

Jill felt the makings of a blush coming on. She just said, "Hi, Simon. It's good to see you again."

"Melinda always has a good sense about these things," he said, "so come on in."

They walked into his office and Jill went straight for the couch. The doctor sat behind his desk and opened her file. "Last time we finished your Irish adventure. You have indicated that you wish to experience another lifetime. That's still the case, I take it?"

Jill simply said, "Yes."

"Any particular time frame you want to shoot for?"

"Just the next life after Ireland, if we can."

"Well," he replied, "if that is where your mind is focused, we should be able to do that. Shall we begin, then?"

Jill didn't answer. She simply lay down on the couch, and soon felt the tension of the last week wash away. Her body slipped into a state of complete relaxation. She listened to the doctor's commands as he brought her under, yet it was as if his voice were a thousand miles away.

She went back. Four years, to a day at the amusement park with Tony and the boys; eighteen years, to a baby shower at the Elks Club for one of her best friends; to the age of three, when her baby sister was born.

"Jill, you are going back to the womb now. You have done this before. It is very easy for you."

"I remember." Her voice sounded almost as distant as his. She paused only for a moment. "I am there now."

"Tell me what is going on, Jill. Are you still at your grandmother's house?"

"No, I'm home now. The time for my birth is close. My mother is on the couch watching television. She is very uncomfortable. She tries not to get up very often, because it's difficult for her. My father is not here, he's working."

"Can you still tell that your parent's want you very much?"

"Oh yes, I know that. I have made a good choice, choosing them as my parents."

"You chose them? Is that how it works, Jill?"

"Of course," she said, as if it should be obvious. "We choose the parents who can best help us learn the lessons we are returning to learn."

"That's very interesting," said Simon. "Now I would like you to go back, farther back. You have told me before about your time in Ireland. Can you go to the life you had after that, the one after Ireland. Do you understand, Jill?"

"Yes, I understand."

"Do that now, Jill." He paused a moment. "Try to find a time in your childhood, a time when you still lived at home with your parents. Take your time, there is no rush."

It took her longer than he expected, but finally she said, "Yes, I have found myself."

He smiled at her choice of words. "Are you a girl in this lifetime, Jill?"

"Yes."

"Tell me what you see around you."

"I'm walking on a bridge, looking all around. There is so much to see here."

Hoping to determine where she was, Simon asked "Do you know the name of the bridge, Jill? Do you see any signs that can help you determine where you are?"

Again he waited as Jill seemed to search for clues. Finally, she said, "There are lots of signs." She paused yet again, and then repeated, "I'm on a bridge. It's crowded with people. People live on the bridge, and there are shops also."

Simon could not recall any bridges in history that people lived on, but history was not his strong suit. "Tell me about one of the shops."

"A mill-something." She tried to say the word again, but failed. "I can only read a little." She was already taking on the characteristics of the girl, her voice even rising in pitch like a little girl's would. "They have a lot of hats in the window."

"A milliner," said Simon. "How old are you, Jill? Can you tell?"

"I'm eight. There's a pastry shop. Everything looks so good. I wish we could go in."

"We? Are you with your parents?"

"No, no parents. There is a little girl with me, just tagging along. She's about five, I guess. I don't know her. She seems very hungry."

"Jill, do you know what your name is?"

"I'm Emily," she said immediately.

"Emily. That is a lovely name. Is there anything you see that might tell you where you are?"

Her head suddenly snapped to the right. "The little girl just tripped a man. He is yelling at us, saying mean things. He says we shouldn't even be allowed on London Bridge."

"So you are in London, Emily," Simon said without realizing he had used her new name.

"London? Yes, that is where I am." She paused. "My father left me here."

"He has let you walk down the bridge while he does an errand?" asked Simon.

"No. He has left me here," she repeated. Then, a few seconds later, she added, "I'm a throwaway."

Chapter Fourteen

LONDON, 1726

The man's loud, angry voice had frightened them. The little girl was now hiding behind Emily, who turned her attention back to the pastry shop window. Her mouth watered. She was starving, she realized.

The girl tugged on Emily's dress. Her face looked as though it hadn't been washed in weeks and her clothes were filthy. There were knots in her hair, which obviously hadn't been brushed in a long time.

The shopkeeper, who had spotted them before the altercation with the man, now came outside. "You two," he scowled, "get out of here now before I give you a boot on yer bottoms."

The girl turned and ran. Emily stared at the man for a moment, stuck her tongue out at him, and then she ran off too.

It had been nearly an hour since her father had left her at the bridge. She was scared but also excited. She had never seen anything like this bridge.

Emily had been born and raised in Guilford, south of London. Her father called himself a trader of various and sundry goods. Most of the people in town called him a junk dealer. Her mother was a beautiful woman with rich black hair, deep blue eyes, and smooth, soft skin.

Ten days ago her mother had died.

No one could say exactly why. She was only twenty-seven years old, yet her heart apparently just gave out. One moment she was in the kitchen, cutting vegetables for the soup she was making. As Emily entered the room, her mother turned and gave her a smile, then suddenly set the knife aside and put a hand to her chest. She uttered a small cry, and Emily watched in horror as her mother silently fell. She was dead before her head hit the floor.

Her father, a gruff, sarcastic man, was fifteen years older than her mother. Emily had never particularly liked him and he had no use for her. He put up with her for a week after her mother's funeral, but that was all.

"I can't afford to feed you no more," he had told her. "You will have to make do on your own." Yet he did not want her staying in Guilford where people knew them. His pride was too much for that. So he said, "I'm going to take you to London. There are a great many people there. You should have no trouble finding someone to take care of you."

She was only eight, but she saw through his lie easy enough; out of sight, out of mind. So she lied right back to him, saying, "I'll miss you, father."

This morning they had traveled by buggy to London. Her first view of the city was overwhelming. She had never seen so many people or so many tall buildings. Even the river amazed her. Her father brought the buggy to a halt. "Cross the bridge to the other side. Go now," he said, and she did, never looking back. She car ried a small sack with an extra set of clothes, plus two tomatoes and half a loaf of bread which she had packed the night before after her father had gone to bed.

She caught up to the little girl and asked, "What's your name?"

"Gina."

"Would you like a tomato, Gina?"

The girl's eyes lit up. They walked to an open spot on the bridge and sat down. Emily kept one tomato and gave the other one to Gina. Before she took her second bite, the girl's tomato was gone.

"More," said Gina.

Emily thought about giving her a piece of bread but decided against it. That was all she had left to eat, and she didn't know when she would be able to acquire any more food. "No more," she said.

Gina got up and walked away.

Emily looked at all the tall buildings on the north side of the bridge and decided to head in that direction. She wanted to explore. In all her life she had never been out of Guilford. She could not have imagined a city the size of London even existed. She slowly walked from street to street, taking in all that she could. There were children everywhere, lying in the alleyways, playing in the streets and roaming the city much as she was.

"What's in the sack? You rich?"

The voice came from behind and startled her. "What?" she said, and turned to face a boy who looked about twelve. "Do I look rich to you?"

"Your dress is clean; you're carrying a sack around with you, so maybe you have some money you'd like to share with me."

She didn't like the look on his face. "Money? I have no money. My father just left me here in London and took off." She could see the surprise on his face when she said this.

"So you're a throwaway?"

"A what?"

"A throwaway. Your parents don't want you, so they throw you away."

"My mother loved me," she quickly cried out. Then, quietly, she said, "but she died. My father had no use for me."

His name was Tom and she quickly changed her opinion of him. He stayed with her all afternoon, telling her things she would need to know to survive. While the grownups called them orphans or street urchins, the kids called themselves throwaways. Tom was twelve and had been living on the streets for five years now. Most abandoned children were far younger. Children three, four, five years old were abandoned because their parents couldn't afford them, or because they were ugly, slow-witted, deformed. Disease and starvation were rampant among them, and most would die long before they ever reached Emily's age.

"The kids' only friends are other kids," Tom told her, "but most can barely take care of themselves, let alone help anyone else."

He told Emily that she had two choices; become a member of a group of kids who would work together to find food, mostly by stealing it, or work alone. "Groups have their ways of getting food, but the older kids usually take more than their share," he said. "However, since you are new here, and still look presentable, you may do better working alone at first. People may not realize you're a throwaway by looking at you, so they may be more inclined to give you a handout if you act politely."

Tom showed her around the city, pointing out Saint Paul's Cathedral, the Stock Exchange, and Westminster Abbey. She learned the river running under London Bridge was called the Thames, and he laughed when he realized she hadn't known that.

As the sun began to set, Emily asked Tom, "So where do I go?"

"Stay out of the alleys," he said. "You'd be robbed every night when they see you carrying that sack. In fact, you need to find a place to hide it during the day. Stay off the streets too. Lots of young kids sleep on the sidewalks and in the gutters, but the drunks and the whores are out roaming at night and you can get hurt real bad."

"So where do I go?" she repeated.

"The parks, or down by the river. Those are your best bets. Someplace hidden, if you can."

"Where do you sleep?" she asked.

"Sorry," Tom said, "I don't share that information with anyone, and when you find a good place, you'd better not either. If you ever need to find me, I'm usually in Hyde Park in the morning." He pointed west, but said no more.

Emily thanked him for his help, then watched him go. She was hungry, and needed to find a place to sleep before it became too dark. From what she had seen, she had misgivings about finding a safe place to stay near the river, so she waited until Tom was out of sight and then headed in the same direction.

She came across a park almost immediately, having no idea if it was Hyde Park or not. However, it did have an area of dense trees which she decided to check out. At one point she came across a copse of hedges directly in front of the trees. She didn't think she would find a better spot this late in the day. After making sure no one was watching her, she slipped behind the hedges and found a clearing large enough for her to lie down.

Exhausted, she opened her bag and took out half of the bread. She wished she had something to drink. That would need to be a priority in the morning. As she ate, she wondered what was to become of her now. She thought of her mother and prayed for guidance. Then, with tears running down her cheeks, she closed her eyes and fell fast asleep.

Emily learned a great deal about London in the weeks that followed. The west side, where she had slept that first night and continued to do so, was populated by the middle and upper class. The lower class lived on the east side.

The area she now called home was St. James Park, which turned out to be a favorite spot for late night amorous affairs of the locals.

While none had yet stumbled upon Emily, she had heard more moaning and heavy breathing than she cared to admit.

Tom had been right about her appearance being a help to her. She stayed on the west side at first and found enough vendors and shopkeepers willing to give her a handout to keep her going. Three weeks into her adventure, however, she knew she was beginning to look a bit ragged. She tried to change her clothes every day, washing them as best as she could whenever it rained. It wouldn't be long though, before it became obvious to all that she was just another homeless waif.

The next morning she awoke starving, so she headed for the closest square where the vendors set up shop. Emily would ask each one if there was some job she could do or perhaps a message she could run for them. It rarely worked, but when it did she might receive a piece of cheese or a crust of bread, which she would hide in the pocket of her dress if she didn't eat it right away. Most of the time she would receive a piece of uncooked fruit, such as an apple, which most people wouldn't eat for fear it would make them ill. Following Tom's advice, she never carried her sack with her. Instead, she hid it where she slept.

Now, as she turned a corner, she heard the call, "Vegetables. Get your vegetables. Fresh today, don't delay." She had talked to this vendor before without success. Emily knew fresh vegetables were a luxury item for the upper and middle classes and odds were he would never give her any.

Running up to him, she said, "Hello, sir."

"You again," he mumbled. "I told you I ain't no sir, and there ain't nothin' you can do for me, either."

A lady approached his cart and Emily stood by as he helped the woman pick out some carrots and potatoes. As she paid the two-pence she owed, she noticed Emily and smiled at her. "A friend of yours?" she asked the vendor.

He looked at Emily with a scowl and then turned to the woman. "Hah. Just a pain in me butt is all that one is. Another street urchin lookin' for a handout."

"Street urchin?" The lady looked surprised. "She doesn't look like an abandoned child to me."

"Must be," he replied. "Comes to me all the time looking for free food."

Emily, happy to hear the lady's words, ignored the vendor and said, "Thank you, ma'am."

"Oh, be gone with you," the vendor cried, chasing Emily away, "and don't come back botherin' me no more."

As she walked away, Emily turned to see the lady still smiling at her.

Three days later, Emily was strolling past one of London's hospitals when it started to rain. Quickly glancing around for a place to stay dry, she spotted a church down the street.

There were only four other people in the church when she entered. She sat in a back row so as not to attract attention. She reasoned she might as well stay until somebody kicked her out. Surprisingly, about twenty minutes later the church started to fill up and Emily realized that a mass was about to begin. She had never been to a church service before. Her father was a devout atheist who refused to let any of his family attend church. "If there is a god, he sure hasn't done right by me," he was fond of saying.

As the church filled up, Emily was happy to see that everyone was sitting towards the front, well ahead of her. One of them appeared to be the lady she had seen at the vendor's cart the other day. Only one man sat in the back near her. He was bedraggled looking, and she determined that he was just getting out of the rain too.

As the service began, Emily mimicked whatever the rest of the congregation did. She understood nothing of what she heard but decided that she liked it. She couldn't explain why, but it gave her a warm feeling.

When the mass was over she wondered what to do. Not wanting to draw attention to herself, she arose and went back outside. The rain was still coming down hard, but she found an overhang on the side of the church that protected her from most of it. She waited until everyone appeared to have left, then went back inside. She found a small room off to the right and tried the door. It was unlocked and she scooted inside. She wanted to take a nap, but the room was simply a closet, too small for her to be comfortable in, so she returned to the bench from which she had watched the mass. In moments she was asleep.

She was awakened some time later by the sound of shuffling feet. She peeked over the top of the bench in front of her, and saw a priest walking slowly around the altar. Emily waited until his back was turned and then quietly headed for the door, only to find it was still pouring outside. She decided to hide in the tiny closet. Within minutes she heard the rain letting up, so she opened the door to peek out. The priest was looking back at her.

"Come out of there right now," he demanded.

Emily thought of making a run for it, but he immediately grabbed her arm.

"Well, who do we have here?" he said.

"I've done nothing wrong," Emily blurted out. "Let go of me."

His tone softened. "It's okay, my child," he said, and as she looked up into his face Emily thought she saw kindness there. "Come, sit and talk with me."

His name was Father Lovell. He was a kindly old man, average in height and overweight. He had thinning grey hair with just a few black strands remaining. He had seen far too many abandoned children over the years and it always broke his heart. He tried to do what he could for them, which he felt was painfully inadequate. He asked Emily what her story was, and she told him.

"You've only been on the streets a month?" he asked as she finished her tale. "That explains why you look so much better than most of the children. It's a bit unusual that someone your age is abandoned. Have you been able to find food and shelter?"

"I have a place to sleep." She thought about her sack and her change of clothes. They were going to be soaked when she returned. "Food, not so much. Very little, in fact. But I haven't stolen anything," she added, thinking that a priest would appreciate that.

He thought for a while, and then Emily saw a smile brighten his face. "You seem like an intelligent girl; got your wits about you," he said. "I may know someone who can help you. Come back here tomorrow at two o'clock. Can you do that?"

"Yes, Father Lovell." Time had not meant much to Emily the last month, but she could certainly find out when two o'clock tomorrow was.

He got up, and she did likewise. "Good girl," he said. "Don't forget, two o'clock."

"I'll remember." Emily walked out the front door of the church and felt the sun shining down on her face.

She returned the next day at noon and sat on the steps. She had no idea what Father Lovell had in store for her, but she was willing to listen to any offers. Already her luck had changed, and she was beginning to think her father was wrong about God.

After leaving the church yesterday she had gone seeking food. She had just arrived in front of a string of stores when she heard someone cry, "Stop him!" She looked up just in time to catch a small child as he was running by her. He was carrying a gilded picture frame which had caught his fancy, but which his mother had told him he could not have. The store owner had done the yelling, but his mother was the one who came storming out of the store chasing him. She thanked Emily, but that was all. It was the owner who made her day after the mother and child had departed.

"Thank you," he said. "There was no way I could have caught the little bugger."

Emily saw the cane he carried and understood. The man had a bum left leg. "You're welcome," she said.

"You saved me a pretty penny there, you did." He looked at her and smiled. "That frame is worth four pounds, what with the gold in it. My wife keeps telling me not to put the good stuff near the door."

"I guess she's right," Emily replied.

"Yes, she's always right, my wife. Got a good head on her. So how can I thank you?"

"Could I have something to drink?"

"Sure, I can get you that. In fact, I can do you one better." He tousled her hair and said, "Come on in."

He gave her a tall glass of cider sweetened with nutmeg, milk, and cream. As she was gulping that down, he brought out the finest feast she had seen in a long time. He set it on the counter, then went to the front of his shop and put a CLOSED sign on the door. "It's been a slow day anyways, and I'm hungry," he said. "I'll be happy if you will share it with me."

"Oh yes," Emily cried, "that would be wonderful."

There was a small piece of brisket, thick slices of bread, and two kinds of cheese. He shared it all equally with her. "My wife went off to see her sister," he explained. "It's nice to have someone to share my meal with."

Now, sitting on the church steps, Emily was starving again. She had been waiting well over an hour when Father Lovell arrived.

"Ah, I see you are already here," he said. "Come inside and keep me company."

Emily followed him down a hall which led to his office. "Sit here," he said, pointing to a chair against a side wall. "Missus Ferguson will be here soon."

Emily sat down to wait. A moment later Father Lovell came out of an adjoining room with a slice of bread and some dried peas. "Here," he said, "you look hungry."

Emily's eyes lit up. "Oh, thank you. I am hungry."

"Have you eaten since yesterday?"

She told him the story of the gilded picture frame while she ate. She finished the peas in short order, but took her time with the bread. She wanted to make it last as long as possible. "I really hate begging for food, father, but it's all I can do."

"It's disturbing." He slowly shook his head as he thought about the situation. "A city this large, with all these people, yet they can't even take care of their own children."

As she listened to him, the door opened. Emily was surprised to see the lady she had seen twice before.

"Ah, Missus Ferguson," said Father Lovell.

She said hello to the priest, then turned to look at Emily. "It is you," she said. "I thought it might be."

Emily noticed the woman seemed happy to see her and wondered why.

"When I saw you in the church yesterday, then received the message from Father Lovell, I was hoping you were the girl he was talking about."

Emily had not realized the lady had seen her in the church.

Father Lovell spoke up. "Missus Ferguson is an extraordinary woman, Emily. She helps a great many of London's abandoned children. I think she can help you too."

"Really?"

Missus Ferguson looked at the priest. "Father, I think I may be able to do better than that this time." Amused by the puzzled look on his face, she turned to Emily. For fifteen minutes she questioned her. Where was she from? Who were her parents? Why was she on the streets?

Emily answered honestly, although she tried to keep the bitterness she felt for her father out of her voice. Finally, Missus Ferguson stunned both Emily and Father Lovell by asking, "How would you like to come live with me, dear?"

For a moment Emily was speechless and so was the priest, who finally muttered, "Oh my."

"I have a house about a mile from here," Missus Ferguson said. "It's quite nice, and I'm sure you would like it. Of course, you will have to help me out with the work, but you would be doing me a great favor if you would accept."

"Yes, yes." Emily spoke the words immediately, afraid this wonderful offer would be withdrawn as quickly as it was given. She was overwhelmed to think she might once again have a home to live in and a bed to sleep in.

"Excellent." Missus Ferguson seemed truly pleased. "I'm sure you will be happy. In fact, I'll see to it."

Minutes later, Emily left the church for her new home. She felt as though she were walking on air.

Chapter Fifteen

Jill was stunned as she sat on the couch in Simon's office. It had been nothing like she thought it would be. She had been homeless. Not just homeless, but homeless as an eight year old. The thought boggled her mind. It did something else, however. It made Jill believe. Maybe not one-hundred percent yet, but the tide had definitely turned, because she knew there was no way she made up that story in her own mind.

Simon was impressed with this past life also. He had never had anyone regress to a life as a homeless child. When Jill had finished, he hadn't been sure she would want to go back to England on her next visit.

She assured him otherwise. "No," she said, "we must go back. Wonderful things are going to happen now that Emily has found this Missus Ferguson. It will be alright. Besides," she paused as she looked at Simon, "I still have to find my Niall in London."

"Perhaps he will not appear in this lifetime," Simon replied.

"Now Simon, don't become pessimistic on me all of a sudden. Niall will show up, and my life in London will turn around. I can feel it."

"You did recognize others," he stated, "so I'm sure you're right."

She had recognized three people in her short month in London. Her mother who passed away at such a young age was her mother now, although she had not recognized the father she hated in London. Tom, the boy who helped her on the streets, was Sean, her youngest son in Ireland who helped her through the post-Niall period. Funny, she had met him twice now in her regressions yet still didn't know who he was in this life. The most surprising person she recognized, however, was Missus Ferguson.

Missus Ferguson was Nuala. Talk about your karmic payback. As Sarah, she had taken Nuala in when she lost both her parents. Now, it appeared that Nuala, as Missus Ferguson, was about to return the favor.

Jill left Simon's office minutes later and headed for The Inner Peace Sanctuary. The sanctuary was the last building on a dead-end street. She parked in the circular driveway and walked up to the front door. It opened just as she was about to ring the bell.

A middle aged woman, tall and lean with lovely platinum blonde hair was standing there. "I thought I heard a car drive up," she said. "How can I help you?"

"Good morning," said Jill. "I was reading one of your brochures and was thinking of taking a class, so I thought I would drive over and check out the place."

"Wonderful, come on in." The lady seemed to exude joy. "My name is Wanda. I am the owner of the sanctuary."

"This home is lovely. Did you buy it recently?" asked Jill.

"Oh no, dear, I built it," said Wanda. "My house is right next door, but it's a typical home. No room for doing any of the things I wanted to do, so I built this place. Now I can run all the classes you saw in the brochure."

"You built it just to run classes? That's amazing."

"I've had a very fortunate life," said Wanda. "Money was not an obstacle. I felt this was the best way for me to give back. Would you like a tour?"

"Yes, thank you," said Jill.

The front door had opened into a large living room. Two plush sofas sat back to back in the middle of the room. They both had a solid oak end table. In front of the most interior sofa was a large, glass-topped coffee table sitting on a giant piece of driftwood. To the left was a small kitchen. "We usually only have appetizers and fruit here," said Wanda, "so I didn't see the need for a table. Larger gatherings are always pot luck, and we have plenty of counter space and card tables for those."

Along the back wall was a sliding glass door that led to the backyard, which was heavily wooded. To the left of the door a bar area had been built with four stools sitting in front. Behind the bar, instead of liquor, was a work station containing a computer, phone and intercom system, and a stereo. There was paperwork everywhere. Jill assumed that was what Wanda had been working on when she drove up. At present the top of the bar was filled with flyers describing a myriad of classes.

"Would you like a drink, dear?" asked Wanda. "I have some fresh carrot juice that I just made; or I have orange juice and some cranberry juice in the fridge."

Jill had never had carrot juice and decided to give it a try.

Wanda handed her the glass of juice, then said, "Follow me."

As the tour continued, Jill realized how well thought out the building of this home had been. To the right of the living room was a hallway. Down the hall on the left were a handicapped bathroom and a door leading downstairs. On the right were two small rooms used for classes, with another room at the end of the hallway. Jill followed Wanda downstairs to find a fully functional basement.

"This is the room we use for any large groups or meetings. Last week a lady from Denmark came and played the harp. It was wonderful."

"I smell a lingering scent of incense, I think," said Jill.

"That's very possible. A group from the Wiccan Society was here last night doing a cleansing ceremony."

Jill wasn't sure what she thought about witches, but she determined the "new Jill" would keep an open mind. Returning to the living room, she followed Wanda up the stairs to the second floor, where there were four more rooms plus another bathroom.

"Up here," said Wanda, "is where the rest of our classes take place. Each room can accommodate eight to ten people easily enough, depending on what the class is. This room," she continued, opening the only door which was closed, "is the massage room, which we leave set up for convenience. I have three different therapists who use this room during the month. They share the equipment and supplies."

Jill felt a wonderful sense of peace in this house and wished her own home made her feel this way. Immediately she started thinking of changes that she could make. Back in the kitchen after the tour, she set her empty glass down on the counter. "That was delicious carrot juice."

Wanda thanked her. "Carrot juice is great for digestion if you are having a big meal. I like to drink some every day. So tell me, what classes were you interested in taking?"

Jill mentioned the meditation class.

"Excellent place to start," said Wanda. "Everyone should begin there."

"Why is that?"

"Because, first and foremost, the spirit needs peace. In today's hectic world it can be difficult to relax. People are always on the go, trying to do three things at once."

Jill had no problem understanding that.

"Meditation helps a person take a step back. It gives them an opportunity to center themselves, to quiet the mind. Everyone needs some quiet time whether they know it or not. So tell me Jill, are you a spiritualist?"

"Well, I'm ..." Jill paused.

"Not sure?" asked Wanda. "Are you a religious person? Do you go to church often?"

"No," said Jill, "I've never been very religious."

"Most people who come here are not very religious. Many have been at some point in their lives, but didn't find the answers they were looking for. Our goal here at Inner Peace is to help people in body, mind, and spirit. That is what all of our classes are designed to do. As spiritualists we believe the spirit lives on after the body dies."

"So you believe in reincarnation?" asked Jill.

"I do, and I believe most spiritualists do. There are some who would debate the issue."

"I see. I guess right now you would have to call me a seeker."

"Well," said Wanda, "we have plenty for you to investigate here." Wanda told her that the Wednesday meditation class met downstairs because it was so popular, usually bringing in twenty people or more. She then went over some of the other classes with Jill, handing her flyers on a number of them.

"This is great," Jill said. "I'll be here tomorrow night for the meditation, and I will look these over in the meantime." With that, Jill said her goodbyes and headed for her car.

The following evening Jill went to her first meditation session. Twenty-three people attended. The meditation was run by a lady named Phyllis, who sat facing them in one corner of the basement. Four small tables placed at the mid-point of each wall held burning candles. The lights in the room were turned off when the meditation began.

Phyllis led the group into a relaxed state, similar to what Simon did, and then began a guided meditation. "I want you to picture a forest," she said. "This forest has a clearing in it, and in this clearing is your own special house. It can be any type of house you want."

Jill pictured a log cabin.

"Open the front door and enter your home," continued Phyllis. "You walk into the living room. It has a soft, cushiony couch in the middle. Sit on your couch."

Jill had no trouble following along. Phyllis asked them to call in their guides, and Jill was quite surprised when she pictured a man entering her room and smiling at her. He was short, with black hair tied in a ponytail and wearing a robe that flowed down to his feet. Phyllis directed them to ask their guide his name and then ask him a question. At once the name Conrad came to her. She thought for a moment and then silently asked her guide how her boys were handling her divorce from their father. An answer arrived almost as soon as she finished asking. She heard it in her mind, although she wasn't sure how.

"They have recovered from the initial shock and have returned to a normal routine. Children are usually more resilient than their parents."

Next Phyllis told them to look to their left, where they would see a mirror on the wall. She told them to go to the mirror and ask another question, then watch the mirror for an answer. Jill tried it, but this time nothing appeared to happen.

"You can go to your special home in the forest any time you want," Phyllis concluded a short time later. "Whether you just want to relax or ask your guides a question, they are always ready to help you."

Jill felt completely relaxed coming out of the meditation. It dawned on her that all the sessions with Simon had prepared her well for this evening. She had slipped into a meditative state easily, and decided she would try to do it at home on a regular basis.

Chapter Sixteen

Jill woke up Thursday morning feeling better than she had in days. After getting the boys off to school, she decided to relax with a hot cup of chamomile tea. She sat down at the kitchen table and noticed yesterday's newspaper lying on one of the chairs. She hadn't had a chance to read it after she had come home last night so she picked it up. *The Willis Sentinel* was usually very small and rarely had much of interest inside. Jill generally just glanced through it. However, this time the headline on the front page jumped out at her.

HOME BREAK-IN, DESTRUCTION STUNS TOWN

Jill was flabbergasted to find that a house barely three miles from hers had been broken into in broad daylight. Everything in the home had been destroyed. Every room, every piece of furniture, every item large and small had been crushed, broken, and ruined. It appeared all that was taken was about twelve-hundred dollars in cash and a lady's diamond ring.

Jill couldn't believe her eyes as she read. Nothing like this ever happened in her small, quiet town. However, the paper said this was the third such home invasion in four months in central South

Carolina. Jill decided to call Lauren to see if she had heard the news.

"Yes, I saw the article in the paper," said Lauren. "Unbelievable."

"Why would anyone do such a thing?" Jill asked.

"Honey, that is rage, pure and simple. Somebody had it out for the guy who owned that house."

"I hope to God I can never hate anyone that much."

"Don't worry, Jill. I don't think it's in you to even think of something like that, much less act on it." They talked a moment longer, than Lauren's first client of the day arrived. "Have to go, sweetie," she said. "Talk to you soon."

An hour later, Tony called. He had to go out of town on business over the weekend and would be unable to take the boys. Jill quickly called the restaurant to get replacements for her weekend shifts, thinking it would be nice to spend time with the children.

When they came home from school that afternoon, however, she found the boys had other plans.

"The Magnuson's are taking their kids to Myrtle Beach this weekend, and they invited us to go with them. Can we?" asked Bret.

Mark added in a long "Pleeeease?"

Jill was disappointed but couldn't blame the boys. It was Myrtle Beach, after all. "Call them now and make sure it's okay," she said to Bret.

The Magnuson's were happy to have the boys come along. It would help keep their three kids occupied. They would be leaving about seven o'clock Friday night, and be home around five Sunday.

Jill suddenly had an entire weekend to herself; no boys, no work.

Saturday turned into a relaxing day around the house. Work had slowed down, and she finished what she had by noon. In the afternoon she did another meditation. She went to her log cabin in the woods and decided to ask the mirror a question. "Is my Niall about to show up in my current life?" She waited as she pictured herself standing in front of the mirror. Just as she thought no answer was going to materialize, an image came to her. It was an airplane landing on a runway. She watched as it pulled up to the gate. Next she saw herself standing in the waiting area, watching as the passengers came off the plane. The mirror then went blank.

When she finished her meditation, Jill thought of the answer she had received and smiled. It seemed that the man of her dreams was about to walk into her life. Or was he? The mirror's image had ended before she actually saw anyone. *Nothing is easy*, she thought.

That night Jill and Lauren went to Sammy Chong's, a Chinese restaurant downtown. They had a half-hour wait for a table, but the food was worth it.

They spent the time catching up on everything that had happened since their last visit, including Jill's regression in London. Lauren was shocked to hear that Jill had lived on the streets as a homeless eight year old. "I don't think I could do that now, as a grown-up," she said. "What do you think will happen next?"

Jill thought for a moment. "Something good, I think. Missus Ferguson seems to be a nice lady."

"Maybe," said Lauren, eyes twinkling slyly, "she is an evil witch who takes kids off the street, never to be heard from again."

"Stop it," Jill said as she laughed along with her friend. "I think things are going to work out just fine."

Later, stuffed from the food and with plenty of leftovers, Jill paid the bill and they headed for the parking lot. As she pulled her keys from her pocketbook, Lauren asked Jill, "So, any plans for tomorrow?"

"None," Jill replied.

"Great. Why don't you come to church with me? Give you a chance to check it out for yourself and discover we are not all crazy psychic people."

Jill thought it over. She knew if she said no, Lauren would be reminding her of her boring life again. "Okay," she finally said, "I'll pick you up. What time?"

"Alright," Lauren practically shouted. "That's my girl. Pick me up at nine-thirty. Service starts at ten."

The next morning's service started out much like any church service, with a song, The Lord's Prayer, and an invocation. Ralph, the guest lecturer, then spoke on intuition and how to become more aware of it. Jill liked some of the ideas and thought she might give them a try. After the sermon, things changed from other church services Jill had been to. First, everyone was invited up to form a healing circle around the altar. They all held hands as Ralph began the ceremony. He said a short prayer, and then told them to imagine white light coming down into the crown of their heads, filling their bodies with healing energy. He then told them to send white light to any friend or family member who was sick or hurting in any way. Jill didn't know if this would help anyone, but she did feel a tingle of energy running through her body which felt very nice.

The final part of the service was the readings. Ralph went around to different people and gave them a message. "People receive messages from the other side in different ways," he said. "I get mine through pictures. Oftentimes they have no meaning for me, but they do for the person receiving the message. I'm just going to tell you what I see and what it means to me. Perhaps it will mean something different to you, and that's okay."

After a few minutes he came to Jill. After asking her name, he said, "Jill, are you new to all this?"

She said, "Yes."

"Okay. I ask because I am seeing a see-saw, and to me that signifies a person groping with an issue: up, down, up, down. It's as though you can't make up your mind about something. Believe, don't believe. You understand?"

Did she ever. Jill just nodded at him, and snuck a quick look at Lauren.

Ralph continued on. "Now I see water, which is spiritual. You are entering into a spiritual phase of your life and it's a real see-saw battle for you. Keep at it, okay?"

Jill said she would, and Ralph moved on. He did three more readings, and then said that was all. Lauren had not received one. After a final song and the benediction, the service was over.

"Now for the good stuff," said Lauren. "Coffee and sweets."

By Tuesday morning, Jill was relaxed and ready to go. She had meditated after the boys had gone to bed Sunday night and then did it again Monday morning. She used the log cabin visualization both times, but not with the success she had previously. Still, after each session she felt calm and peaceful. She was determined to meditate at least three times a week besides her Wednesday night class.

She greeted Melinda with a hearty hello as she arrived at Simon's office.

"My, someone is in a great mood," Melinda said. "Ready for your next trip to Neverland?"

"I sure am," she said. "I can't wait to get started." She and Melinda talked about the home invasion and how awful it was. Minutes later, the young girl Jill had seen before came out of the back room, made another appointment, and left.

"Your turn," said Melinda.

Jill entered Simon's office, and after a short chat with him, she laid down on the couch, waiting to go back two-hundred fifty years in the blink of an eye.

He took her through their normal routine and noticed her body relaxing. "We have seen you in London as a little girl, Jill. You have met Missus Ferguson. Now I want you to try to find that same life as a grown-up, around the age of thirty. Let's see what has become of little Emily. Can you do that, Jill?"

As Jill lay on the couch, she exhibited no signs of strain or worry, but it did seem to be taking her longer than usual. Finally, she said, "Not there."

"What do you mean, Jill? Have you left the London area?"

This time she responded immediately. "Not there. Gone."

"Have you left England?" he inquired. "Are you in another country now?"

"Dead," she quietly said.

I should have realized sooner, Simon thought. "Okay, I understand." Where to go now? He wanted to advance the story, not just return to her meeting with Missus Ferguson. Then it came to him. "Jill, in your previous life you had a husband named Niall. Can you find that entity in your London life? Is he there?"

"Oh yes," she said, and the smile that overtook her face was a wondrous thing to behold.

"How old are you when you meet him?"

"Seventeen."

"And what are you doing?"

"I'm in the park with Mabel."

Chapter Seventeen

LONDON, 1735

Emily was tired, but not nearly as tired as Mabel. They had been shopping in Piccadilly since early morning: linens, a wash tub, a new set of fine silverware to replace the aging set at home. That and much more was being delivered to the Ferguson residence at this very moment. The final items they purchased were cheese, bread, and some slices of duck and partridge, which they now carried with them as they entered Hyde Park.

They found a lovely patch of grass away from most of the crowd and settled down to eat. They were just about to begin when a young man walked by, a girl by his side. Emily looked into his eyes as he passed, and he looked right back. She couldn't take her eyes off him. The girl walking with him never noticed, but he did, and so did Mabel.

"You're going to go blind looking at someone that long, my dear."

"Huh? What?" Emily hardly knew she was speaking.

"Over here, Emily." Mabel was waving a hand in front of her face.

"Oh my! What just happened?"

Mabel was grinning from ear to ear. "I think you were just struck by a love bug, if I'm not mistaken. I've never seen that look on your face before."

Every instinct Emily had told her to run after the man. Instead she picked up a sandwich and took a bite.

"My goodness," cried Mabel, "have you gone fluffy in the head?" When Emily looked at her, baffled, Mabel said, "Honey, you are eating my sandwich. Yours is right in front of you. You don't even like duck."

Emily looked at the sandwich and then handed it to Mabel. "Sorry," she said. "Did you see him?"

"How could I not, with you staring at him like that?"

"He was gorgeous." Emily's voice still had a dreamy quality to it.

"He was a very attractive man. I suggest if you see him again, you do a little more than just stare." In all the years she had known Emily, Mabel Ferguson had never seen her like this. Emily had precious little time for boys growing up and didn't seem to care. Her work with Mabel took up most of her time.

"What would I do?" Emily asked.

"You could start by saying hello."

"I'll probably never see him again." Emily sounded dejected. She went back to eating her sandwich, but her mind remained on the stranger.

Ten minutes later, as they were finishing their lunch, he came back. He walked up to Emily with no sense of fear and said, "Hello, my name is Jared. Would you like to join me for a walk to Piccadilly?"

Emily was startled, but she managed to sputter, "Yes." Then, as if her mind had just clicked on, she said, "But we've just …"

"She would love to join you, Jared," Mabel cut in, "and since we have just had the pleasure of meeting you this instant, I shall follow along a few paces behind."

It was not an offer, he knew, but a condition. He quickly accepted.

After cleaning up, Mabel and Emily headed back to Piccadilly for the second time that day, this time with Jared. Mabel kept to her word and soon dropped back about ten paces.

Once Mabel was out of earshot, Jared looked at Emily and said, "No one has ever looked at me like that before."

Emily was now completely back in her senses. "I've never done that," she said, "but I'm sure many girls have looked at you that way. Maybe you just never noticed before."

Jared smiled. "I've seen plenty of girls looking at me. Just not like that. It was as though you were in a trance."

"Did you feel a spark?" Emily asked. "It was as if I were being hit by lightening."

He nodded in agreement. "It was very strange. I've never had an experience like that before. Suddenly the girl I was with seemed like a sister to me."

The mention of the other girl gave Emily a sudden pang of jealousy. "Are you seeing her?"

Jared laughed out loud. "I was just being funny," he said. "That really was my sister."

Emily breathed a huge sigh of relief. "In that case you must tell me all about yourself."

His name was Jared Halstead. He was an apprentice carpenter, learning the trade from his uncle, who was one of the finest carpenter's in all of London. Jared was not tall, barely five-eight, but he was fit and obviously strong. He had blonde hair and blue eyes that seemed to twinkle whenever he looked at her.

"Enough about me," he said after a while as Emily directed him towards the Ferguson home. "Tell me something about yourself."

"Where to begin?" said Emily. She started with the passing of her mother and her father's leaving her in London. "I lived on the streets for about a month, then Missus Ferguson took me in, and my life hasn't been the same since."

"You survived the streets?" His voice sounded incredulous. "You're one of the fortunate ones."

"I know. Mabel Ferguson is one of the most wonderful people you will ever meet. Her entire life is devoted to helping homeless children. Anyway, she took me in and gave me two educations."

"Two?"

"First, she took me out onto the streets with her every day to help the kids. She showed me things even I hadn't seen. Of course, I had only been out there a month, mostly in the good side of town. Second, she made sure I was educated. I had four years of schooling."

"Wow, she really saved your life," said Jared.

"Now I help her save as many kids as we can, and I am training to become a nurse. One day we hope to open a shelter for the homeless children of London."

He stopped to look directly at her. "I knew when I first saw you that you were someone who helped people. The fact that it is London's homeless makes you even more special in my eyes."

Emily had never been happier.

AUGUST, 1743

Emily watched as the men hung the sign on the hooks over the door.

FERGUSON'S FOUNDLING HOUSE

She thought it looked rather nice. Mabel's dream come true. As long as Emily had known her, Mabel had wanted to open a home to help the orphaned and abandoned children walking the streets of London. For the longest time it had appeared that it wouldn't happen, but two years ago a man Emily fondly knew as "Captain Tom" had opened a home for children, and now Mabel was following suit. She had saved Emily from a life on the streets; now she would be able to help hundreds, perhaps thousands more.

Harold Ferguson, who ran an import-export business, had many connections high in government, both Tories and Whigs. Neither side had ever cared to talk much about the homeless problem over the years. They had done even less. However, the idea that a thriving, cosmopolitan city like London should have babies dying on its streets eventually became an embarrassment. Captain Tom, with Harold's help, finally convinced the government to do something. Once the captain's foundling house had opened, Mabel began pushing for her own place.

It had been well over a year before Mabel received the go ahead for the project. On the night it came, Emily couldn't stop cheering; Mabel couldn't stop crying. They gave her a building in Cheapside, just two blocks from the Guildhall. It was so rundown that it took another year to renovate. Now it was set to open in the morning.

The entrance to Ferguson's Foundling House led to the registration area. The first step would be to collect as much information as they could about each child, and then the children would be examined. After the exam, the children would be placed into one of four categories: Reasonably Fit, Needs Attention, Needs Infirmary or Can't Help. Those deemed to be in the Reasonably Fit category were sent to the cafeteria, situated on the first floor to the right of registration. After eating they would be sent back out onto the streets, under the assumption that they were healthy enough and old enough to take care of themselves. No one under the age of seven would be placed in this category. Each day they could come into the cafeteria, show a special card they were given, and receive a meal.

Children in the Needs Attention category would be fed and then given a place to sleep on the second floor. That was divided into two sections, one for boys and one for girls. Those children who needed medical care were placed in the Needs Infirmary category. They would be given a bed in the infirmary, which took up the remaining space on the first floor to the left and behind registration. Children who were obviously close to dying, whether from malnutrition, disease, or some other cause, would be put in the Can't Help category and sent on their way. Sadly, no food could be wasted on them. The process was a long way from perfect, but Emily thought it was better than the lottery system that Captain Tom used.

After making sure the sign had been hung properly, Emily ventured inside. Mabel was in the process of thanking the countless guests who had been invited to see the building before tomorrow's opening. These people had donated their time and money to help Mabel see her dream to fruition.

Emily found Mabel in the cafeteria. "Sign's up," she said, and saw a beautiful smile come over Mabel's face.

"That's wonderful, dear. How does it look?"

"Terrific." Emily watched as Mabel waved to a group standing on her right and noticed Captain Tom was among them.

"I must talk with the Captain," said Mabel. "He's helped us so much."

As Mabel started to walk away, Emily said, "Have you seen Jared?"

"I think he's upstairs. Some last minute equipment problem he's fixing."

Emily headed for the second floor.

Jared came out of the boy's dormitory just as Emily arrived. "Hey there," he said, "I was just about to go looking for you."

She grabbed him around the arm. "Well you've found me now, haven't you?"

"Want to see the finished product?"

"Sure." She realized she had not been upstairs in over two weeks, instead spending all her time getting things ready in the infirmary.

In the years since their initial meeting in the park, Jared and Emily had been together whenever possible. Even if he worked all day and half the night, Jared would stop by the Ferguson home just to say goodnight to Emily. Their love had blossomed into a deep, abiding affair of the heart. A year after their initial meeting, Jared rented a small apartment and Emily had moved in with him. When Mabel began work on the foundling house, Jared volunteered all his free time. Even his mother, whom Emily had become ever so fond of, had joined in.

Now Jared led her back into the dormitory. Over two hundred small beds and cots were neatly arrayed, yet cramped around the huge room. They had squeezed in as many as possible while still leaving room to walk around. Unlike the infirmary where the walls had been white-washed, and would be regularly, the walls in the dorm were a light yellow. The floors were tiled for easy cleaning just as they were in the infirmary. There were eight windows around the room, which would provide for good light and ventilation. In the far left corner, a hole had been cut to the outside, then a shaft built leading to the ground. It was through here that the human waste of the children would be disposed of.

"It's wonderful." Emily was beaming with pride, happy in the knowledge that she had helped in some small way to make Mabel's dream come true. "Tomorrow is going to be such a wonderful day," she declared. She then looked at Jared, gave him a big smile, and said, "Was there one bed in particular you wanted to show me?"

"What?" he asked, looking at her. Then he said, "Oh," as he understood her meaning. "We shouldn't. There are too many people around."

"The only two people in the boy's dormitory are you and me," Emily replied, "and I want you. Now."

Jared shook his head and laughed, then led her to a bed in the far right corner, which might hide them if someone entered. If they were quiet. Which Emily never was.

MARCH, 1745

Emily awoke to find Jared already gone. She stared at the ceiling of their bedroom. They had moved to a new, larger apartment just off of Tottenham Court Road six months ago, and Emily loved it. She had never been happier. Jared was the love of her life. He worked hard, drank little and doted on her whenever he could. He was a carpenter on his own now, always busy and always in demand, yet he managed to make sure he took time for Emily. She did the same for him while working long hours at the foundling house. Like most young people in London they had not married. She knew he had snuck out quietly this morning so as not to wake her, because she hadn't been feeling well lately.

As she arose from the bed Emily started coughing and had a hard time stopping. When she did, she saw blood in her hand. She also realized that she had a fever. She began walking towards the kitchen, took four steps, and passed out.

Mister Wiggins, who lived upstairs, heard the noise of Emily's falling and decided he had better check it out. He received no answer to his knock on her door, nor did he hear anything when he called out her name. Worried now, and certain the noise had come from Emily's apartment, he opened the door and went inside. He found her lying on her bedroom floor. Wiggins, a big man, picked her up and laid her back on the bed. He then ran outside, found a young boy passing by, and sent him with a message to the foundling house.

Mabel arrived forty minutes later and came charging up the stairs. After checking out Emily, she sent Mister Wiggins to find Jared.

Emily's condition worsened throughout the day and into the night. She had short periods where she was awake and fairly alert, but as her fever rose she became delirious.

Jared arrived later that morning and stayed by her side the entire time. "Emily," he would whisper to her, "just rest. I'm here for you."

She would stroke his hair for a moment, then lose energy. Still, she managed to smile at him. He had always made her smile and she wouldn't stop now. "My Jared. How I've loved you so."

"I love you also. We will have many more years together, but now you must just concentrate on becoming well."

"No," she said. "I'm a nurse, my love. I know what is happening to me."

"Don't say that. You will get better."

She saw the fear in his eyes. "Jared, my Jared. You have made my life complete. When I was on the streets as a little girl, I thought my life was over. Mabel helped to keep me alive. But you gave me life. You gave me joy. I will always watch over you."

He was crying. "Emily, please, you must get better."

She didn't hear him. She had already fallen back to sleep.

Chapter Eighteen

"I awoke for only moments at a time after that," Jill said. "The next day I quietly passed over. It was a peaceful passing. My spirit had left my body earlier. I was just watching. Jared was overcome with emotion. For days he was inconsolable; Mabel too. Losing me was like losing a daughter to her, but she had seen so much death in her life, she understood it. She was a strong woman and she had her work to keep her going. Even Harold, who was in Spain, broke down when he heard the news."

"How do you know that?" Simon asked.

"I saw him."

"Didn't you cross over shortly after your death?"

"Not this time. I owed so much to Mabel and Harold, and I truly loved Jared. I stayed near them for some time. When I heard Mabel say she had sent word to Harold about my passing, I thought of him, and instantly I was there with him in Spain. I had never seen Harold cry before, but I did then."

"You can travel easily as a spirit then?"

"It's very strange when you first pass over. Your thoughts are powerful. You think of Paris, and *wham*, you're in Paris. Think of a particular person and next thing you know you are standing next to them. It takes a while to learn to control it."

Jill had never spoken of this part of the afterlife before, and Simon was excited to continue it. He wanted to hear more, learn more. Unfortunately, Jill had other ideas.

"I'm ready to return now," she stated, and Simon brought her back.

As he had after her Irish lifetime had ended, Simon asked Jill to take a seat at his desk when she was ready. "You must be surprised that your London life is over so soon," he said.

"I'm shocked," Jill replied. "I thought of dozens of scenarios of what was going to happen, but an early death was not one of them. It seems like it is over so quickly."

"Back in those days many lives were short. If you lived to be fifty or more you had a good, long life back then. There were plagues, of course, and medical treatment was basically a stab in the dark. They had no idea about viruses, and no medicines to treat them."

"I died of typhus."

Simon looked surprised. "How do you know that, Jill? You didn't say anything about that in your regression."

"I must have realized it when I was looking over my body. I just didn't say anything."

Simon opened her folder and took out the questionnaire. "It's interesting, Jill," he said. "On the question of where overseas you would like to visit, your first two answers were—"

"Ireland and England," she finished for him.

"And do you remember the next one?"

"I think I put down the Holy Lands, but with more time to think about it, I believe Greece would be my third choice."

"So, assuming you wish to come back again, perhaps you may soon be running around the streets of Athens."

Jill thought for a moment. She was intrigued by these sessions with Simon, but perhaps it was time for her to concentrate on this life. She wondered if all the daydreaming she was doing about her past lives was stunting her growth in this one.

No, she decided. She was making progress. She had started her meditation sessions at the sanctuary, she had gone to Lauren's church, and she had attended a channeling session. Plus, she was enthralled with these remembrances of her former lives, even if they never materialized as she thought they would. She was hooked.

"I do wish to continue," she said.

Simon was delighted. He didn't want to lose his best client now. He was certain that Jill was going to be the primary subject in his book. "Excellent," he said, and meant it.

As Jill left Simon's office, she was pleased that her regressions were going so well, but somewhat saddened, as her loss of Jared brought back feelings she had before at the loss of Niall. What an interesting life it had been, short as it was. What characteristics of that life had she brought over to this one, she wondered?

Her decision to continue with the regressions felt right to her. Simon had said it was probable she had another life between London and now. After all, she had died over two-hundred sixty years ago. She realized that now she believed, and wondered where the next life would take her.

As Jill daydreamed on, she inadvertently cut off a beat up old Plymouth wagon as she turned a corner. The driver blasted his horn, and then gave her the universal sign of unhappiness as she looked at him in her rear view mirror. "Sorry," she muttered. Jill headed home, having no errands to run. Ten minutes later she parked in the driveway and walked into the house.

She did not notice that the brown Plymouth wagon had followed her home.

Jill felt a sense of lightness and joy in the days that followed. It was as if a weight had been lifted slowly off her shoulders. She did not dwell on her early death in London or the short time she had with Jared. Instead, she was delighted that she had learned about another past life.

She believed now. How she could have changed her position on the subject so fast, so completely, she did not know. There was something thrilling about knowing the lives she had lived before. What else had she been in previous times: a queen, a monk, a disciple of Jesus? She often wondered.

Her meditations were helping with the sense of peace she felt. She attended the Wednesday night session at the sanctuary again and began making new friends. She also started what she hoped would be a regular regimen at home, meditating at eleven o'clock every morning. She unplugged the phone; shut off the television, radio, and her cell phone; closed the door to her room; and relaxed. She decided to start with twenty-minute sessions. She found calming her mind was easier said than done, but figured it would get better with practice.

Thursday night her mother called. She and her father wanted to visit on Saturday. Jill was delighted. She called Tony, who agreed not to pick up the boys until Sunday morning. She then called work and was able to swap her Saturday night shift for one Sunday afternoon.

David and Helen Mooney pulled into the driveway just past noon on Saturday. They had moved to Charleston three years ago after living in Willis all their lives. Back in 2000, Jill's mother had started an Internet business selling collectible figurines. She had done it to help pass the time and make a little extra money. The business had taken off. Before she knew it, she was spending two hours a day online filling orders. Soon that increased to three hours. What she had hoped would be a thousand dollars extra spending money every month or so turned into a booming business. David took early retirement from his job with an accounting firm and stayed home to help. Together they started three more websites, selling office supplies, jewelry, and perfume. They were now grossing well over two-hundred thousand dollars a year. Helen's sister Mary lived in Charleston and they had always enjoyed the city when they visited, so one day they packed up and moved onto the same street Mary lived on. Last year they helped Mary set up her first website.

Jill had always enjoyed her parents. They were lively, easy-going people who knew how to get a party started. They loved their grandchildren and the kids always looked forward to seeing them.

"We come bearing gifts!" David bellowed as he walked in the front door. He was carrying a large box wrapped in Christmas paper with a giant red bow adorning the top.

The boy's eyes lit up. They ran to him, almost knocking him over.

"Whoa, boys," he said, "let me put it down first." He then went back out to his car and brought in a second box just like the first one.

"Dad," asked Jill, "what is going on?"

"It's Christmas in May," yelled Bret, looking at the Santa Claus on the wrapping paper.

"Something like that," said his grandfather. "Now everybody take a seat."

The boys jumped on the couch, eager to obey so they could open the gifts as soon as possible. Jill and her mother both took seats as David knelt on the floor by the boxes.

"Things have been going pretty well for us lately," he said, "and we wanted to share our good fortune with our favorite people."

Bret and Mark were beaming, wondering what could be in the very large boxes.

"One for you, Bret," he said, motioning to the box on his left, "and one for you, Mark."

The boys tore the paper off the boxes faster than Jill could say, "Easy, boys." In seconds they were opening the cardboard flaps and staring inside. Each box contained a complete computer system: monitor, tower, speakers and printer, keyboard and mouse.

"Fantastic!" Bret yelled. "No more waiting for my brother to get off the computer."

Jill was just as stunned as the boys. "Dad, you shouldn't have."

"Nonsense," he replied. "I can't begin to tell you how well things are going for us right now. This is no problem, and I don't want you to worry about it. Now the boys will each have their own computer, and so will you."

He spent the afternoon setting up the new systems in the boy's rooms and moving the old computer into Jill's bedroom. Jill hadn't seen the boys this excited since the real Christmas. She was certain they were happier now than they had been back then. *One perfect gift can be so much better than ten pretty good ones*, she thought.

They went out to eat that night at her father's insistence. He took them to The Willis Steak House, his favorite spot. By the time they arrived back home everyone was stuffed. Bret and Mark headed for their rooms to sign on to their new computers.

Jill poured glasses of merlot for her parents and herself. They sat around the living room, relaxing after their big meal. After a few minutes of small talk, Jill said, "I'd like to tell you what I've been doing lately."

"We would love to hear it, dear," her mother said. "How has life been treating you recently?"

Jill smiled. Wait until they hear this, she thought. "To begin," she said, "let me ask you a question. Do either of you believe in reincarnation?"

She saw her parent's give each other a startled look, then thought she noticed a slight smile in the corner of her mother's mouth. Instead of answering, her mom said, "Tell us why you ask."

For the next hour Jill told them about Simon and his past-life regression work. She told of her lives in Ireland and England and about Niall and Jared with as much detail as she could remember. She also told her mother that she had also been her mother in England, and how she had died so young. Jill then realized for the first time that Emily had died at the same age as her mother.

They listened with rapt attention, asking almost no questions as Jill rambled on.

As Jill spoke, she wondered what they were thinking. "That's why I asked if you believe in reincarnation. Now before you answer, let me fill up our wine glasses."

Jill went into the kitchen, brought out the bottle and refreshed each glass, then sat back in her chair. "So what do you have to say?"

"How very interesting that you asked us that question now," her mother said. "You see, about two months ago we met a couple at your Aunt Mary's. They live about a mile away. We hit it off, and the next week we went to the theater with them. That was when we saw Riverdance. I told you about that on the phone."

Jill remembered how much her mother had enjoyed the Irish step dancers.

"Anyway," her mother continued, "they have become good friends of ours. Their names are Peggy and Emanuel Dennis, by the way. Well, Peggy's favorite television show is that John Edward program. Have you heard of him?"

Jill had seen part of his show once at Lauren's suggestion. "That's the guy who has an audience all around him and brings in messages from the other side, right?"

"Yes. Peggy loves that show. Never misses it. Tapes it if she can't watch it. She talked about it so much that your father and I decided to watch it one night. At first you have to wonder, but then he gets so many details right you have to pay attention. Anyway, we watched a few episodes and he really seemed to bring through some amazing information, things only family members in the audience would know. Well, one day Peggy calls and says there is a man in Charleston who does the same thing, and would we like to go."

"Are you serious?" Jill asked. "You actually went to see him?"

"We did. David," she said, looking at her husband, "tell her what happened."

Jill laughed inside. Her parents did this often. One of them would start telling a story, then for no particular reason the other one would take over.

"Well," her father started, "there were only about twenty-five people there. I don't think this gentleman had been doing this for very long, although he said he had been receiving messages from the other side since he was a little boy. He had been speaking for about twenty minutes when he suddenly said, 'There is a man here who has just stepped in. He's very excited. He has elbow patches on his suit coat.' That made me think of my father, of course. He wore that stupid coat long after it went out of style. We couldn't get him to throw it away. Anyway, next he says 'the man is holding an accordion.' Well, then I knew it had to be your grandpa, Jill. He loved to play his accordion, which was almost as annoying as the suit coat, considering how poorly he played it."

"Your grandfather had a message for us," Jill's mother chimed in.

Jill sat, mesmerized.

"It was about you," her father added.

"Me?" Jill shot straight up in her chair. "What did he say about me?"

"He told us you would be going through some profound changes in your life, beginning soon. He said we needed to keep in close touch with you and encourage you to go through them, because your eyes were going to be opened to a whole new way of life, and he wasn't sure you'd believe what you were hearing. He wanted you to know you shouldn't be afraid. Follow your heart," he said. David looked at his wife. "Did I get that all right, mama?"

"You did fine, dear," she answered.

"Should we tell her the last part?" They had a twinkle in their eyes as they looked at each other.

"What is it?" cried Jill.

"I think it will be okay," said her mother.

"You tell her," said her father.

"Well, Jill," her mother said, "your grandfather also told us one other thing. He said you would be meeting your other half, your soul mate, very soon."

Jill couldn't believe what she had heard.

The next day, she was asked out on a date.

Chapter Nineteen

Jill was working her makeup shift at The Ravenwood Sunday afternoon. It was a much different crowd than the one she was used to seeing on Friday and Saturday nights. Older. It was about four o'clock, a slow time for the restaurant. The lunch crowd was long gone and the dinner crowd was still an hour away. She was standing by the front entrance, filling the basket of complimentary peppermint candies, when a gentleman approached her.

"Excuse me," he said.

Jill looked up to see a man about her age, perhaps a little older. He had black hair combed straight back and dark eyes, almost a bluish-black. He appeared to be about six-two, and must have been close to two hundred pounds. She had greeted him when he came in and escorted him to his seat. "What can I do for you?" she asked.

"I couldn't help noticing you," he said. "You're very attractive. My name is Neal, and I was wondering if perhaps one night this week I might be able to take you to dinner?"

Jill was so stunned she almost couldn't answer. It had been a long time since anyone had asked her out. "Oh," she finally managed to say.

"I know this is sudden and you don't know me or anything, but I've eaten here before, and whenever I see you I always want to ask you out." He knew he was rambling, but couldn't help himself. He paused, and then asked, "You're not married, are you?"

"No." Jill looked at him and realized he was just as nervous as she had suddenly become. *This dating thing isn't easy for any of us*, she thought. "No, I'm divorced. Dinner, you say?"

"Any night you want."

And suddenly Jill realized she wanted. "Thursday?" she asked.

His smile lit up the room. "Thursday would be great. Where would you like to go?"

"Anywhere but here," she said. Since she didn't know Neal, she didn't want to give him her home address. She told him she would be browsing in Desmond's Book Shop at six o'clock and he could meet her there. He gave her his phone number in case anything came up, and then he exited the restaurant, whistling a happy tune as he went.

Jill could hardly believe what had just happened.

Tuesday morning snuck up on Jill. For once it seemed as if it had arrived too quickly. She had spent all of Monday thinking back and forth between two subjects. The first was the incredible information her parents had told her. Grandpa Dale, who had died last year of a massive heart attack, had come through with a message encouraging her in the changes she was making. She had talked with Lauren about it Sunday night, and Lauren told her about synchronicity; things happening in a specific order for a specific reason. Jill added that to the list of items she needed to investigate.

The second subject, of course, was Neal. He had certainly seemed like a nice man, and Jill was tingling with excitement wondering how her date with him would go. Was he the Niall of Ireland, the Jared of England? Perhaps, she concluded, he was simply a nice guy looking for some female companionship.

Thus, as she readied for bed Monday night, it had dawned on her that she had a meeting with Simon in the morning. Jill was shocked to realize that she had forgotten all about it these past few days.

She arrived at the office just minutes before nine.

Melinda greeted her with a big smile, as always. "Still showing up," she said. "That's a good sign. How was your week?"

The May morning was a bit chilly. As Jill was taking off her light jacket to hang on the coat rack she turned to Melinda with eyes wide. "You," she stated emphatically, "would not believe my week."

"That good, huh?"

"I think my life is becoming infinitely better, and it's all because I started coming here."

"Wow, I never heard that before. I think you just made my day, and it's only nine in the morning."

Just then the door to the doctor's office opened, and the young girl Jill had seen twice before came out. She looked subdued this time.

"You okay, Gail?" Melinda asked.

"That was hard," Gail replied. "I just watched myself die in the great San Francisco earthquake. It happened so fast. One minute I was living a wonderful life, the next minute gone."

"Would you like to make another appointment?"

"No, not right now. Maybe in awhile."

"That's fine," Melinda said. "Just call when you're ready, and I'll be happy to set you up."

"She's not coming back," said Melinda after Gail left. Before Jill could reply, the buzzer rang on Melinda's phone, and she said "Your turn. Go on in."

Minutes later Jill was relaxing on the couch, preparing for another trip back in time.

Simon brought her through their usual routine. "Have you found your next lifetime, Jill?" he finally asked.

She answered almost immediately. "Yes, there I am."

Again he smiled at the way she phrased things. "Can you tell me where you are, Jill? What are you doing?"

"I'm at a party. It's a wonderful time: singing, dancing, lots of drinking."

"Do you know what country you are in?"

"No. I'm in a large building of some sort. I believe it might be a theater. Don't know what we are celebrating, but it sure is a good time. Everyone's all dressed up. I think we are in the States."

"Do you mean the United States, Jill?"

"Yes."

"Can you tell where?"

"No, but ..." she paused, and when she spoke again Simon noticed a change in the sound of her voice, "I may be a bit tipsy."

BOSTON, 1851

Charlotte Adelaide Pechel was more than a little tipsy. Her twin sister Camilla said, "You're stark raving drunk, Charlotte."

"Am not," Charlotte tried to say, but it was obvious to everyone remaining at the party that she was indeed four sheets to the wind.

They were attending the Lion's Ball at the Boston Theater. Outside snow was beginning to fall. Inside it was warm, thanks in part to the three-hundred fifty people who had attended this first major ball of the season. Charlotte had been thrilled to meet Nathaniel Hawthorne, who was one of the loveliest men she had ever met. He had spent twenty minutes talking with her about his many books, and had even let on that a new book was to be published in a few months. Charlotte promised to read it, although she had never read any of his work.

The food had been spectacular. Lobster, lamb, and buns with currents had been served. Plates with poultry and hot stewed oysters could be found in every corner. Eating was the number one priority for many of the guests. Now, as February turned into March and the clock neared three a.m., most of the revelers had left for home.

Charlotte had been the life of the party for the last half hour. If the others weren't listening to her they were talking about her. Edwin, her husband, had been off in a corner speaking business with some other gentlemen. Now he was making a beeline for his wife.

"My dear, you are causing a scene," he said as he took her by the arm and not so gently tried to pull her away from the group around her, his face becoming redder by the second. "Are you trying to embarrass me?"

"Embarrass you?" she said, her words slurred, her eyes blurry.

It was obvious to Edwin that she was about to pass out. He asked Camilla to call for his carriage.

"Running from the scene of the crime, Edwin?" asked Camilla.

Charlotte, drunk as she was, noticed the smirk on Camilla's face. Her sister had never liked Edwin. After five years of marriage, Charlotte was beginning to agree with her. She turned to Camilla. "Yes, slave girl, get my ride."

Camilla always played along with her sister no matter the circumstances. She bowed deeply, as a man would, and said, "I shall do so directly, my queen."

Ten minutes later, Edwin and Charlotte were heading home. The ride to their apartment on High Street was relatively short, but Edwin used the time to berate his wife, even waking her on one occasion to continue his tirade. "How dare you make such a scene? Do you have any idea who was listening to you? You are going to make a laughingstock out of us."

All she could do was look at him through sleepy eyes. She would remember none of his words when she awoke sometime the next afternoon. "Poor Edwin," she sighed drunkenly, "do you hate me?"

"I love you," he said, finally calming a bit, "but you must use some judgment once in a while. I was talking business with two gentlemen who could help me immensely when Mister Dalton ran up and told me you were talking about the Irish again. Why must you harp on that matter so?"

Of all the things that annoyed Charlotte, the subject of the Irish in Boston was number one. They were coming to her city in droves, destitute people who could do nothing for the place she called home. Like many Bostonians, she wished they could all be shipped back to Ireland, potato famine or not.

As the carriage arrived at High Street she passed out once again. Edwin carried her up the stairs and put her to bed.

Charlotte was born in Germany in October of 1824, twelve minutes before Camilla. They were the only children of Rudolph and Anna Schultze. Rudolph had been a policeman but hated the job. One day his uncle, who had traveled to America, sent him a letter telling him about this wonderful country where anyone who worked hard could become rich. Jobs were plentiful, his uncle wrote, and Rudolph believed him. Anna had not wanted to leave Germany, however. It took him three months to convince her that moving to the United States would be good for them.

They set sail four months before the twins' seventh birthday, and arrived in New York on July first, 1831. They hated New York. It was much larger than their small hometown, and more people were arriving every day. They stayed four months before Rudolph heard about a small community of German settlers in Boston. They moved just before the snows of winter hit. Rudolph found a job in the shoe industry as a salesman. He traveled throughout New England selling his wares and was good at it. Before long the Schultze family was well off.

Rudolph and Anna couldn't have had two more outgoing children. Charlotte and Camilla could enchant anyone. They would put on plays at a moment's notice and people would think they had rehearsed them for weeks, when the truth was they were all ad-libbed. Like many twins, they always seemed to know what the other was thinking and often finished each other's sentences.

By their eighteenth birthday, the girls had developed into lovely young ladies, with long brown hair, light brown eyes, and large mouths with full lips. They were five-foot five, with large breasts and shapely legs. They had their pick of gentlemen friends and changed them often. Marriage, they both agreed, couldn't possibly be as much fun as they were having. They frequently double-dated, and often switched partners halfway through the evening. They never told and were never caught.

They had lost their virginity on just such a date shortly after turning fifteen. Charlotte slept with a tall German boy named Herman while Camilla slept with a Norwegian lad named Sven. A half hour later each slept with the other man. Herman and Sven, happy as larks, had no clue.

Charlotte also discovered alcohol when she was fifteen. Her father kept a cabinet full of bottles, mostly for special occasions. Rudolph rarely drank, and Anna never did. One day the girls were home alone and Charlotte decided they should see what alcohol tasted like. Camilla took one sip, gagged, and didn't touch another drop for five years. Charlotte took a sip and was hooked. It made her feel warm all over. She took another swallow, then two more. She might have died from alcohol poisoning that day if Camilla hadn't stopped her. Soon she was making excuses to stay home just to hit the liquor cabinet. Their taste for alcohol was the first difference between the girls. Five years later a greater split occurred.

In the winter of 1844 Boston Harbor froze over. It was sheer ice from the wharves all the way out to Boston Light. Charlotte and Camilla ventured out to see and decided to take a walk on the ice. Moments later, Charlotte hit a slick patch and lost her balance. Her arms began windmilling as she started to fall backwards. Half way down she suddenly felt two arms catching her from behind.

"Whoa there lady, let's not have your pretty little head hitting the ice."

Charlotte turned and saw a beaming oval face, cheeks red from the cold. It was her first glimpse of Edwin Pechel. "You may have just saved my life," she said.

Camilla had come rushing over. She looked at Edwin and said, "Nice catch."

They chatted for a while, and he invited the girls to a small shop down the street for hot chocolate and biscuits. The girls agreed.

Edwin Pechel was a publisher with offices on Congress Street. It was a small company but growing quickly. He was twenty eight and married only to his job. His family had emigrated from Germany forty years before the Schultze family. Although never a ladies' man, he was immediately taken by the twins.

Edwin was not the type of man Charlotte and Camilla usually dated. He was a little too stuffy and straight-laced, the sort of fellow Camilla referred to as a "dump and run." An hour over hot chocolate was enough for her.

For whatever reason, Charlotte saw him differently. She didn't think it was because he had saved her from a nasty headache, or worse. He was polite, good-looking, and seemed kind. He wasn't too tall, maybe five-nine, and probably not much over a hundred fifty pounds. His light brown hair was already thinning, and he wore small round glasses with gold frames.

When they stood up to leave, Camilla said, "A pleasure to meet you, Edwin," then shook his hand and turned to go.

Charlotte lingered. "Thank you again for catching me," she said.

"Right spot at the right time," he replied.

It seemed as though he were going to let it go at that, so Charlotte spoke up. "Perhaps you would like to see me again, without my sister?"

He looked like the idea had never occurred to him, but said, "That would be nice."

"When do you have some free time?"

Camilla was shocked. Why would Charlotte want to see him again? He certainly didn't seem like the fun type.

He quickly determined the work he had planned on doing the following night at the publishing house could wait. "Would tomorrow night be too soon?"

"That would be wonderful," Charlotte had agreed.

To Camilla's chagrin, Charlotte started seeing Edwin once or twice a week, along with other men she was dating at the same time. After a month, she resolved to date Edwin exclusively. Camilla never understood, and the more she came to know Edwin, the less she liked him. However, in June of 1846, Charlotte Schultze and Edwin Pechel were married.

After four years of marriage, Charlotte had begun to think that her sister had been right. Edwin worked long hours, often returning home late at night and leaving first thing in the morning. His love-making lacked passion, and he was usually too tired to take the time. Charlotte wasn't about to give up on their marriage, but she needed some spice in her life. She began to drink more than ever. Nights on the town ended in drunken fights with Edwin. She made a scene at the opera on one occasion, and he refused to go back for a year. He began to fear taking her anywhere in public.

As 1851 began, both knew their marriage was in trouble. Edwin grew tired of going to functions alone and having to explain her absence. However, taking her anywhere that served alcohol was out of the question. She had begged him to take her to the Lion's Ball, promising to behave, and he had finally relented. She had done well for most of the evening. It was only after most of the guests had left that she had started drinking in earnest.

The day after the ball Charlotte awoke about two in the afternoon. Her head was pounding. She tried to eat but couldn't keep anything down. She finally realized she needed to change. The drinking was going to kill her if Edwin didn't do it first. She had to stop. How many times before had she said that after a night on the town? Too many to count, she knew, but it was now or never. "Decision made," she said.

She sat at the kitchen table and pulled a newspaper toward her. It was a two-day-old copy of the *Boston Pilot*. She browsed through the pages with bloodshot eyes. A new Verdi opera was coming to the Howard Athenaeum. Edwin would want to go to that, she thought. She continued glancing through the paper; the pages were full of "Missing Friends", Irish people looking for long lost loved ones. She read:

OF PATRICK GOUDY, native of Coolcra, parish of
Two-Mile-Burrows, co Tipperary, who sailed to NY
five years ago on the Nestor, then went to Pennsylvania.
Wife's name Maria. Information will be received by his
brother, Daniel Goudy, at the post office in Lynn, MA.

Charlotte was unsure why she hated the Irish so much. She knew the famine in Ireland was killing thousands, and the only good food they could grow was taken by the English. Why didn't the English feed them, she wondered?

As she tried to recall last evening, she wondered how outrageously she had been talking. Other than meeting Nathaniel Hawthorne, she didn't remember much. She wasn't even sure how she had arrived home.

NOVEMBER, 1856

The common was crowded with people. It was election week and everyone was in a festive mood. Charlotte and Edwin took their time walking along Park Street as they headed for the food booths. They had been on the common all morning and both were starving. Edwin found a booth selling a plate full of oysters for six and a quarter cents and bought two plates. Charlotte bought baked beans and a steaming slice of brown bread, and then they headed for the drink carts. Edwin purchased some ginger beer for himself and lemonade for his wife, and they finally settled on a bench under an old elm tree to eat.

"Don't you just love election week?" asked Charlotte.

"I'd like it better if my candidate won occasionally." Edwin smiled as he said this, no bitterness at all in his voice. It was a running joke that he always backed the losing candidate.

"Someday, Edwin, your man will win." Charlotte ate her beans and stared out at the crowd.

They had celebrated their tenth anniversary five months earlier. Their lives had changed a great deal since Charlotte had given up drinking. It had been a tremendous struggle for her, but she had held firm. She hadn't touched a drop since that night at the Lion's Ball. Edwin and Camilla were both incredibly proud of her.

Charlotte remained close to her sister, although she didn't see her as often as she used to. Camilla had finally married two years ago on their thirtieth birthday. Her husband was an actor named Forrest Garrison. The stage company he was with performed throughout the northeast, and he and Camilla spent many months traveling to New York, Philadelphia, and Washington. Edwin was still the only subject that came between the two sisters.

"He's lousy in bed," Camilla would say.

"You don't know that," Charlotte would always answer, even though she had told her sister exactly that more than once.

Besides the changes she had made with her drinking, Charlotte had also changed her attitude towards the Irish. Edwin had helped her with that. Once he realized she really did intend to stop her drunken ways, he took it upon himself to open her eyes to the Irish situation.

"I have two Irish men working for me, you know," he said to her one day.

"Really?" The Irish people she saw on the street didn't look like they wanted to work.

"Truly," he said. "Patrick Delany works in the printing room, setting copy. Hugh Brady, who started with me as a janitor four years ago, now spends most of his time repairing the equipment that is constantly giving us trouble. Turns out he has a knack for it, and if I'd asked him the right questions when I hired him he never would have been a janitor. They are both hard workers."

"I didn't know," was all Charlotte could think to say.

"That's part of your problem. You have these strong opinions regarding things you really don't know anything about. These are people who had to flee their homeland because they were starving to death. Many of them lost family members to disease and hunger. The English are treating them brutally and with seeming indifference. They have come here trying to survive."

Charlotte just stared at her husband, not saying a word.

"I don't mean to yell at you. I'm sorry."

"There is no need to be sorry," she said. "I have been in the wrong here, and I am grateful to you for pointing it out to me. I want to change, I really do."

"Come to the office with me someday and meet them," he said. "You will find they are not the villains you make them out to be."

She had only been to his office a handful of times since their marriage, but she took him up on his offer. A week later she met Patrick Delany and Hugh Brady. They were standoffish at first, for they knew all about her opinion of them. She realized it immediately, and told them so. "I've been unkind to the Irish because of my stupidity. I hope you can forgive me. I am going to change all that."

She began going to Edwin's office on a regular basis. She learned about his work, saw the effort he put in, and became intrigued by the entire process of publishing. She made it a point to see Patrick and Hugh whenever she was there, and over time they thawed towards her. Three months after they first met, she invited them and their families over for dinner. It had been a marvelous time, and Charlotte couldn't believe how cruel and naïve she had been in the past. From that point on she began apologizing to all her friends whenever she met them, telling them what a fool she had been on the subject of the Irish.

"Ready?" Edwin was looking at her, his two plates full of oysters gone, his ginger beer finished.

"What?" Charlotte realized she had been daydreaming. "Oh, almost. I just have to finish my brown bread. It was really very good."

Charlotte took his hand as they began the walk home. Her life had changed in so many ways these past five years. However, one big problem still remained, and she had known it for a long time now.

She just didn't love him.

Chapter Twenty

Jill was horrified. "I was a terrible person," she moaned.

Simon had seen this reaction before from other clients. "I'm sure we have all had past lives that we would rather forget," he said. "Just remember, you are a good person in this life."

"I was a drunken tramp," she rambled on, "and I hated the Irish. What was that all about? And Tony! I'm married to Tony, my ex-husband, for goodness sake. And he's nice, while I'm rotten."

Simon needed to slow her down. "Okay, Jill, now I want you to take a deep breath and calm down."

"But—"

"Right now," Simon demanded.

Jill did as he said. She realized she had been rattling on and remained quiet.

Simon gave her a smile. "There," he said, "that's better. Let's try to stay focused on the fact that you are Jill, not Charlotte, and from everything I know about you, you are a wonderful person.

"Charlotte wasn't," she mumbled.

"Perhaps not. Maybe it is too early to tell. Let's just focus on what we can for now. You say that Edwin is your former husband Tony?"

"Yes. Why would I marry him two lifetimes in a row? And why was he so rotten to me this time when it appears he was an okay guy back then?"

"Perhaps the question should be why did *he* marry *you* this time?"

She looked up at him, a bit startled. Then she thought about it for a moment and said, "Good point. As awful as I was in Boston, why would he marry me again?"

"Precisely. Another example of karma, I assume, although we don't yet know what the future holds for Charlotte and Edwin. Who else did you recognize?"

"My sister. Camilla is still my sister, though we are not twins now, of course. Rudolph and Anna are my parents again too. It seems the whole family has come back together."

"Certainly not uncommon," Simon noted.

Suddenly Jill blurted out, "I knew Nathaniel Hawthorne. That's the first famous person we've come across in my regressions."

"Have you read much of his work?"

"No. I think the only book of his I've read is *The House of Seven Gables*. I liked that book. It was one of the few books they assigned in high school that I actually read."

"Perhaps he will show up again in your next regression. In the meantime, I would like you to go home and take an honest look at what you have just learned. You weren't a tramp, Jill. From what I heard you were loyal to your husband, even against your sister's wishes. You apparently overcame a drinking problem. As for your opinion of the Irish, you certainly were not alone in that respect. They were outcasts in Boston for years as I recall."

"But I used to *be* Irish," she said.

"You didn't know that though, did you? You used to be English also, and they treated the Irish terribly during the famine years. Each life is different, Jill. Less than two months ago you were unaware of any past lives. Don't beat yourself up over something you cannot change. "

Melinda buzzed the doctor to let him know his next client had arrived. He looked at Jill. "I know these were not the regression memories you were looking for. However, it was your life. I hope you want to come back and continue the story."

"Could it get much worse?"

"There's only one way to find out, Jill. Come back next Tuesday and we shall see."

"I wish I knew if Niall/Jared was going to show up." It was after all the main reason she had continued these sessions in the first place.

"Do you need time to think about it?" Simon asked.

As unhappy as she was with the way her Boston saga had started, Jill wasn't ready to give up on it just yet. "I'll be back," she said.

Tuesday night Jill called Lauren. She needed to talk about her regression and hoped her best friend would help her find the silver linings. Instead, Lauren seemed to get a kick out of Jill's story.

"My goodness, you were a floozy," Lauren said. "Your sister, too. That part about you two sharing lovers was priceless. There's a daytime soap opera for you."

Jill was less than amused by Lauren's description of her. "Hey," she said, "I'm not proud of it. I'm looking for some help in understanding it."

"Jill, chill out." Lauren realized Jill was taking this way too seriously. "Listen, I told you before we have led many lives. In some we may have been Good Samaritans, famous people, wonderful leaders. In others, we walked on the other side of the street: murderers, scoundrels, cheats. It's how we learn, how we grow as a spiritual being. So you spent your youth as a drunk and a floozy. So what? Look at how many people are leading lives like that right now. You obviously learned something from that life. You drink responsibly. You don't sleep around. You are a good person, Jill, and one of the reasons you are is because of the lessons you've learned in your past lives."

"I guess you're right," Jill finally replied. "I was just hoping for a much better story."

"Who's to say it won't get better? Hey, maybe you had an affair with Nathaniel Hawthorne."

That brought a smile to Jill's face. "He was cute."

Jill thanked Lauren, and a few minutes later they said their goodbyes. Jill was lying on her bed, staring at the computer. She knew there were parts of her Boston life she could look up online, but decided not to start any of that tonight. Talking about the cute Mister Hawthorne had made her think of the date she had coming up with Neal. She was looking forward to seeing him.

Wednesday night she went to the Inner Peace Sanctuary for her meditation session. She had trouble calming her mind at first. The events of her regression kept popping into view, but finally she was able to relax and concentrate. She was beginning to feel a part of the group and was pleased that she was finally getting out of the house and meeting new people.

Thursday night she made supper for the boys a little earlier than usual and told them she was going out on a date.

"You're going out again?" Bret asked.

"Are you going to miss me? I thought you enjoyed being home alone."

"When will you be back?"

He seemed so serious, Jill had to laugh. "Why, do I have a curfew?"

Bret suddenly decided to play the part of the man of the family. "You be in by eleven," he said, shaking a finger at her, "or you will be grounded. Do you hear me?"

Jill ran her hand through his hair and mussed it up. "I'm sure I will be home by eleven. You make sure nothing goes wrong while I'm gone, okay?"

Bret agreed, and ten minutes later Jill was in her car heading for the bookstore. She arrived a few minutes before six. The store had a small coffee area off to the left, and she saw Neal seated there. "Hello," she said.

Neal stood up, appearing apprehensive. "Hi. I'm glad you came."

"I've been looking forward to it," she replied.

He pulled out a chair for her and Jill sat down. He was drinking a mocha latte, and asked if he could get something for her.

"No, thank you."

They chatted for a while, and then discussed where they should go for dinner. They decided on Italian, and Jill suggested Amelio's.

"That would be fine," said Neal. "It's close by, and I'm starving."

Amelio's was busy for a Thursday night, and the aromas that floated around the dining room made Jill's mouth water. They ended up with a corner table in a side room, giving them some privacy from the rest of the crowd. Neal suggested a bottle of Chianti, but Jill said one glass would be enough for her, so they ordered separately. When the wine came, they placed their order, and then Jill said, "Why don't you start by telling me about yourself?"

He told her about his job as an insurance agent, a disastrous first marriage, and his second marriage and the two wonderful daughters he had with his second wife. Tragically, his wife had died four years ago in a car crash. Where this was Jill's second date in two years, it turned out to be his first date in four.

"It took me a long time to get over it," he said. "My dad had just passed away six months earlier. I had my mother move into our home with us. She pretty much raises her grandchildren while I work. I guess we helped each other cope with our losses."

Jill then had her turn recapping her life, and she saw a sympathetic look on Neal's face when she told of Tony's betrayal.

The food came and they dived in. They were getting comfortable with each other, thought Jill. It felt nice. They made small talk about movies, the kids' schools, and the state of politics in Willis. When they finished eating, they drank the last of their wine and sat back to let the food digest.

It had been a pleasant evening, and when Neal suggested they go out again, Jill said yes. He took her back to her car in the bookstore parking lot, where they hugged each other and said goodnight.

She made it home well before Bret's curfew.

Chapter Twenty-One

The next morning Jill awoke in high spirits. She was humming as she made the boys their breakfast.

Bret gave Mark a soft kick under the table, nodding at her. "Mom must have had a good date last night, Mark," he said. "She's humming old people music."

"Maybe her date was old," replied Mark, and both boys broke out laughing.

"Alright, you two, that's enough picking on mom." She was pleased the boys seemed okay about her having a date.

"Was he nice?" Bret asked.

She knew how important this was to them. She didn't think they really wanted another man in their life competing with their father. "Yes, he was very nice, Bret."

"Are you going to see him again?" Mark asked.

"I believe so, probably this weekend." She thought they took it as well as could be expected. She had never really talked with them about seeing other men because she hadn't dated since their father left. She determined that it would probably be a good thing to do. Maybe Sunday night after the boys came home from their dad's she would sit down and talk with them.

At noon, Kim, a fellow hostess from The Ravenwood, called asking if she could take Jill's shift that night. "My husband broke his hand yesterday on a construction site and he's going to be out of work for awhile," Kim said. "I could really use the money."

Jill was happy to let her have the shift. *My set schedule sure is getting changed a lot lately*, she thought. With a Friday night free, Jill considered the possibilities. She decided to call Lauren and see if she wanted to go out.

"It's my friend the floozy," Lauren said when she heard Jill's voice. "Oh wait, that was your last life."

"Very funny," said Jill. "I have the night off from work. Would you like to go out and do something?"

"Hey, good timing. Bill has gone out on a photo shoot, and won't be back until Sunday morning. I'd love to get together, but I do have some things I need to get done later. How about if I pick you up around eight? Maybe we can catch a late movie."

"Sounds good to me. I'll be ready."

Jill finished a new batch of work that she had picked up yesterday, and then spent the afternoon reading the latest Stephen King novel. She enjoyed his books, but tried not to read them at night. Sometimes they just scared her too much.

Tony picked up the boys at quarter past four and Jill decided to go to Sammy Chong's Restaurant for some take-out food. She figured she would have some quiet time before Lauren picked her up.

She figured wrong.

The man in the brown Plymouth wagon watched Jill leave her home. Right on time, he thought. He had been following her for ten days now, ever since she had cut him off. He hated when people did that to him. It was one of the ways he found his victims. Idiot drivers deserved the wrath he brought.

His name was William Allen Zink, but most people knew him as The Snake. In high school, he had a snake tattooed on his right arm. The tail of the beast started just above his wrist and wound its way up to a hissing head situated at his shoulder. He thought it was an impressive sight and gave him power.

Nothing else about Zink was impressive. He was short, barely five-seven, and had never weighed more than a hundred forty pounds. He had black hair that was course and unmanageable, and the cream he used to try and control it gave him a greasy look. His face had been pock-marked by a severe case of chicken pox as a child. His attempts to make friends in high school had been rebuffed. He had been alone and angry his entire life and he spent most of his time getting even.

His criminal life started with shoplifting when he was twelve. He had been arrested twice on that charge, so he began robbing people on the street; mostly elderly women whom he didn't think would fight back. Unfortunately, his description was easy for people to remember, particularly once he had the tattoo. He ended up serving six months in an Oregon prison. He was released early due to overcrowded conditions at the jail, moved to California and resumed his ways. Caught again, he spent four years behind bars before escaping from a work release assignment. He decided to head east, and spent ten years in Iowa and Indiana before moving to South Carolina and resuming what he had started in those states: home invasions.

Not when anyone was home, of course. He tended to get hurt in any altercation he was in, so he took great joy in ruining people's lives while they were away. He would take whatever money or jewelry he could find and simply destroy everything else. The next day he would joyfully read about his handiwork in the newspaper, and then cut out the articles and put them in his scrapbook.

The idiot lady who nearly ran him off the road was going to be his next victim.

He always followed his prey for a while to get down their routines. This one was pretty simple. A quick peek into her mailbox had given him her name. She didn't seem to work much, just some weekend shifts. The ex-hubby came by and took the kids over the weekend, which made his job easy. He had called the restaurant where she worked yesterday to make sure she was on the schedule for tonight, and the airhead who answered the phone had told him all he needed to know. Jill Palmer was working a five-to-midnight shift. He would have plenty of time to go through the house for valuables.

As he watched Jill leave for work, a smile came over his face. He decided to go grab a bite to eat. Then, around seven, when the neighborhood had quieted down, he would strike.

Jill returned home just after five, parked her car in the garage and closed the door. She wouldn't need it again tonight since Lauren was picking her up.

After eating, Jill headed upstairs to her bedroom. She wanted to look up some things about Boston before Lauren arrived. She went over her regression, trying to remember as much as she could, and decided to start with Nathaniel Hawthorne.

There were a plethora of links for Hawthorne. She found one in particular that gave a wonderful biography of his life. After reading his story, Jill perused the list of all the books he had written. She had been unable to remember a single one other than *The House of Seven Gables*, but now she saw *The Scarlet Letter* listed. He wrote that, she thought? She had certainly heard of that one. As she read on, she discovered that *The House of Seven Gables* was a follow-up to *The Scarlet Letter*.

"I guess I should read that sometime," she spoke aloud to the computer screen. Then she looked at the dates the books were published and the hair on her arms went straight up.

THE SCARLET LETTER, 1850

THE HOUSE OF SEVEN GABLES, 1851

She thought back to her regression and was certain she remembered it correctly. The Lion's Ball was in 1851. She had talked with

Hawthorne, and he told her his new book would be coming out soon—*The House of Seven Gables*. The only book by Hawthorne she had read in this life was the same book she had told him she would read in that life. There had to be some subconscious connection there. Once again, Jill was amazed by the things her regressions brought out.

She spent some time trying to find something about the Lion's Ball, but came up empty. She checked out her name, her sister's name, and that of her husband, but found nothing. A few more minutes, she thought, and then she needed to get ready for her night out with Lauren.

Twenty seconds later, she heard something shatter in her kitchen.

The Snake was in a happy mood. He always was whenever he was about to embark on a destructive tirade. He had parked the wagon in the lot of a playground half a mile away. From there, he jogged to the Palmer residence. If anyone saw him, he was just one of those countless morons out for a run.

As he reached her driveway, he stopped. Anyone seeing him would think he was just catching his breath. He discreetly looked around the neighborhood and didn't see anyone watching. He waited for a moment as a car passed on the main road, and then he put his plan into effect. He waved, as if he had seen someone in the Palmer house, ran up the driveway, slipped by the side of the garage and entered the backyard. He didn't bother to check the garage for a car because he had seen her leave and knew she was not home.

A quick glimpse told him the backyard was empty. He went to the back door and was prepared to pick the lock, but first tried the handle. The door opened. He couldn't believe his good fortune. "The idiot lady doesn't even lock her doors," he mumbled. She deserved what she was going to get for being so stupid. This, he felt certain, was going to be a perfect evening.

He passed through a small foyer, entered the kitchen, and gazed around the room. On occasion he would be lucky enough to find a stash of cash in the freezer or in some old mason jar, but not often. The fun of the kitchen came when he threw the food all over the place, covering the walls, cabinets and floor. He always felt giddy doing that. He usually saved it for last, however, because it made such a mess.

He searched the room, freezer and all, but found no money, so he began looking for the first piece to be destroyed. He liked to choose the first piece carefully because it began the night's festivities and should be something noteworthy. He was about to leave the kitchen when he saw it sitting in a corner, partially hidden by the microwave.

It was a vase. It looked like the real deal, but you can never tell. He picked it up and turned it over. Waterford. A glow came over him. It was not only the real deal, but top of the line. He thought it was a fantastic item to start his night of destruction. He examined the vase closely, running his hands over the edges. If he was one to steal larger items, he would definitely take this. It was beautiful. Instead, he raised his right hand high and smashed the vase on the kitchen floor.

Upstairs, the crash made Jill jump. "What in heaven's name ..." she said, stunned by the jolting sound. She thought it came from inside the house, but that was crazy. She was home alone. What could it have been, she wondered? She was about to head for the door when she suddenly had a feeling she knew what had made that noise.

Her Waterford vase. Crystal always sounded different from regular glass when it broke. But how could that be? It was not near the edge of the counter where it could fall. She stood motionless for a moment, listening for any more sounds. Fear replaced shock, and Jill realized her heart was pounding. Was someone in her home? She reached the doorway when she felt ... what? Something caused her to stop, and moments later the next crash came.

The Snake walked over the broken pieces of crystal as he headed towards the living room. The rest of the kitchen he would save for last. He looked around the living room and was impressed. The lady had a nice home. Good stuff, not cheap. All the better, he thought. Now the order of destruction didn't matter. Just break everything. He walked to the far end of the room where a lamp sat on an end table. He picked it up and smashed it on the floor. Then, as he turned to look for the next object of his desire, his instincts kicked in. What was that? Houses always made strange noises, he knew: drafty windows, refrigerators turning on, creaking floorboards. Yes, that was it. It sounded like someone walking on a creaky floor. But it couldn't be. There was nobody here but him. They probably had a pet that he had startled. Still, it didn't pay to take chances. He had better check it out. Besides, it would be best to do the upstairs first.

He noticed the stairs leading up to the second floor and headed that way.

Jill started shaking when she heard the second crash. It was definitely inside the house. Someone was here, breaking things. All at once she remembered the article from the newspaper. For a moment she was glued to the floor, afraid to move. They must not know I'm here, she thought. Sweat beaded on her forehead and her hands turned clammy. Her mind went blank for a second and she couldn't decide what to do. Then she heard a soft sound, slowly repeated a second and third time. It was a sound she had heard a thousand times. Someone was coming up the stairs.

She quickly closed and locked the bedroom door as quietly as she could. She was thankful to be in her bedroom. It was the only room on the floor, besides the bathroom, that had a lock. Tony had put it on so the kids wouldn't walk in on them during their lovemaking sessions.

Jill tip-toed to the cordless phone by her computer and dialed 9-1-1. The phone was answered on the third ring.

"9-1-1, what is your emergency?" The voice sounded semi-bored.

Jill whispered softly into the phone. "My name is Jill Palmer. 28 Clearwater Road. There's someone in my home."

The dispatcher, Delores Sullivan, woke up in a hurry. "Someone in your home? Do you mean an intruder?"

"Yes. He's breaking things."

Now Delores really perked up. Everyone in the station had been talking about the home invader. She repeated Jill's address to verify it.

"Yes," cried Jill, still trying to keep her voice down. "Hurry, I don't think he knows I'm here yet, but he's coming upstairs."

"I'm sending help right now," Delores said. "Can you stay on the line?"

"I'll try."

"You say you're upstairs. Can you tell me where?"

"My bedroom. Front of the house, right-hand corner as you look from the street."

"How many intruders?" asked Delores.

"I don't know, but one is coming upstairs," she repeated, the urgency in her voice picking up, making it sound thinner and higher pitched.

"Keep this line open, but stay quiet. I have two police cars on the way."

"Thank you," Jill said so softly she doubted the dispatcher heard.

Then there was a loud knocking on her door.

The Snake walked slowly up the stairs, gazing at the floor above as he did. He still believed the noise he heard must have come from an animal of some kind, but he wasn't sure. If it was a dog, it should be barking. What else could it be? Another burglar, he mused, and chuckled to himself. At the top of the stairs he checked the layout. There was a bedroom on his left, obviously one of the kid's rooms, a bathroom, and then another bedroom. All of the doors were open. Reaching the top of the stairs, he turned to check out the front room. The door was closed.

He made a quick check of the open rooms, and noticed that each kid had his own computer. They looked new. Apparently this lady was rich and didn't have to work much. He looked forward to smashing the computers. First things first, though. He headed to the closed door, which had to be the master bedroom.

He listened for a moment as he reached the door and thought he heard something. Very slowly, he turned the door knob and found it locked. Now that wasn't good. Fraidy-cat dog—he smiled at his play on words—would not be locking the door. A fraidy-cat person, well now, that was another story entirely. Someone was here. He listened again and thought he heard the faintest sound of a whisper. What to do? He could just walk out of the house and no one would see him. Still, this was a new situation for The Snake. He knew there was no man of the house, so who could it be? He decided to find out.

He banged on the door.

Jill jumped and let out a gasp.

Hearing the noise over the phone, Delores asked, "What was that?"

Jill spoke into the phone, louder now. "He's knocking on the door."

The dispatcher made a quick call, and then said, "Hold on, honey. The police are two minutes away. Do you have anything to defend yourself with?"

Jill looked around the room. What could she use to defend herself? She saw a leaded glass paperweight on her computer table. *I could throw it at him,* she thought, *or bash his head in.* She took one step towards the desk when she was startled by the sound of snapping wood. She dropped the phone. The intruder was kicking in the door. She jumped back, looking for the phone, but it had bounced under the bed where she couldn't see it. Just then the door flew open. "He's in the room," Jill hollered.

The Snake strode into her bedroom and heard her yell. He was surprised to see it was Jill Palmer. "Thought you went to work," he said. "Who you talking to?"

He was now closer to the computer than she was. The paperweight was not going to help her. She backed away against the far wall, glancing around for anything she could use to defend herself. She grabbed a wire hanger that was lying by her nightstand, thinking that maybe she could poke at his eyes with it. The man was moving slowly around her bed, taking his time, enjoying the moment. She determined that she would fight him with all she had.

The Snake was excited by this turn of events. She was actually a very attractive woman, he noticed. Whatever thoughts he had of running away disappeared when he saw her. "I think we're gonna have some fun tonight," he said.

"Honey, what's happening?" The dispatcher suddenly shouted into the phone, loud enough for both of them to hear.

"What the …" The Snake bent down, saw the phone under the bed, and suddenly realized he should have run when he had the chance. "Oh no," he cried. He took a knife from his back pocket and opened it up. "I'm gonna cut you up," he snarled at Jill.

As he started towards her, Jill heard a sound and saw movement on her right.

"Freeze!" An officer in the doorway had his gun trained on The Snake. "Drop the knife!" he ordered as a second officer entered the room.

The Snake complied. The knife bounced on the floor and landed by the phone, and then the second cop handcuffed The Snake.

Knowing she was safe, Jill collapsed onto the floor and broke down crying.

Chapter Twenty-Two

As Lauren drove over to Jill's, she was debating where they should go. There was a Sean Connery movie at the cinema and a new nightclub opening in Spring Valley. She decided to leave it up to Jill. All of these thoughts quickly scattered when she turned onto Jill's street and observed the commotion.

There were police cars everywhere. Two were in Jill's driveway, another was on the street. A state police car was parked in a neighbor's yard, and she even saw a van with the NEWS 7 logo on the side. *What was going on*, she wondered. She noticed the neighbors standing in their front yard, staring at Jill's house. She had to park four houses down, and then she sprinted as fast as she could. An officer stopped her in the driveway.

"Is Jill okay?" she asked the cop breathlessly. Her heart was beating rapidly, much like Jill's had been less than an hour ago.

"Who are you?" asked the cop.

"I'm Lauren Masters. Jill Palmer is my best friend. Is she alright?"

"Miss Palmer is fine."

"What happened? Can I see her?"

"A man broke into her home not realizing she was there," he said. "We've been hoping to catch this guy for a while now. Thanks to your friend, we did."

"Can I see her?" Lauren asked again.

"She did mention you were coming. Let me see if she is finished giving her statement," said the officer. "You stay here."

Two minutes later, he came to the door and motioned to Lauren. "Come on in," he said.

Jill was sitting at the dining room table with two other officers. Lauren saw a smile, or maybe it was more a look of relief, come over her.

"Lauren," Jill called, getting up from the table. The two friends ran to each other and embraced.

"Are you okay?" asked Lauren.

"I'm okay now," Jill said. "It was awful. Come with me." She led Lauren to the table and introduced her to Sergeant Jeffrey Anderson and Officer Paul Wheeler. "They saved me from a terrible ordeal."

Both officers arose and shook hands with Lauren. "I think we have enough for now, Miss Palmer," the sergeant said. "If we have any more questions we will contact you." He handed her one of his cards. "If you think of anything else, just give me a call anytime."

"Thank you both so much," said Jill, and she gave each of them a hug.

Jill turned to Lauren and said, "First of all, I need a drink. Second, can I stay at your place tonight? I don't think I want to be here alone."

Lauren quickly agreed. "I have a full bottle of Captain Morgan's at my house. What say we just go straight there?"

Jill thought that was a great idea.

Stories of the home invasion and the capture of William Allen Zink were on the local news channels at ten o'clock. Jill called the boys after arriving at Lauren's house to tell them what happened and assure them she was okay. After finishing that call, she spent another hour on the phone with her parents, her sister, and Neal. Even though they had only been on one date, she didn't want him to worry if he saw the news.

The next morning Mark called her after seeing the story in the newspaper. "Mom, you're a hero," he said. "You're on the front page."

"I saw it," she replied, "but the police were the heroes, Mark, not me. I was just fortunate they came as fast as they did."

"Were you scared?"

"I was scared to death, honey. I hope you never have to go through anything like that."

Bret grabbed the phone from Mark. "Hey mom, did you get any sleep?"

"I slept fine, Bret." In part because of the very strong rum and Cokes Lauren made.

"I read the paper," said Bret. "You did great. I'm glad you're okay."

After finishing her call with the boys, Jill sat down and ate a small breakfast of pancakes and bacon that Lauren had made for her. Lauren was already at work with her first customer of the day, who had arrived while Jill was on the phone.

Jill left Lauren's after finishing her breakfast and headed home. She was nervous when she opened the door, and called out "Anyone here?" as she entered. She walked into the kitchen and looked around. She saw some small pieces of crystal still shining on the floor and vacuumed them up, then did the same in the living room, making sure there were no remnants of the table lamp on the floor. Another thin slice of fear invaded her as she went upstairs for the first time. The scene was still very fresh in her mind, and she knew it always would be. She had some uneasy moments throughout the day whenever she heard some unknown sounds. It seemed her hearing had suddenly become acute. After work that night, she slept in her bed, but sleep didn't come easily.

Sunday morning a reporter named Tim Davidson from the local paper came by to have her give a first-person account of the incident. Jill really just wanted to forget it, but he was persistent.

That afternoon she met Neal at the Broad Street Diner. One of the patrons recognized her and hollered out to everyone in attendance, "Hey, there's Jill Palmer, our local hero." She had to go over the whole story again with Neal, and was thankful when the food arrived so she could stop talking. Gratefully, Neal recognized her unease and led the conversation in other directions.

Sunday night her boys came home and it started all over again. They asked countless questions and pestered her until she couldn't take it anymore. Tony even came in when he brought them home just to tell her how happy he was that she was safe. He winced when she told him the intruder had broken the Waterford vase. He had bought that for her on their fifth anniversary and filled it with roses.

Monday Jill stayed home. She took the phone off the hook for most of the day and shut off her cell phone. She tried meditating in the morning, but her mind was just too active. That night she went through her new routine--locking every door and window in the house.

By Tuesday morning, Jill couldn't wait to get back to Simon's office for her next regression. The last few days had been crazy, but as she opened his office door she felt happy and relaxed. This was the place to be. *Want to get away?* she thought to herself in the car on the way over. *How about Boston, a hundred and fifty years ago?* It seemed like a great idea to her.

"There she is," Melinda called out as Jill walked in. "The woman of the hour."

"Please," Jill replied, holding up a hand indicating stop, "I've had enough. I just want to forget about it all for awhile."

"But you're famous!" Melinda shouted. "This is your fifteen minutes of fame." Jill said nothing, but Melinda saw the look of anguish come over Jill's face and turned serious. "I'm sorry," she said. "It must have been just awful for you."

Jill gave her a nod of agreement. "Thanks, Melinda. It was. I just want to move on. I've never wanted a regression more than I do today."

Ten minutes later, lying on the couch, Jill's wish came true.

Chapter Twenty-Three

BOSTON, 1858

Charlotte sat with Edwin in the Joy Street Church listening to the speaker, a fair-haired gentleman, somewhat gaunt yet with a lively voice. Jarvis McKay from New York was a leading anti-slavery spokesman. He had been brought to Boston by the local movement because they had heard wonderful comments about his speaking. He wasn't letting them down. Charlotte paid rapt attention as he continually banged his fist on the lectern to help make a point. Who would have believed such a strong voice could come from such a skinny human being?

"Slavery," McKay bellowed, "is an abomination in the eyes of God!"

Charlotte agreed. She took more interest in the world around her now, and the slavery issue was important to her. "Emancipation of the slaves is the only answer that God desires," McKay proclaimed. "If the cause is just, God will be on our side. And our cause is just!" he shouted. A great cheering broke out among the crowd. Charlotte came to her feet along with many others, clapping and yelling for more. McKay spoke for another two hours.

As they left the church that evening, Charlotte and Edwin decided to walk home. It was a crisp, clear summer night in early July. Charlotte loved Boston. The streets were narrow, too narrow for the bustling traffic which was growing all the time, yet they gave the city a homey feeling. The city was growing upward also. Every building now seemed to be five or six stories high. She wondered where it would end.

"It was a fine speech tonight," Edwin said to her.

"I agree," she said. "He was a wonderful speaker. The crowd seemed to be hanging on his every word."

"It's an important message. This country may be torn apart by the slavery issue, but it is worth fighting for."

She smiled at him. They had come to a peaceful understanding over the past few years. He loved her more than ever now that she was sober. She was still a beautiful woman, and he delighted in showing her off.

For her part, Edwin was more like a close friend. Their sex life was almost non-existent. They made love once a month or so, and as always with Edwin it was not in any way exciting. Charlotte often wondered if that was the way it was to be for her. She wished she could change him, teach him to be more outgoing and wild in bed, but he worked so hard he was often too tired to care much about sex.

"I almost forgot," he said, "we have been invited to the Pierpoint Farm this weekend. It will be partly business for me, but you will have all day to enjoy."

She had been there before on several occasions and always enjoyed it. "That will be nice," she said.

They finally arrived home and went inside. Ten minutes later, Edwin Pechel was sound asleep in his bed.

Pierpoint Farm was in Kingston. They had to take the train to get there, then a short buggy ride to the farm. It was a large place, well over two hundred acres. The main house consisted of thirteen rooms, and they needed every one of them. The Pierpoint's had nine children. A barn was located down a short hill from the house. In the other direction, Winston Pierpoint had built a meeting house, one large room that could hold two hundred fifty people comfortably. He held gatherings of all kinds there. On this day dozens of tables were set up with the finest china and silverware to feed the one hundred twenty people who had been invited.

The meal was scrumptious. Charlotte and Edwin had their fill. "I'm going to need to walk this off," she said to him.

"Plenty of walking to do around here," he replied. He gazed into her eyes, and she knew that he loved her in his own way. "My meeting should start soon. Stroll around the grounds, and have a good time. I'm probably going to be a few hours."

"Okay. I'll probably head down to the lake."

The farm had an adjoining lake about a mile to the north. Charlotte enjoyed spending time there listening to the loons and geese, so as soon as Edwin left for his meeting, she walked outside and headed that way.

It was another beautiful day, warm sunshine occasionally blocked by a high, puffy cloud. There was a slight breeze that ruffled her hair and helped her stay cool enough. She found the path to the lake and tried to remember the one spot she had always liked. It was a secluded area surrounded by maple trees and high growing brush. It was a wonderful place to become lost in.

The brush had grown much higher than her last visit, and she almost walked by the small opening. Using her left hand to guard against any branches whacking her, she slowly entered the clearing. She was about fifty feet from the edge of the water. To her left a string of trees blocked the view from outsiders, and thirty feet to her right the brush was so dense no one could possibly see through it. It was as though God had made a special outdoor room just for her. Anyone who didn't know where the entrance was would never find this place unless they arrived from the lake.

Charlotte walked halfway to the water and stopped. The view was delightful. The early afternoon sun was shimmering off the water as a sailboat gently glided by in the distance. There were ducks, dozens of them, floating on the surface of the lake.

"Good afternoon."

The voice came from behind and startled Charlotte. She turned to see a man sitting behind an easel, looking her over from head to toe. He was tucked back against the hedges, yet she was still surprised she hadn't seen him upon entering. "My goodness, you startled me," she said.

"Sorry about that. I hadn't expected company."

"Nor I." She noticed his easel and supplies. "I take it you're painting."

He smiled a soft smile that made him seem younger than his years. "Good guess. It's a fine painting of a sailboat on a lake. Now I may have to include a lovely lady by the shore."

She felt herself blushing. He was an attractive man, maybe thirty-five, with thick wavy light brown hair. He seemed to be in good shape, although not overly muscular. "How did you find this spot?" she asked.

He resumed his painting as he spoke. "It's my favorite spot on the lake. I come here often."

"How did you get here?"

That smile crossed his face again, and his eyes seemed to sparkle in the light. "My rowboat," he said, pointing off to the left. Charlotte turned and saw the boat pulled up on the shore, under a tree. "Easier to find this spot from the lake than it is from the path. I take it you have been here before?"

"Yes, several times."

"What's your name?" he asked as he dabbed another stroke of paint onto his canvas.

"Charlotte Pechel."

"Lovely name for a lovely lady."

He was flirting with her. She felt a warm tingle through her body. "And who might you be?"

"My name is Grey."

She laughed, thinking it funny. "Grey is a color, not a name."

He laughed with her, taking no offense. "Apparently my parents didn't realize that. Perhaps they knew I would be an artist."

"Are you?" she asked.

Indeed he was. Grey Talbot was one of the leading painters in New England. "You've seen the portrait of Mister Pierpoint in the main house?"

She had. It was a beautiful work of art, some five feet by three feet. "Yours?"

"I cannot deny it," he said. "Next month I am to do one of Missus Pierpoint."

"May I see what you are working on now?" Charlotte asked.

"Not yet." He brought her the stool he had been sitting on. "Here, take this and go down by the water's edge. Look out over the lake, if you would."

She did as he requested. For nearly an hour she sat quietly, gazing out at the horizon. Occasionally she would ask, "How's it coming?" He told her each time to just be patient. Her back to him, she pictured him in her mind. She wondered if he were married, then chided herself for thinking about such foolish things.

"Finished," he finally said. "Come and see."

She walked towards him, looking at him with eyes she hadn't used in years. She gave him her biggest smile, and he never took his eyes off her. As she reached him, he held out his hand to her and led her around to the painting.

She gasped. It was wondrous. He had in fact added her into the picture, not sitting on the stool but standing and looking out over the lake. "It's beautiful," was all she could think to say.

"Thank you. It was just a picture until you came along. Now it is a work of art."

"Do you flatter every woman you meet in such a manner?" she asked.

"I've never met a woman worth flattering until now."

She stared into his eyes and wished that were true. "Oh, I could get into a great deal of trouble with a man like you."

He brought her to him, and kissed her gently. She didn't resist. After all the years of pent-up frustration with Edwin, her body quaked with excitement. She let him kiss her again, more deeply this time.

He walked to his rowboat and took out a blanket and a basket of food. He spread the blanket on the ground, and beckoned her over.

She pointed at the basket. "I'm not hungry," she said. "I ate at the house."

"Good," he replied, "then we can move on to the dessert."

And they did.

Charlotte's affair with Grey Talbot began like a bolt of lightning and grew into a firestorm. His youthful good looks hid the fact that he was actually forty-four years old. She didn't care. Their lovemaking reminded her of cats in heat. It was vibrant, alive. She received more pleasure from him in the first month than Edwin had given her in twelve years.

When she wasn't with Grey she thought of him the whole day. He had a home in Ipswich and a small apartment in Boston. If she could get away, Charlotte would take the train to Ipswich. It was tricky, but she told Edwin she had a new girlfriend she liked to visit. Meeting Grey at his Boston apartment was much easier. Soon after Edwin left for work, she would go over and spend hours with Grey. They made love first thing in the morning, after lunch, in the afternoon.

"My painting is lagging behind," he would say to her, "but I don't mind. Making love to you is better than any picture I have ever painted."

After seeing Grey for a month Charlotte realized her sister had been right all these years. What was she doing with Edwin? She loved the house in Ipswich, which was right by the ocean. On the left as you entered was Grey's studio, the largest room downstairs. There were paintings everywhere, and works in progress that he was doing from his imagination. "When I'm too lazy to go out," he would say. Upstairs were three rooms that used to be four. Grey had taken down a wall and made one huge bedroom for himself. Outside the sandy beach almost looked white in the sun. At high tide the water was about seventy yards from his back door, which led out onto a deck. Grey loved to hold intimate parties of six or eight people on the deck in the summertime.

Charlotte loved being invited to those parties when she could get away. Initially she attended as "Grey's friend." Her marriage precluded them from being too open about their true relationship. It wasn't long, however, before people in Ipswich were talking about the beautiful lady who regularly came by train to visit their famous artist.

The apartment in Boston was much different. It was a small apartment on the second floor. The largest room was mostly occupied with dozens of paintings and supplies. A small easel stood by the back wall, but Grey rarely painted here. It was more a gallery to show interested people his work. The apartment had a small bedroom with just a bed and dresser.

"I don't actually live here," he had told her on their first visit, "but I sell more paintings to people in Boston than I do Ipswich, so I needed some place to store them." After meeting Charlotte, Grey spent a great deal more time in Boston.

Charlotte had been amazed when she first discovered where this apartment was—barely a block from where Edwin worked. How had she never run into Grey Talbot before?

It was two months before Edwin had his first suspicion. He had suggested they have sex before going to bed, but Charlotte had quietly demurred. He couldn't recall the last time she had said no, if ever. It occurred to him that they hadn't made love in some time, and she had not been nagging him about it. He began looking for signs, but found none. She still attended the local events with him, but her mind seemed to wander off a great deal. When they finally did make love, she seemed unenthused and glad when it was over. Something was definitely wrong, he thought, but what it was, he had no idea.

It was six months to the day when it all came apart for Charlotte. Grey was at the beach house. She hadn't seen him in four days and couldn't wait any longer. As soon as Edwin left for work, she headed for the train station. She felt invigorated. Her relationship with Grey was better than she ever imagined a relationship could be. She was sure Edwin had no idea. Her being married was a problem, of course, and one day she would have to come to grips with it, but for now she was having too much fun. As she boarded the train, her thoughts were on Ipswich and the rendezvous with her lover.

She didn't know she was being followed.

It had taken Edwin time to figure it out, and he didn't want to believe it. He loved her so, and thought she felt the same, but it had become obvious to him that something was wrong. She didn't seem to want to be with him. As shocking as it was to him, he finally came to the conclusion that Charlotte was having an affair. The thought dumbfounded him.

Edwin boarded the train two cars down from Charlotte. He knew she was on her way to see her friend in Ipswich. He hoped it would be a female friend as she had told him, but deep down he doubted it.

When the train arrived at the station, Charlotte disembarked and started walking. Grey's house was a mile away. He often painted first thing in the morning and didn't eat, so she stopped at a bakery and bought croissants and strawberry jam.

Edwin was following one hundred yards behind her. He watched as she walked up to the front door and went in without even knocking. Unsure what to do, he slowly approached the house and then passed by. From the street he couldn't see anyone inside. He sat on a rock across the street and waited. After ten minutes, a local came along.

"Lost?" the man asked.

"No, I'm just resting. Looking at that home there. Nice place."

"Sure is," the man said. "That's the artist's place. I was inside once, and it's beautiful."

"Artist?"

"You don't know?" The man happily filled in the details. "That's Grey Talbot's house, one of the finest painters in all of New England. Why, just the other day I heard he sold a painting to the Worcester Museum for nine thousand dollars. Can you believe that?"

It was a huge sum of money for anyone to pay for a painting, but the only thing Edwin really heard was the word *he*. "Does anyone else live there?"

"No. He's always lived there alone. Bought the place about ten years ago, as I recall. They do say," the man continued, "that lately there has been an awfully good-looking woman visiting him on a regular basis. Lucky guy, huh?"

Twenty minutes later, Edwin Pechel was waiting to board the train back to Boston.

Charlotte learned everything when she returned home late that afternoon. Edwin was there, which greatly surprised her. When she entered the apartment and saw the look on his face, she knew instantly her secret life was secret no more. The hurt in his eyes was real and she saw it plain as day. She also saw four suitcases packed and ready to go by the front door. She guessed correctly that her clothes were in them.

"Edwin," she started, but then knew not what to say.

As he was in everything else he did, Edwin was straightforward and matter-of-fact. "I followed you today to Ipswich."

She was surprised, but said nothing.

"If I had to guess, I would say about five months now. Am I right?"

"Six." The pained expression on his face grew worse. She swore he was aging in front of her eyes.

"Where did you meet him?"

Why don't you just throw me out now, she thought. *Why go through this exercise in futility?* She gave him an abbreviated version of all that had transpired from the day at Pierpoint Farm until now. He took it all in, not saying a word. She thought at least this would make him mad, cause him to yell and curse at her. Instead, he did nothing. Same old stoic Edwin. When she finished, he asked his last question.

"Why?"

What should she say? Not wanting to explain, but also not wanting to hurt him further, Charlotte simply said, "It was time, Edwin. We had run our course. We probably stayed together longer than we should have. It just took me a long time to realize it, and I guess you never did."

"I loved you, Charlotte. I would have loved you forever."

She saw the tears forming in the corners of his eyes and knew it was time to go. She picked up two of the bags and brought them outside. After hailing a cabbie, she went back in for the other two. Edwin hadn't moved. She looked at him and felt a deep sense of pity. "You will survive, Edwin. Your work is what you are married to. It's what will get you through."

She grabbed the bags and walked out as Edwin gently closed the door behind her. As he did, she heard him burst into tears. *Finally*, she thought, *some deep show of emotion.*

Too late.

Chapter Twenty-Four

Jill awoke to a strange melancholy. In Grey Talbot, she had found her Niall, her Jared. The man she now truly believed to be her soul mate. A man she had yet to find in this life. Yet she also realized the instant she was back in the present why Tony had done what he did. She had done it to him first. If what she had learned about karma were true, Tony cheated on their marriage in this lifetime because she had done it to him in their last lifetime.

The thought did not please her. All the hurt, all the anger she had felt towards him must have been what he felt like in Boston. The idea depressed her. Was his new wife his soul mate? Had Jill just been a stepping-stone to her? The regressions were starting to become very complicated.

She saw Simon looking at her. "I'm not really liking Boston a whole lot," she said.

He correctly guessed what was going through her mind. "Not all lifetimes turn out to be fun and games, Jill. My guess is you will learn more about yourself from this Boston experience than you have from either of the others."

"I was a good person in Ireland. I would have been a good person in London had I lived. Why didn't I carry all that goodness over to Boston?"

He could see how anguished she was. "Jill, you must remember we are only touching upon a few brief periods of your past life. There is a great deal we will never uncover. We don't have the time. You are simply recalling periods of a life in Boston that you, your subconscious, deem important. While all you may see when you look at it is a 'bad person', the truth is more likely that you were a good, normal woman trapped in a bad marriage. It happens now, it happened back then."

She tried to take his words to heart, but it was difficult. She needed time.

"I take it Grey is your mate then, your Niall?" he asked.

She gave him a slight smile. "Yes. Could I have possibly fallen for him any faster?"

"Those who say love at first sight is a myth simply never had it happen to them." Simon looked down at the notes he had taken. Then he looked back up to her and asked, "Have you ever been to Boston?"

"No, and it is not on my list of places to visit, either."

He took out her questionnaire. "Ever been to the northeast at all?"

"Philadelphia is as close as I have come to Boston. I'm a southern girl," she said to him, smiling for the first time since the regression had ended.

"You may want to add it to your list. You might recognize some buildings or places where you used to go."

"Maybe." Jill looked at her watch. "Oh my, we went over a bit today. I have to get going."

"That's fine." He looked her straight in the eye. "You will be back next week, right?"

"I'll be here," she said, "although I hope it gets better than it's been so far."

"I would prefer it," he said, "if you didn't look up anything about Grey Talbot. Let's not influence our next session, okay?"

She agreed, reluctantly.

Tim Davidson's article on Jill came out in the Wednesday edition of the *Sentinel*. Once again, she found herself on the front page, this time with a picture of her. The boys were excited to see their famous mother in the paper again. Jill could have done without it. She thought it made her out to be more than she was.

"All I did," she tried to explain to them, "was call 9-1-1, then wait for the police to arrive. Other than that I was just cowering in the corner. I'm no hero."

Bret and Mark would have none of it. "You're on the front page!" Bret yelled out. "You helped the police catch a wanted felon."

"Yeah," Mark chimed in, "and you saved all our stuff from destruction. Imagine if he had destroyed our computers and television. What would we have done then?"

"Our home insurance would have paid us for our loss, and we would have bought all new stuff," she told them.

"Our computers *are* new," Mark said.

"And the television is fine," added Bret. "We don't need new stuff. We just don't want to lose the stuff we have."

Jill felt a sense of pride in both of them and told them so. She then decided that instead of going to her Wednesday night meditation session, she would take them out to eat anywhere they wanted. They chose Applebee's.

Thursday morning Lauren called. "Brenda is having another channeling session tonight. Want to come?"

"Sure," she said. "It was pretty interesting last time. I'd be curious to hear what messages I receive tonight."

"Great. We'll meet you there. Bill is coming with me."

"Okay, but …"

"I know, I know. I won't let him bring you a date."

They both laughed.

Jill arrived at the church just after seven and was glad to see Lauren and Bill had saved her a seat. There was a good-sized crowd, much larger than the last time, and they were sitting on the opposite side of the room from last time.

"We'll be the last ones they get to for questions," Lauren said as she sat down. "Not good."

However, Martin was happy to see such a large crowd. As soon as his voice came through Brenda's body, he said, "Good evening. I'm happy to see so many of you here tonight."

Jill wondered how he saw, since Brenda's eyes were shut firmly once again. She assumed spirits from the other side could use some of their senses, like sight, but others they needed help on, like speaking.

"Tonight I am going to speak about your government," Martin began.

That sounded interesting to Jill, so unlike her first visit, she paid close attention to what Martin said. She was surprised to find the spirit world took such an interest in what transpired on planet earth. They worried that one madman could blow up the world and worked behind the scenes to see that it didn't happen.

Martin finished his fifteen-minute lecture by saying, "We can only do so much. We cannot interfere with people's free will. In the end it is up to you, the inhabitant's of the planet, who will determine its fate."

"Whew," Jill whispered to Lauren, "and here I thought my biggest concern was getting the kids through school."

As Lauren had said, it took a long time for the questioning session to come around to them. When it did, Bill was first. He asked about the future of his photography work. He was pleased when

Martin told him that his business was about to pick up and he would be traveling a great deal more.

Lauren wasn't sure she liked the traveling part when she heard it, and jokingly asked Martin, "Will I being going with him?" She was surprised by Martin's answer.

"Indeed. I see the two of you going on a great many adventures together."

"But what about my business?" she said. "I can't just up and leave. How am I going to handle traveling when I have such a full schedule of clients?"

"Ah yes," said Martin. Jill could swear she heard a chuckle in his voice. "I see you are a woman who has always known what she wanted and went after it. Why do you think this will be any different?"

"Well …" Lauren mumbled, but went no further.

"You are a strong woman. You always have been. You always will be. The time will come when being with the gentleman seated next to you will be more important than your work. When that time comes, you will find traveling to be very easy for you."

Jill watched as Lauren's mouth fell open. She also noticed the wonderful look on Bill's face. He had obviously enjoyed the message.

Now it was Jill's turn. "Good evening, Martin. This is Jill," she said.

"Jill, my new friend. You have had an exciting week, have you not?"

What? Even he knew about the break-in and all the publicity? "Yes I have," she answered.

"I want you to know you were not alone."

"What do you mean?" Jill asked, wondering if they were talking about the same thing.

"From our side, we can see events that are about to happen, and we can oftentimes help out. As I said earlier, we cannot interfere with a person's free will. We can, however, offer subtle influences in a situation such as you faced."

"What did you do?" Jill wanted to know.

"When you started to leave the upstairs bedroom, we held you back. Two of your own spirit guides and I were standing in the doorway. As you neared the door, you felt our presence, did you not?"

Jill remembered when she had been about to leave the room, then had stopped.

"Something told you to stay in that room," Martin continued. "Had you left that room, the ending of the story would have been much different, I'm afraid. People oftentimes feel the presence of a loved one in their home. Once in awhile they may see a wisp out of the corner of their eye, or an outline of someone sitting on their bed when they wake up in the middle of the night. Spirits visit often, particularly when there is danger around, or when one of their loved ones is about to cross over."

"So you helped save my life?" asked Jill.

"Let's just say we all helped you to have a better ending. Yet even with our help, it was a very close call. Do you have a question for me tonight?"

Jill's mind was in a fog with all Martin had said. Of the hundred questions she had been contemplating while awaiting her turn, none came to her now. Her mind was a blank. "Do you have a message for me?" was all she could think to ask.

"You are a wonderful child of God," he began. "Kind, giving, a loving mother. Your world is beginning to open up in ways you had never thought possible. You are seeing with new eyes. Be bold. Be open. Take in all you see without judgment. One day you will sit down and decide what you will take as truth and what you will discard. For now, enjoy the ride. Do you understand, my child?"

"I do, Martin, and thank you."

It was just after eight-thirty when the session ended. Lauren suggested the three of them go out and relax over a glass of wine, but Jill wanted to get home to her boys. "You two should be alone," she said.

They ended up talking in the parking lot for fifteen minutes. "So where are you two going to go?" Jill asked.

Lauren, who had a streak of bright orange in her hair tonight, spoke first. "Slow down, girlfriend. I'm going to have to do a little thinking about this before I figure out what I'm doing. Bill's message came out of the blue, even surprising him I think."

Bill shook his head in agreement. "That's for sure."

"Maybe you don't need to cut back," said Jill. "Perhaps you just need to start scheduling some vacations into your time. When is the last time you took a week off?"

"Well, let me think." Lauren scrunched up her face, trying to remember. "I guess it has been a while."

"Over a year, I'll bet. So you better start, because now you have someone to go on vacation with." Jill turned to Bill. "You would like to take Lauren on a nice trip, right?"

"Absolutely," he said, "but remember, they are going to be working vacations for me. I may be photographing coyotes in Alaska, staying out in the freezing cold for thirty-six hours at a time just to get the right shot." He looked at Lauren, and asked, "How's that sound, babe? Want to bring me hot chocolate every hour or so?"

Lauren stared at him as if he were crazy, then finally said, "I'll be in the hot tub."

Now Bill looked at Jill. "So what are the things you are becoming involved in that Martin was talking about?"

Jill looked at Lauren. "Have you told him anything?"

"About your regressions? No."

Which means she probably hasn't told him about her own regression, Jill thought. Better not bring up that one. Jill told him about her sessions with Simon without going into much detail. She did inform Lauren that she had met her soul mate yet again in Boston. "He's an artist, sort of like Bill."

"And you haven't met him in this life yet?" asked Bill.

"Not yet. Soon, I hope."

Bill turned back to Lauren. "You should do one of these regressions, honey." He saw the look the two girls gave to each other, and the big smile on Jill's face. "Or have you already?"

Jill bit her lip waiting for Lauren's reply.

"Oh, there is so much about me you don't know yet, my dear," said Lauren, "but it's getting late. I think we should save it for another night."

"Chicken," Jill whispered under her breath.

Friday, just after the boys left with their dad and just before Jill was about to leave for work, she heard a car in the driveway. For a moment her heart caught in her throat, and then she remembered that The Snake was still in jail, unable to make bail. Looking out the window, she saw her parents walking up to the front door. She opened it just as they were about to ring the bell. "What are you two doing back here so soon?"

"Hello dear," her mother said. "We thought maybe you wouldn't want to be alone this weekend after what happened, so we came to keep you company."

What a lovely gesture, thought Jill. "I was just about to leave for work."

"That's okay," her dad said. "When you come home and see the lights on, you'll know it's just us."

"That's really thoughtful of you." It dawned on Jill that coming home to a dark house around midnight just may have scared her to death. Knowing her folks were going to be here was a great comfort to her. "You two are the best, you know that?"

When she arrived home from work, Jill saw a present wrapped in beautiful paper on the kitchen counter. Her mother entered the room, and Jill said, "Hi. What's this?"

"We went shopping tonight and bought you a gift. Bring it into the living room and open it. Your father is watching the sports."

Jill did as asked and sat down in the rocking chair. "You didn't have to buy me anything," she said.

Her father just grinned. "We're your parents. We can buy you something anytime we want."

"I think you will like it," her mother added.

Jill slowly tore the wrapping paper off the box. There was a picture of the item on the outside panel. "You didn't have to do this," she said.

"We wanted to," her dad replied. She noticed the pride in his voice.

Jill opened the box and took out her new Waterford crystal vase. It was exactly like the one that had been smashed on her kitchen floor. "You guys are too much," she said, and a tear ran down her cheek.

Chapter Twenty-Five

Jill's phone rang early Monday morning.

"Jill, its Melinda. We're going to have to cancel your appointment for tomorrow. The doctor has had a death in the family."

"Oh no," said Jill. "Was it someone close to him?"

"One of his uncles," Melinda replied. "He flew to Colorado last night."

Life is always changing, thought Jill as she hung up the phone a moment later.

Neal called on Wednesday just as Jill was about to leave for the sanctuary. He was hoping they could go out the following evening. She checked with the boys, wanting to let them know they were part of the process.

"We don't mind if you go out," Bret told her.

She picked up on the *we* right away. "So have you two been discussing my dating?" she asked.

Bret gave her a long stare as Mark looked at him. Finally, Bret said, "We've talked about it. You deserve to have a life outside of us. But ..." he stopped, looking to his brother. Then, summoning up new courage, he said, "You're not going to get married again, are you?"

"Married? Heavens, no. Why would you think that?"

"We don't really want a step-father," he said

Wow, thought Jill, they really have been thinking about this. "Honey, people don't get married after just a few dates, at least not very often. It takes a long time to get to know someone. I assure you, I am never going to rush into a marriage, and if I ever think about getting married again, I will certainly discuss it with both of you beforehand."

"That's good." She saw the relief on their faces. "Go out tomorrow, and have a nice time."

The next night Neal picked her up just before seven. The boys were upstairs on their computers, and Jill just called out a goodbye to them as she left. She thought it was too early in the dating process for them to meet Neal.

After she slid into the passenger's seat, Neal told her there was someplace special he wanted to take her. Jill couldn't wait to see where it was. It turned out to be the local theater in Claremont. Open Thursday through Sunday, they ran only movies that were at least thirty years old. Jill had heard of the theater but never been. Tonight they were showing *Casablanca*.

"I remembered you mentioning how much you enjoyed Bogart movies," said Neal.

Casablanca was her favorite Bogart movie. She had seen it at least a dozen times and never grew tired of it. It turned out that Ingrid Bergman was one of Neal's favorite actresses. Jill was delighted, because she had never seen the movie on a big screen.

When the movie ended, they went to PJ's Winery for a drink. After ordering, Neal said, "I had a wonderful time tonight. I just love that movie."

"Me too," said Jill. "Bogie is just the best."

They discussed other films that either Bogart or Bergman had been in as the waitress delivered their wine. After they had each taken a sip, Neal said, "Jill, I need to talk to you."

Jill felt her danger signals jump. I hope he's not getting serious already, she thought. She remembered her talk with the boys the day before. "Sure," she said, "what's up?"

He suddenly looked a little nervous, and as he took another sip of wine his hand shook slightly. "I miss my wife," he finally said, a quiet statement that spoke volumes to Jill.

"That's perfectly understandable. It's awful to lose someone in the manner that you did."

"What I mean is ... I don't think I'm ready to start dating yet."

"Oh." Jill was surprised by the comment but recovered rapidly. She liked Neal. He was a lovely man, and she had enjoyed their few times together. On the other hand, he had not started her blood boiling. He was not her Niall, and Jill knew it.

"I should be over it by now," he said. "It's been four years. I thought I was ready, but ..."

"Its okay, Neal." Jill reached over and took his hand in hers. "There isn't a time limit on something like that. You obviously loved her very much."

"She was my life."

Jill saw his eyes starting to water.

"Do you believe in soul mates?" he asked.

Jill had never mentioned her regressions to him, and Neal had never said anything to make her think he was a believer in the ideas she had just started investigating. This was coming from his heart. "Yes, Neal, I do."

Her answer elicited a small smile. "I do too. I believe she was mine."

"You're probably right," Jill said.

"What do you do when your mate leaves you so soon in life?"

What indeed. What did Jared do after Emily died? How did he carry on? Did he ever marry, or find someone else? He must have, Jill thought. He was so young. To Neal, she could only say, "I don't know." She looked into his cyes, and his sadness was palpable. "I guess that you need to concentrate on taking care of yourself and your children. Hopefully that will help you through your period of mourning. You're still mourning, Neal."

"You're right. I'm sorry. I really do enjoy being with you."

"Neal, you are a wonderful man. I've enjoyed every minute I've spent with you, but up to this point I don't think there has been a spark between us. That tension that tells you you're with that someone special."

He just bowed his head.

"And that's fine," she continued. "I feel I have made a terrific new friend, and I hope you feel the same way."

Neal perked up a bit. "Oh, I do. You're wonderful, Jill."

"Thank you. Perhaps we can stay in touch and maybe meet for a drink on occasion."

He didn't answer directly. Instead, Neal said, "It's strange. I feel like I'm cheating on her by being with someone else."

Twenty minutes later he took her home. "Come see me at the restaurant once in a while," she said.

Neal looked at her, but it was like he wasn't there anymore, and Jill was pretty sure she would never see him again.

Saturday morning found Jill working at her computer. The kids were at their dad's, the house was quiet, and the doors were all locked. When she finished her work, she wanted to look up Grey Talbot on her search engine, but she honored Simon's request not to. She had decided that Tuesday's visit to his office would be her last. She wanted to see how the Boston life ended, but she was also ready to move on.

It had been an amazing ride. Two months ago her best friend had taken a chance and set up Jill with Simon. She recalled sitting outside his office debating whether or not to go in. She almost hadn't. One small decision, yet how that decision had changed her life. Had she simply gone home, she still wouldn't believe in past lives. She wouldn't have had the home invasion, because she never would have visited the Inner Peace Sanctuary. There would be no weekly meditation sessions. Had she backed out of that parking lot and driven away, her life would be just as it had been two months ago.

Instead, she had entered Simon's office and her life had changed forever. Now she was certain the events of her past lives were in fact real. The winds off the water as she stood on the cliff overlooking Bicksby were real to her. So was dying at a young age in London before she could become the nurse, the healer, the hero to some other child whose fate was much the same, or much worse, than hers. And Boston? What was she in Boston: a floozy, a good wife, an adulteress? Why had she followed up the previous lives with this strange affair in Boston? What was she learning, and why did she come back in that manner to learn it? Boston was not giving her any answers, other than her karmic circle with Tony.

She wasn't sure if it mattered anymore. She was ready to stop. That realization had hit her shortly after Neal had driven off on Thursday night. She found the regressions interesting, exciting, sometimes mind-blowing, but now it was time for her to return to this life. It was time to move forward. Her eyes had been opened. There was so much out there she didn't know, so many things she didn't have a clue about. It was time she learned.

The sanctuary had a number of classes on interesting topics. Jill had been reading up on them, and quite a few had aroused her interest. She would not believe anything automatically, but she would be open-minded about everything. She would talk with Lauren about the classes and choose where to begin.

One thing Jill wanted to do was travel. The sanctuary ran trips three or four times a year to exciting places around the globe including Stonehenge, the pyramids of Egypt, and Machu Pichau, a spot everyone at Inner Peace seemed to love.

Thinking of ancient sites brought Jill's mind back to her past lives and the people she had known, particularly those who had been with her in multiple incarnations. Her mom and dad had been in the same roles in Boston. Her mom had also been her mother in England, but she hadn't seen her dad in that life. She wondered why? Bret and Mark had been her sons in Ireland, but hadn't appeared since. Her other son in Ireland, Sean, had reappeared in London as Tom, but had not been seen yet in Boston or in this life. Nuala had turned into Missus Ferguson. It's strange, she thought, how it all plays out.

Finally there were the channeling sessions. Martin had warned her on her first visit to be aware of her surroundings. He knew she was in danger from The Snake but couldn't come right out and say it. During the invasion she had been about to leave the bedroom, but felt something stop her, and Martin had told her he and her guides were protecting her. As farfetched as it may have seemed a few short weeks ago, how could she not believe in the abilities of Reverend Doran now?

Now, staring at the screen in front of her, Jill realized there was nothing else she needed to know. She turned off the computer and went for a walk.

Jill decided to go to church on Sunday morning. She hadn't talked with Lauren about it, but Jill hoped she would be there. She wanted to find out if attending the church on a regular basis was something she wanted to do and hoped Brenda would be leading the service. She had enjoyed being around her both times she had met her. Brenda seemed down to earth, easy to get along with, and she had an energy about her that Jill found interesting.

She arrived at the church about five minutes after the service had started and spotted Lauren's car outside. The congregation was in the middle of a hymn when she entered, and Jill was happy to find a seat next to Lauren in the front row.

"Hey," whispered Lauren, "what brings you here?"

"Last minute decision." She could tell her friend was pleased.

Jill was happy to see Brenda in the lecturer's chair. Five minutes later, after a few prayers and some announcements, Brenda was introduced. Jill relaxed as Brenda spoke on listening to that still, small voice in each of us for guidance. The sixth sense, she called it, and Jill thought of the movie starring Bruce Willis. Brenda gave examples of how her sixth sense had helped her out in the past, and Jill realized that she too had been through experiences like that. Some were little, like thinking of a person and having them call a minute later. Others were more important. Jill remembered the time she had an uncontrollable urge to visit her aunt and found her at the bottom of the stairs. She had fallen and broken a leg, and would have been there for hours if Jill had not shown up. When asked why she had come, Jill had just said, "I had this feeling that I needed to be here." That feeling, she now understood, was her sixth sense.

After the sermon and another song, the group stood and gathered in a circle for the healing ceremony. Everyone held hands. Lauren was on Jill's right, and a man she didn't know was on her left. Brenda led the ceremony, and it was similar to what Ralph had performed the previous time Jill had come.

After the healing circle came the message part of the service. Jill was dismayed when she was not chosen to receive one. The service ended with another song and the benediction, and then everyone headed for the dining area.

Jill joined Lauren for coffee and snacks. There were four others at their table, talking about a variety of subjects. One of the older ladies mentioned Lauren's hair, which today had a streak of blue. The man from the healing circle was again on Jill's left, occasionally asking her questions about herself, but she paid him little attention. Jill heard stories of tarot card readings, a summer solstice gathering that was taking place soon, and a retreat to someplace in New York called Lily Dale that a group of parishioners were leaving for in two weeks.

Jill wanted to speak with Lauren alone, and suggested they go somewhere after church.

"No can do," said Lauren. "Bill and I are heading to Coleman's Pond. It seems that a bald eagle was spotted there recently. Bill hopes to get a picture of it. I'm going to lie in the sun while he tries."

Ten minutes later Jill headed home. The service had been interesting, she thought, and she made a decision to go to the church regularly for the next month to see if it resonated with her.

It was six-thirty that night when Lauren called her. As soon as she answered the phone, Jill could hear the excitement in Lauren's voice. "Your phone is going to ring in the next few minutes."

"What do you mean?" Jill asked.

"Michael Harmon just called me asking for your phone number."

"Who is Michael Harmon?"

"The man from church," said Lauren. "He sat next to you during coffee hour and stood by you during the healing circle."

"Why does he want to talk to me?" Jill couldn't fathom a reason.

Lauren nearly yelled into the phone. "He wants to ask you out!"

"What? Why?"

"Jill, I've known Michael for nearly a year now. That's when he started coming to church. He's really very nice, and he's interested in you."

"We hardly talked," said Jill. "How could he be so interested in me?"

"Get this. He said he was 'taken with you' as soon as he saw you walk into the church."

A man was "taken with her"?

"I just wanted to warn you," said Lauren, "now hang up."

As soon as Jill hung up the phone, it rang again.

"Is this Jill?" a man asked. He seemed confident, and she liked the sound of his voice.

"It is."

"My name is Michael Harmon. We met at church today. I sat next to you in the dining room."

"Yes, I remember." Jill was so excited she could barely speak. Was this man she had ignored this morning about to ask her out?

"I called Lauren, and she gave me your phone number. I hope you don't mind, but I was really taken aback when I saw you today, and to tell you the truth I have been thinking about you all afternoon. I was hoping we could get together someday and maybe have lunch."

Jill couldn't believe it. He had come right out and said "taken aback." No one, not even Tony, had ever said anything like that to her before. She spoke with Michael for a few minutes, and the flow of the conversation became less nervous, more routine. He seemed nice, and he made sure she understood how interested he was in her. Finally, she decided to take the plunge and set up a date with him for lunch on Wednesday at Amelio's.

When he said goodbye, he sounded like the happiest man in the world.

Chapter Twenty-Six

Tuesday morning Jill prepared for her final regression with Simon. She was not sad that it was ending. It had been a wonderful journey, but it was time to move on. The day was warm and sunny, not a cloud in the sky. *Ending on a high note*, she thought.

She entered the office and found Melinda cheery as always. "It's graduation day," she said to her.

"What?" Melinda looked puzzled.

"Graduation day," said Jill again. "My last visit."

"Are you sure?" asked Melinda.

"I'm sure."

"Has it been fun?"

"Fun?" Jill thought for a moment. "Let's see, it has been interesting, surprising, and unbelievable. I've been shocked, saddened, and had my mind blown more than a few times. If a wild ride like that can be called fun, then yes Melinda, I'd say it has been a blast."

"The wild rides are the most fun," Melinda said, and Jill guessed she was right.

Simon entered the room and Jill offered her condolences.

"Thank you," he said. "Come on in and make yourself comfortable."

Jill sat on the couch, so plush and comfy that she wished she could take it home with her. "This is going to be my last visit," she told him right away.

"I thought that might be the case," he said. "It's doubtful you had another life between Boston and your current one. If you did, it must have been short. So then, are you ready for your final foray into the past?"

"Absolutely."

"Did you do any reading ahead?"

"None at all. I wanted to," she admitted, "but kept my word and didn't."

"Thank you." Simon took out her folder and scanned through it as he had many times before. "When we are finished today, we will go through this together and see what jumps out at us. Jill, I want to thank you once again for having the courage to come in that first day and for continuing these sessions for the last two months."

"It's been an eye-opening experience."

"So are you ready to go back to Boston?"

"I am," she said. She relaxed on the couch as Simon brought her back for the final time.

He went through the relaxation process, and then began the regression. "Go back to your teenage years. Find a time that you remember well, one that was a pleasant episode."

"I'm fourteen," said Jill.

"Where are you?"

"At home. It's my birthday. Mom lets me invite my friends from school over. I have lots of presents, but my parents just give me an envelope. I thought they had just given me money, and I was going to be embarrassed in front of all my friends, but I open the envelope and it has tickets to Disney World inside. I'm so happy. I've always wanted to go there, and they always said it was too expensive."

"So you were not embarrassed after all, I take it?"

"Oh no, it was a wonderful gift. The best present I ever received."

"That was a nice memory for you. Now I want you to go back further, back to when you were just a toddler, maybe age two or three. Can you do that for me, Jill?"

It took just a moment for Jill to find another time she was exceedingly happy. "Yes, I am three. We have gone over to my grandparent's house."

"The same house you remembered before from the womb?"

"Same house. I'm playing a card game on the floor with grandpa. War, I think. I'm not really sure about all my numbers yet, and I don't know the face cards very well, but grandpa helps me out, and I always win. He is laughing, having a gay old time, and he tickles me when I least expect it. I try to tickle him, and he pretends it does, even though I don't really know how to do it very well. It was a wonderful day."

"Let's go back again, Jill, back to the womb. You've told me about the day at your grandparent's home a couple of times from the womb. Can you find a different day this time?" Simon watched as Jill lay on the couch, her eyes moving rapidly as they always seemed to do when she was in a regression. Finally she was ready to speak.

"I'm not in the body," she said. "I'm just watching from above."

"Your mother is pregnant, but you're not in the body?"

"No, I'm just watching. I can enter and leave at this point. She is only five months pregnant. It is a long time until I am born. I can enter my body that is forming for short periods of time to get used to it, and then I can leave."

"Why do you do that?" asked Simon.

"I'm still preparing to be reborn. My guides that I have chosen for this lifetime are still training me, helping me get ready. I spend a few hours each day in the body, but most of the time I'm still on the other side."

"Can you tell that your body will be healthy?" Simon asked, amazed at what he was hearing. None of his patients had ever gone this far back in the womb before.

"Yes, I have chosen a healthy body. I am happy with it."

"What would happen if you were not happy?"

"I could decide not to enter the body. My mother's guides would then help her to miscarry. I can also change my mind at any time, if I or my guides think that I have made a mistake. Sometimes people rush to come back to the earth plane, and when they realize they are not ready, they back out and the mother miscarries. Oftentimes they will return to the same mother two or three years later, when they really are ready."

"So the baby that the mother miscarries and the baby born three years later is actually the same baby?"

"The same spirit, yes."

"This is fascinating. Can you tell me more?"

Jill was very still on the couch. Simon noticed the eye movements slow considerably. He waited over a minute, and suddenly worried something was wrong. "Jill, are you okay?"

"Yes. It is time to move on."

"Time to go back to your Boston period?"

"Yes."

Later, when he was listening to the tape again, Simon noticed a change in Jill's voice while she was giving her womb message, and he suspected that one of Jill's guides had come in and spoken to him through her to give him the information he had received. He would never know for sure.

"Okay then, Jill, I want you to go back to your previous life in Boston. Can you do that?"

"Already there," she answered, and Simon could swear he saw a smirk on her face.

"Very well," he said. "Can you tell me where you are, and who you are with?"

"I'm with Grey, of course." She said it as though he were foolish to think she might be anywhere else. "He and I are always together now."

"That's wonderful," he said, then switched to her Boston name. "Charlotte, where are you?"

"We are walking down the street, arm in arm. It's a lovely day in May. Quite warm."

"Can you tell me what year it is?"

"1864."

"And are you walking down the street in Boston?"

"No, we are in Ipswich, downtown. We've come to pick up some groceries for the home, but we run into Grey's good friend Willy Zanger. He's crying right there on the street."

"Why is Willie crying, Charlotte?"

Grey reached Willie a moment before Charlotte. "Willie, what's wrong?" he asked.

Willie looked up at them, his eyes red from crying, tears still running down his cheeks. He was an elderly man in his seventies, with gray hair all askew on his head. He had been a friend of Grey's long before Charlotte had met him. He turned to Grey and said, "Oh, it's awful." He started to cry again, new tears forming.

"What's awful, Willie?" Grey asked.

Charlotte put her arm around Willie. "What has happened? Can you tell us?"

"It's Nathaniel," sobbed Willie, "he's gone."

"Gone where?" Charlotte asked, but the answer hit her before Willie replied.

"D-died." Willie stuttered. "Nathaniel died y-yesterday. He was on a trip to the White Mountains and ..." he couldn't continue.

"Oh, no." It was all Grey could think to say. He looked at Charlotte, and then he too put his arm around Willie. The three of them hugged in the street. "Come back to the house with us, Willie," Grey finally said. "I think we could use a drink."

, They had known Nathaniel Hawthorne had been sick, but they hadn't expected this. He had been a good friend over the years, coming to the house in Ipswich numerous times, usually when Grey threw one of his artist's parties. Nathaniel loved to walk along the sandy beach with his pant legs rolled up, letting the water splash over his feet. The coldness of the water never seemed to bother him. Charlotte never understood how he could stand it.

She had grown very fond of Nathaniel and found him to be a bright, articulate man. He was always engaging at Grey's parties and many people came simply because he was there. On a few occasions she had walked with him on the beach, or around Ipswich proper, when Grey was busy with work. She often asked him about his writing, how he came up with his ideas, how he researched his subjects. In return he always inquired about her, seeming genuinely interested. He was happy his friend Grey had finally found a good woman. Charlotte was going to miss Nathaniel very much.

They arrived back at the house and Grey poured scotch for Willie and himself. Charlotte still refrained from alcohol. They gave a toast to Nathaniel, and then Grey poured another round. "Do you know what happened, Willie?" he asked.

Willie said, "He had been sick for quite a while. His son told me he knew he was dying. He didn't want to be around Sophia when it happened, so he planned this trip to the White Mountains. He was sure when he left that he would never see her again, and I guess she knew it too. It's just so tragic."

They returned to the apartment in Boston the next morning and made plans to attend the funeral. Charlotte recalled the first time she had met Nathaniel at the Lion's Ball. She hadn't known Grey then and didn't know the two men were friends. How handsome he had looked. He never changed, a beautiful man right to the end.

Charlotte and Grey had married just last year. She had not expected it, assuming that he was happy with the way things were. She didn't much care whether they married or not, as long as he was with her. Then one day he came back to Ipswich after a trip to Boston. He walked in the front door, gave her a great big bear hug that lifted her off her feet, kissed her hard on the lips, and blurted out, "Let's get married! I think it's time."

She was astonished. "What brought that on?"

"I hope that's not your answer." He held her at arm's length, trying to look upset, but he wasn't. He knew her answer.

"My answer is yes, of course." A moment later they ran up the stairs to the bedroom, clothes flying in all directions.

The July wedding had been held in Ipswich. It was the first time Anna and Rudolph had been to the beach house, although they knew Grey well. He had accompanied Charlotte on visits to her parents' home numerous times. Just before the ceremony started, Charlotte was startled to see Camilla come running in. She had no idea her sister would attend. She had hardly seen Camilla in the last ten years. She and her husband had been moving constantly: up and down the east coast, over to France for a year, then to Germany. They now lived in New York City. Charlotte was thrilled to see Camilla, and her sister was delighted that Charlotte was finally marrying someone she approved of.

After Nathaniel's funeral, life returned to normal. Grey was constantly commuting between Ipswich and Boston. Charlotte stayed in Ipswich more often than not. She loved the ocean and enjoyed her free time when he was not home.

Camilla came to visit shortly after the funeral and spent a month with them. She left her children, two boys and a girl, with her husband's parents. He had volunteered for the Union Army and was somewhere around Washington.

"What's he doing?" Charlotte asked.

"Damned if I know. I can't get a straight answer out of him. He's probably some kind of spy."

Charlotte was bemused by this. "Well, he is an actor, so he would probably make a very good spy."

Camilla agreed, and then said, "I just hope he comes home safe. I've seen so many war wounded return, and it's just heartbreaking. The injuries those boys sustain are just unimaginable."

Charlotte had seen her share of the injured in Boston and knew full well what Camilla was talking about.

She loved her month with Camilla. "It seems like old times," she said.

"Only we are not quite as wild," Camilla chimed in.

"You married well, sister; a loving husband, three children. You must be very happy."

"I am, and you have married well also. When I first heard you were dating Grey Talbot I couldn't believe it. His work is everywhere in New York. I know of one man who has four of Grey's paintings in his living room. He loves to show them off. My sister, the rich girl," laughed Camilla.

"Rich?" Charlotte honestly didn't know how true that was. "I guess we do okay."

"Okay? Honey, haven't you ever asked? Grey is worth a fortune, I swear."

Charlotte didn't much care. She only knew she wanted to be with him for the rest of her life. Rich or poor, it didn't matter. Love mattered, and she had found her love in Grey.

BOSTON, NOVEMBER 1872

The day was gorgeous, not a cloud in the sky, and warm for early November in Boston. Grey and Charlotte had taken the first train in that morning. Even though Grey's business had grown by leaps and bounds over the past few years, he still kept the same small apartment. It was now bulging with paintings, so many that it was hard to move around in.

Grey had a client coming over at noon, so Charlotte took a walk. She made her way to Tremont Street and saw the Old Granary Burying Ground next to Park Street Church. She had been in the church on numerous occasions, but had never wandered the grounds of the cemetery. She thought it was about time she did.

She knew the names of many who were buried here, and resolved to find their gravestones. In short order she came upon the final resting places of John Hancock, Robert Paine, Paul Revere, and Samuel Adams. The tall obelisk in the center signified the burial site of Ben Franklin's parents. As she was about to leave, she came upon the grave of Crispus Attucks, who was killed in the Boston Massacre.

As she walked back to the apartment, Charlotte's mood had been subdued by her trip through the graveyard. *Someday Grey and I will be lying side by side*, she thought. She wondered where, but wasn't worried. They still had many years of wedded bliss ahead of them. Her mood picked up as soon as she saw him. He was bubbling over with joy.

"Great news, honey," he said. "I sold three paintings to Mister Baron, and he says he has some friends who would be greatly interested in purchasing more."

Charlotte was thrilled for him. "That's terrific, Grey." She didn't ask how much he sold them for, and didn't care. She was simply glad that he was so happy.

"I want to celebrate," he said. Needless to say, the celebration started in the bedroom. He made love to her three times in the next hour. When they were finally finished, they were both starving. "Let's go to the Oyster House," Grey suggested, and Charlotte was more than happy to second the motion.

They spent the next two hours dining on Oysters on the half shell, sea scallops, and fresh cod. As they sat back relaxing after the meal, Grey suddenly said, "Let's take a vacation."

Charlotte was amused. He was acting like a kid with money burning a hole in his pocket. "Where would you like to go," she asked.

"No, no, no mademoiselle," he said, shaking a finger at her and trying to imitate a French accent, "the question is, where would you like to go?"

She thought on that for a moment. She had never really dreamed of traveling much. Her little corner of the universe was fine with her. However, since he was asking, she said, "Let's go to Europe."

"Where in Europe?"

"Anywhere, I don't care. I've never been anywhere, so it will all be new to me."

"Perfect," he said. "I will take you everywhere in Europe. We will be gone for a year, and maybe we will never return."

"Grey, of course we'll return. I like our beach house. I can't leave it forever."

"Okay," he said, his face beaming with joy. "Anything for you, my love. I will make the arrangements tomorrow. Let's leave as soon as we can."

They left the restaurant talking about all the places they wanted to visit and headed for the theater district to see what was playing. The beautiful day was turning into a lovely, mild night. They strolled down the streets of Boston, two people obviously in love. They came upon a small ice cream stand, and they each ordered a dish of vanilla and chocolate. The vendor heard them talking about the theater.

"There's a nice little comedy at the Boston Museum," he said. My wife and I went last night. It's only a dollar to get in."

The show was well worth seeing. Charlotte found herself laughing uproariously, and she could tell that Grey was enjoying himself also. By the time the show ended at nine o'clock, Charlotte was marveling at what a wonderful day it had been. She couldn't imagine a better one.

As they stood to leave the theater, a slow murmur began spreading though the crowd. The buzz spread as they drew closer to the exit, and it finally reached them. They were as startled as everyone else, and a sense of dread nestled into Charlotte's being. When they reached the door to the street, they knew the rumor was true. The heavy fragrance of smoke was in the air.

Boston was on fire.

Charlotte saw flames licking the skyline. The fire was northeast of the theater and didn't look to be more than ten blocks from where they stood. They knew immediately this was no small fire.

"Look at the smoke," said Grey, "and those flames. It must cover two or three blocks by now."

"But they can put it out, right?" Charlotte hoped she knew the answer to that question.

"They're in trouble," he said. "Come on."

They headed towards the fire. At ten o'clock they were standing outside of Trinity Church with a large crowd of onlookers. She heard someone say that the Beebe Building was gone, and that the fire had started near there.

By midnight the fire had reached Boston Harbor, and Charlotte knew the apartment she and Edwin once shared had gone up in flames. She was thankful he had recently moved to Quincy.

As the new day turned towards two a.m., they realized Grey's apartment would soon be in danger. "I don't think they can stop this thing," he said. "We have to get to the apartment and move my paintings."

Grey rushed off. Charlotte hurried to keep up with him, jostling though the crowd of onlookers. Everywhere she turned she saw frightened faces. In the fire zone she could see people on rooftops, trapped by the flames below them. Others were coming towards her who had escaped the inferno, many with burned clothes, their faces full of soot, ashes in their hair.

"Grey," she called as he began to slip from her sight.

He turned and waited for her, and when she caught up he grabbed her hand and started running again. They had just reached the doorway to his building when they heard a tremendous explosion. The shocking sound caused Charlotte to trip on the stairs. "What in heaven's name was that?" she hollered.

"Dynamite," he said. "They're blowing up buildings."

Charlotte was stunned. "Why?" she asked.

He reached back to help her up. "It's an attempt to stop the fire."

She didn't understand how blowing up buildings could stop the fire, but now was not the time to ask. She raced up the stairs after him. "What are we going to do?" she asked. "We can't carry all the pictures out."

He was already in the back room, quickly sorting through his inventory to determine which ones to save. She knew he hated to part with any of them. His paintings were like children to him. How did you choose?

He pointed to half a dozen he had set aside and said, "Take these down to the bottom of the stairs."

"But Grey, how are we going to move them? We can't carry that many."

"Run outside," he said, "Find a cab. We'll load the cab with as many as we can. Hurry."

She made three trips up and down the stairs, leaning the paintings against the wall by the door, and then ran outside to look for a cab. She didn't think there was any chance she would find one, but she would try. She was shocked to see the fire seemed so much closer than it had just minutes ago. She jumped as another explosion rocked the neighborhood.

A man standing in front of her building said, "That was less than a block away."

She looked at him and yelled, "How many buildings are they going to blow up?" but received no reply.

Charlotte ran down the streets of the neighborhood looking for a cabbie. She found none. "What can I do, I have to do something!" she screamed, then wondered if she were losing her mind. As she turned the corner onto Devonshire Street, she finally spied one.

"Please help," she cried to him. "We need to move paintings from our apartment. Let us use the cab. Please," she begged.

"One hundred dollars," he said to her, "payable now."

Charlotte couldn't believe it. "What! That's crazy."

"Look around you, lady," the cabbie said. "The whole night's crazy."

Charlotte knew Grey kept some extra money hidden in the apartment at all times. She felt sure he must have a hundred dollars stashed away. "Okay," she said, "hurry." She ran back to the apartment, never thinking to get in the cab. He followed her to the front of the building.

Charlotte ran to the stairs and noticed Grey had brought down at least three dozen more paintings. She grabbed three and brought them out to the cab.

"Money first," he reminded her, "and you'd better hurry. This fire is coming mighty close, and I'm not putting my life on the line to save a bunch of pictures."

She ran back inside and saw Grey coming down the stairs with two more paintings.

"Where have you been?" he yelled.

She ignored the question. "I have a cab," she said. "He wants a hundred dollars right now."

"What?" Grey was as astonished as she had been. "That's crazy. Find someone else."

"There is no one else, and no time either. The fire's coming closer. It's going to be here soon. If you want to save your paintings, find the money."

He could tell she was serious. He turned and went back to the apartment. He came out a minute later and handed the money to Charlotte, and then said, "Start loading the cab, and make sure he stays."

She ran back outside and gave the cabbie the money.

"You don't have much time," he said to her, and pointed to the top of her building. Cinders blown by the breeze had landed on the roof.

"Please help us load the cab," she said to him, pointing to the pictures. She ran back to Grey and found him on his hands and knees in the bedroom.

"I had a second stash of cash back here," he said to her. "I figured if robbers found the first box, they wouldn't look for a second one."

"Grey!" She looked at him in exasperation. "We need to go now."

"Okay. I'm just going to double-check what's left behind. Get that cab loaded and I'll be right out."

Charlotte turned, walked out of the apartment and started down the stairs. As she neared the bottom she realized the cab was nowhere to be seen. The area outside the doorway seemed brighter than before. Then, with a whoosh, the front of the building seemed to burst into flames. The fire had jumped to her block, and the building caught like kindling. She watched wide-eyed for a moment as flames licked Grey's paintings at the bottom of the stairs, then turned and ran back into the apartment, screaming his name over and over.

He came out, took one look at the stairway, and then slammed the door shut. He threw a blanket under the door to try and keep the smoke out. They had no other exit. They could have run up to the roof, but that was already on fire. The window in the bedroom, on the side of the building, was their only hope, but that blew in a moment later.

They were trapped, and they both knew it.

"I'm so sorry," said Grey, holding her in his arms. "We never should have come here."

She cried sobs of tears in his shoulder, saying nothing.

"I put my paintings ahead of you. I'm so sorry," he said again.

"It's okay," she was finally able to say. "We didn't know. We thought we had more time." Charlotte couldn't believe how hot it was getting. Through the open window, she heard people shouting on the street. Someone cried "get out", and she wondered if they were calling to her. The smoke was heavy now, and they both started coughing. She turned to face Grey, to look him in the eyes one final time.

"I love you, Charlotte Talbot," he said.

"I'll always love you," she replied.

Then, with a loud crack, the ceiling split open, and a large beam fell straight for them.

Chapter Twenty-Seven

"I left the body," said Jill.

Simon spoke in a smooth, calm voice. "You're now floating above the scene, just watching it unfold?"

"Yes," said Jill. "I'm out of the body, looking down."

"That's fine, Jill. There is no need to be afraid. Can you tell me what is happening? Does the beam hit you or Grey?"

"Me. The beam hits me on the shoulder, knocking me down. I think it broke my collarbone. My head hits the floor hard, and I almost lose consciousness, but not quite. Grey dove out of the way just in time. Now he's trying to help me. The beam is on top of me, over my waist. He's trying to lift it off, but it's on fire and he burns his hands. He's crying."

"He's crying because of the pain?"

"No, he's crying because he can't save me. More of the ceiling comes down, and a large piece lands right by my head. Burning embers bounce onto my face. Grey tries to cover me, putting his body over mine, but it doesn't matter anymore. The roof caves in completely. We are covered by debris. I pass out from the smoke and the dust the rubble makes. I never wake up again."

"You're okay, Jill. Remember this is just a recalling of your past. You are in my office, and you are okay."

"I know."

Simon had one more question before bringing her back. "Grey also dies in the fire, is that right, Jill?"

"Yes. He died lying on top of me."

"Okay, Jill. Now I'm going to bring you back to the present. We are going to leave the past behind, where it belongs." Simon began the process of Jill's return, and moments later she sat up on the couch. "Welcome back, Jill."

"Wow," was all she said.

"Indeed. You have the most remarkable regressions." He poured her some water and brought it to her.

"That was amazing," she said, "but ..." she paused, looking at him. "Was it true? I've heard of the great Chicago fire, Mrs. O'Leary's cow and all, but I never remember hearing anything about Boston burning down."

"Well then," said Simon, "this is wonderful verification that your regressions must contain some truth to them."

"You mean Boston did burn down?"

Simon nodded yes. "As I recall, it was just a few years after Chicago. Nearly half of Boston was destroyed, I believe."

"So how come I've never heard of it. If Chicago is so famous, why not Boston?"

He thought that was a good question, but he didn't have an answer. "Maybe they just couldn't come up with a good cow story."

Jill laughed and realized she was happy to be back in the present. She asked for a second glass of water. "I'm still trying to put the fire out," she told him, and it was his turn to chuckle.

Simon refilled her glass, and then asked her to relax for a few minutes. He went out to the waiting room, and she heard Melinda ask, "How did it go?" before the door closed.

Jill leaned back against the couch. *It's over*, she thought. No more regressions. It's time to move on. She wondered if she would miss coming here, but she didn't think so. She took a moment to look back on the life she had just left. She really had been a friend, perhaps a close friend, of Nathaniel Hawthorne. Imagine that. He was the only historical figure she had come upon that the average person would know; so much for everyone being Cleopatra. She came to the conclusion that as bad as her Boston life had started, she had turned out to be a pretty good person after all. She was sure she had learned some valuable lessons in that lifetime, and hoped she could figure out what they were in the days ahead.

The door opened and Simon returned. "Feeling back to normal now, Jill?"

"I'm fine."

"That's my girl. Come have a seat at the desk, if you would."

She took her usual place opposite him and watched as the ever present questionnaire came out of the folder one final time. Instantly she remembered one thing. To the question, "What form of dying do you fear the most?" she had answered FIRE in capital letters. She couldn't imagine dying that way. Now she knew why. She mentioned that fact to Simon.

"Yes," he said, "I was aware of that. When I first read your answers I assumed you must have died by fire in a previous life. It was just a matter of when."

"I guess we found out when."

"You said you have never been to Boston."

"No, never, but I bet if I went to that old cemetery, I'd know where every famous grave was located. I can still see them in my head."

"Amazing. Perhaps you should plan a trip there."

Jill's eyes widened. "What, to the place where I burned to death? I don't think so, at least not for a while."

"More memories might come back to you if you did. Good memories. It might give you an opportunity to say goodbye to that life. You didn't have a chance while you were living it."

"Maybe someday," was all she was willing to commit to. "It's funny. That had been such a wonderful day. We made all those plans about traveling through Europe, and a few hours later we were gone. You just never know how much time you have."

"Very true," said Simon. "Whenever something like that used to occur, my mother would always say 'Ah, the mysteries of life.' It occurs to me that over the course of these visits we have looked over your questionnaire pretty thoroughly. I'm not sure there is much left we haven't already examined." Simon was gazing up and down her answers, confirming what he said. "I had Melinda make a copy for you so you could take it with you. Maybe when you look it over you will find some more interesting tidbits. For now, however, I think we are finished."

Jill looked at him, and knew she was looking at a friend. "Simon, I want to thank you for all of this. It's been a wonderful, eye-opening experience. It certainly has given me a great deal to think about, and it has helped me to understand more about myself."

"It has been my pleasure, Jill. Of course, you can always come back for more if you wish to."

She held a hand up to him. "No, that's quite alright. As much fun as it has been, it is time for me to move on. You've taught me to open my mind to new ideas, and I'm going to do just that."

He stood up and came around his desk to walk her out.

She gave him a big hug. "Thank you," she said again. "I hope you will keep me informed about how your book is coming."

"Of course," he replied, "and you will be receiving the first autographed copy."

As she left she gave Melinda a big hug also. She thought Melinda might start to cry.

"Don't be a stranger. Come visit us once in a while for old time's sake."

"I will, Melinda." It was one of those things you say to someone without really meaning it, but Jill intended to try.

Chapter Twenty-Eight

When Jill arrived at Amelio's just after noon on Wednesday she saw Michael Harmon waiting for her right outside the door. He was about six feet tall, slender, black hair with a touch of grey beginning to show, and wearing tan slacks and a button down shirt. Jill thought he looked handsome and wondered why she had not paid much attention to him in church.

He smiled as he saw her exit her car and greeted her with a warm, "Hi there, I'm happy you came."

"Nice to meet you again," she said. "Sorry I was so preoccupied at church Sunday." Jill wasn't sure how this lunch date would go but she was anxious to find out. She still had goose bumps whenever she thought of his saying he was "taken aback" with her. What a lovely thing to say.

He opened the door for her and they entered the restaurant. A hostess named Holly brought them to their table. It wasn't busy yet, and the waitress came right over. Jill asked for coffee and Michael did the same. She gazed into his eyes as they made small talk. Could she see glimpses of Niall? Was Jared lurking behind those hazel peepers, or Grey? She didn't know. She could tell that Michael Harmon was very happy to be with her, and that was fine with Jill.

She ordered chicken cacciatore and gobbled it down as though it would be her last meal. He had the chicken scampi, but only managed to eat half of it, taking the rest home with him when the meal was over.

Michael worked for State Representative Wallace Greene, running the local office in Willis. "It really doesn't pay much," he said, "but it is an interesting and rewarding job. I'm able to help people with their problems, at least most of the time."

Jill was curious. "Give me an example."

"One of the dilemmas I have always been concerned about in Willis is the condition of our parks and playgrounds. They've been a mess, neglected for a long time. Last year I convinced Representative Greene that it would be a good idea for him and the town if we did something about it. So he started up a local committee, we held fund raisers, and we received a small grant from the state. Eventually we had enough money to begin renovations, and just last week we re-opened a playground over on Winter Street. It was so rundown and overgrown with weeds that no one had been using it. Now it looks brand new, and the kids in the neighborhood love it."

Jill could see how proud he was of the work he was doing. Their conversation fell into an easy banter, and she couldn't believe it when she looked at her watch and saw the time. "I have to get going," she said. "Kids will be coming home from school soon, and I still have an errand to run."

"I had a nice time," he said. "I hope you enjoyed your lunch."

Jill couldn't believe how much she had eaten. "I did, but didn't you like yours?" she asked, pointing to the doggie bag.

"I have a hard time eating when I'm nervous," he said, smiling a boyish grin at her.

He hadn't seemed nervous to Jill at all, and she told him so.

"Nervous on the inside, I guess," Michael replied. "Hoping this would go okay. Did it?"

She was surprised yet delighted by his admission and his question. "Yes, it went fine."

"Then I can call you again."

"You better," said Jill, and she meant it.

Saturday Jill asked Lauren to come over the house for dinner. "It seems I've been eating out quite a bit lately," she had told her over the phone. "How about tonight I make us a nice home-cooked meal and we catch up on the latest gossip?"

Lauren thought that was a great idea, but asked, "Aren't you working?"

"That's one of the things we need to catch up on," Jill replied.

When Lauren arrived just after six, she found the table covered by a linen tablecloth and two place settings of Jill's best china. "What's all this for?" she asked.

"Well, I thought I owed you," said Jill. "Every month I receive this fantastic massage from my best friend and I never pay her back. Not only that, but she is always trying to help me out with my life …"

"… Like bad blind dates," Lauren said, and they both laughed at the thought of Dusty.

"You know what I mean. If it hadn't been for you getting on my case, I would still be stuck in the same old rut." She looked at Lauren with all the sincerity she could muster. "I mean it, girl. I owe you a great deal."

Jill said they had plenty to talk about, but the final regression and her date with Michael could wait until after they finished supper. She had other news to tell Lauren over dinner.

She had been working in the kitchen most of the day preparing the meal. Home-made minestrone soup. Fresh baked bread from the bread machine that Tony's parents had given them for Christmas one year, and which Jill had never used. Spinach salad with hot bacon dressing. Chicken parmesan with linguini. Tiramisu for dessert—another first for Jill—which came out divine. They had a bottle of Chianti with the meal, which was empty by the time they finished.

As they ate, Jill brought Lauren up to date. She had been busy since her lunch with Michael on Wednesday. That evening she went to her meditation at the sanctuary. While there she had spent some time talking to Wanda. It turned out Wanda was looking for an assistant, someone to help her coordinate all the different classes and functions that were ongoing, particularly when she ran her New Age Fairs every month. Then there were the flyers that needed to be printed for all the classes, plus organizing all the trips the sanctuary set up. Wanda was finding it too much to handle by herself.

As soon as she understood what Wanda was saying, Jill had said, "I'd love to help you out with all that." While she was still new to the sanctuary, the place had grown on Jill. She loved the energy it gave off, and how it made her feel. She often came home from the restaurant feeling keyed-up, on edge. She liked Wanda, and was sure they would work well together.

"That would be wonderful," Wanda had said, and Jill suddenly realized that Wanda had wanted her for the job all along.

Jill called the restaurant as soon as she arrived home that night and quit her job. No notice, which she was sorry about, but she knew they had enough girls on the schedule to cover her shifts without a problem.

"Goodness," said Lauren when she heard the news, "my girlfriend is ready to take on the world again."

"It's time," said Jill. "You were right that day you sent me to see Simon. My life was boring. I was stuck in a rut of self-pity, thinking my life was basically over because my marriage had ended. How stupid was that?"

"I tried countless times to get you out of that shell," said Lauren. "You just weren't ready to listen. That's why I made the appointment for you. I was down to drastic measures. To be honest, I never thought you would go."

"It was probably the best thing you have every done for me."

When they finished eating, Lauren said, "That was spectacular, better than any restaurant meal I've had in months."

Jill made tea for them, and they moved into the living room to relax. She put some background music on the stereo, which rotated songs between Enya, Loreena McKennitt, and Kenny G.

"Okay, I'm nice and comfy now, so let's move on to the good stuff," said Lauren. "I want to hear all about your final regression and your date with Michael. Tell me everything."

Jill took her time. She talked about Hawthorne's death, which prompted Lauren to say, "Can you believe it, Jill? You were a friend of Nathaniel Hawthorne's. How cool is that?" Jill spoke about life with Grey, finishing with the wonderful last day which had ended in a deadly fire.

"Did you know Boston had a fire much like Chicago's?" asked Jill.

"Never heard of it. Did you look it up on the Web?"

"I spent much of Thursday online. Eleven firemen died in the blaze, and an unknown number of civilians, including Grey Talbot and his wife. I also looked up Grey, of course. I had never heard of him, yet he was considered one of the finest painters in New England at the time. They have a couple of his paintings at the Museum of Fine Arts in Boston."

"You should go," said Lauren. "Maybe you will look at one of his paintings and remember it, like déjà vu. That would be unreal. You could say, 'Oh yes, that used to hang at our beach house in Ipswich.'"

"What would be even cooler," replied Jill, "is if I saw a painting that he did of me."

Lauren agreed. "Do you know if he did any of you?"

"I only recalled the one on the day we met, and that just showed my back."

After talking about Boston a while longer, Lauren asked, "So, have you figured out what you learned in that lifetime, and what traits you brought over to this life?"

Jill had thought a great deal about just that subject the last few days. "I have, although I'm still processing it. I was angry at myself when I found out I had cheated on Edwin. The truth is I stayed with him a good deal longer than I should have. I guess that showed perseverance, sort of a stick-to-it attitude. I think I was a good friend in that lifetime, which I hope you will agree I carried over to this life."

Lauren just smiled brightly at her. She could see happiness in her friend's face as she spoke, and it made her happy. *Jill is once again back among the living,* she thought.

"I know more will come to me, but like I said, I'm still processing it."

"I only have one complaint," said Lauren. "You never saw me in any of your regressions, did you?"

"No, I didn't. I thought that was odd also. However, I do remember thinking after the very first regression that you might have been Mary Whalen."

"Really?"

"Yes," said Jill. "I never actually saw Mary in the regression. I was simply at her funeral. There's no way to prove it, of course. As I said, it was just a feeling."

"Now," said Lauren, "tell me about Michael."

"Before I do, I'd like to hear what you think of him. After all, you've known him a great deal longer than I have."

"I told you on the phone," Lauren protested. "He seems like a nice guy. He's quiet, polite, helps out quite a bit in church cleaning up and all. And in all the time he's known me, he never asked me out once. Then he sees you and needs to have your phone number the same day. Heck, when I first heard him on the phone I thought he might be calling to ask me out." She laughed. "Good thing I was already taken. So I say, go for it girl."

"We had a nice time," said Jill. "It was just a lunch date, but it gave us a good chance to get to know each other. He called last night, and tomorrow we are going to the movies. That new Tom Hanks movie is out, so I think we'll see that."

When they were finished talking about Michael, Lauren brought Jill up to date on her life. "I've planned three vacations into my schedule between now and the end of the year."

"It's about time," said Jill. "You've been working way too hard."

"Don't get too excited. My initial vacation is the first week of August, so you're going to have to change that month's appointment."

"The least I can do," said Jill.

An hour later the party ended. Lauren said goodnight, and Jill watched from the front door as Lauren walked to her car. They gave each other a final wave, and then Jill closed the door behind her—and locked it. *Funny how you can change your habits almost overnight,* she thought. She was tired, all the cooking of the day having caught up with her. Still, she felt … what? Vibrant, restored, like a new woman. She had a wonderful family, a terrific best friend, an exciting new job, and maybe a new love interest, whom she may have known forever.

Epilogue

They drove slowly along the Irish coastline. Jill was glad that Michael had driven overseas before, since she was a little leery about driving on the left-hand side of the road. The day was overcast and breezy but warm as they passed through small towns with names like Bundoran and Killybegs. Last night, the tenth night of their honeymoon, they had stayed in Sligo. They walked downtown, saw the famine memorial, and had beers in a pub. Jill was disappointed that nothing seemed familiar to her

Their wedding had been a small affair, held at the former department store church that they now attended regularly. It had been mostly family, but with a few special guests. Lauren and Bill were there, of course. They were still single, but enjoying each other's company. Jill thought they would be getting married soon, but Lauren simply said they would know when the time was right.

Michael's daughter Stacy was there. She was nineteen, a sophomore at the community college in Willis. She adored her father. Jill had spent a good deal of time with Stacy over the past two years, and when she looked at her she sometimes wondered if it was Nuala looking back. Stacy, Bret, and Mark all participated in the ceremony as their parents became one, and Reverend Doran had been honored to officiate.

Simon Taylor was there with his wife, whom Jill was happy to see again. They had first met the previous December, when Simon's book, *Past Life Memories*, was first published. In three weeks it was on the New York Times Best Seller list. Two months later it reached number one. Jill's story was the focal point of the book. In it he changed her name to Caryn W. Jill's identity had remained fairly well hidden until they appeared on Oprah together two months ago. It had been the only interview request she had granted, much to Simon's dismay.

Melinda was also at the wedding, beaming brightly. Jill had called her out of the blue one day and invited her to lunch. Since then, they had become good friends, and the next time Melinda had a girlfriend's vacation planned Jill was invited to come along.

Jill and Michael started their honeymoon in England, landing at Heathrow and staying in downtown London for five days. They acted as most tourists do, visiting Buckingham Palace to watch the changing of the guard, riding the London Eye, and seeing an exhibition at the Globe Theater. They visited Saint Paul's Cathedral. It was a beautiful church, and Jill lingered there, hoping for some spark of recognition. It hadn't come, and she was disappointed. They shopped in Piccadilly and walked in St. James Park. Still no vision of a life as Emily came to her.

From London they had flown to Dublin and spent three days roaming the capital city. They rented a car and drove south, visiting Blarney Castle, where they kissed the stone and bought sweaters at the Blarney Woolen Mills. They proceeded west to Killarney and toured the Ring of Kerry, which was mostly fogged in while they were there, and then they began their journey up the west coast.

"Just one thing," she had said to Michael. "All I want is for one place to look familiar."

They stopped at the Cliffs of Moher and spent three hours in Galway. They traveled to the shrine in Knock, where Michael gathered holy water in a small plastic flask while Jill prayed for a memory of the past. From there they had driven to Sligo.

Now, as the honeymoon neared its conclusion, Jill was becoming more business-like. They had turned off the main highway to follow the coastline. Jill was certain she would remember the town of Bicksby when she saw it. The only problem, of course, was that there was no Bicksby in Ireland. She had hoped an Irish map would include more cities and towns in its index than the one she had purchased after her first regression, but it didn't. Whenever they stopped she would ask the local residents if they had ever heard of Bicksby. None had. Still, they had come this far. She knew she would recognize the town even if the name wasn't right.

Michael was thrilled when he first found out about Jill's regressions. He had been a spiritualist for many years, and had dabbled in a variety of New Age subjects, much as Lauren did. A past-life regression had not been one of them, however, and he was not tempted to visit Simon on his own. If he and Jill had been together through many lifetimes, that was great. All that was important to him was that they were together now.

Jill also had not returned to see Simon. She was happy with the way her life was progressing, and had no desire to double-check to find if Michael was "the one." Besides, she had become involved in so many new and wonderful things at the Inner Peace Sanctuary that her schedule was full. She was currently studying Reiki healing, and felt a deep connection with it. She wondered if subconsciously her nursing training as Emily was resurfacing.

From Killybegs they drove to Clooney, and then Dunglow. There they stopped to eat, finding a pub where the lunch crowd was just thinning out. They were seated at a table by the window, where they could look out over the bay. Jill loved to listen to the accents of the Irish people, which she found delightful. Michael kept talking about the dozen shades of green in Ireland, and how beautiful they all looked.

When the waitress came they both ordered Irish stew and iced teas, and Michael said, "Not even married to you two weeks and here I am having the exact same meal as you. My lord, what have you done to me?"

They both enjoyed the meal. When the waitress, whose name was Erin, came by to check on them, Jill asked, "Have you ever heard of a town called Bicksby?"

"Bicksby?" she replied, as had everyone else in Ireland.

Jill had seen that look too often, but wasn't about to give up now. "I believe it used to be in this part of Ireland, but I can't find it on any map."

"Can't say as I've ever heard of it," said Erin. "Hang on, though. I'll ask the cook. Liam knows everything."

Jill thanked her as she wandered off. "Don't worry," said Michael. "Whether we find Bicksby or not, this has been a fantastic honeymoon."

"True," Jill said, but she was really hoping for some kind of confirmation that she had once lived here. It had been over two years since her last regression, and even though Simon's book was a huge success, Jill had started to wonder if it was really true, or if she had just been caught up in the moment.

Minutes later a short, rotund man wearing a grease splattered apron approached their table. "Hi there," he said. "My name is Liam. How was your lunch?"

"It was wonderful," they replied in unison.

"Excellent. I've been making that stew for forty years. It was my mother's recipe."

Michael introduced them, and he and Liam shook hands.

"I understand you're looking for a place called Bicksby?" said Liam.

"Yes." Jill felt her hopes rise just a bit.

"Wherever did you hear that name?"

"It's a long story," said Jill.

Liam looked at her and grinned. "Anyone ever call you Caryn W?"

Jill was stunned by the question. "How did you know that?"

"I do a lot of reading when I'm not working. The wife died six years ago, and ever since then …" he said, trailing off. He pulled out a chair and sat down. After a moment, he resumed. "That was quite a book the doctor wrote."

"But it won't be released over here for another month. How did you get it?"

"Oh, you can get anything on the Internet these days. I noticed an ad for the book, read the blurb, and saw where it mentioned a past-life in Ireland, so I bought it. When I saw the name Bicksby, I didn't think it could be a hoax. Nobody around here remembers that name, but I know of it. You see, there's a journal in my family that's been passed down for generations now. I possessed it once, and then I gave it to my son. Someday soon he will give it to his daughter, as he has no son. Anyway, in that journal the man who wrote it said he had a grandmother who was born in Bicksby. I'd never heard of the place, so I did some research on it. It took forever. A town as small as Bicksby was doesn't make many history books."

Liam looked at Jill like a father about to confer a precious secret to his child. "The Scots changed the name when they took over. You're almost home, my dear."

"What?" Jill hoped she had heard him correctly. "What do you mean?"

"Follow the coast road north for fifteen kilometers." He put his hand on Jill's shoulder and gave it a little squeeze. "The town you're looking for is named Brannagh Harbor."

Jill felt her whole body trembling as Michael drove north. They were close now, having just passed a sign reading "Brannagh Harbor 3 km." Even Michael was anxious, knowing how much this meant to his wife.

"Quite a honeymoon," he said.

Jill could only raise her eyebrows to him, too excited to speak. Her eyes were glued to the road.

A few minutes later, Michael said, "Here's the town up ahead."

He drove slowly as they entered, letting her look all around. The waters of the bay were on their left, close by. Dozens of boats were anchored in the shallow waters, rocking gently in the breeze. It was obvious this was still a fishing village. However, you could do plenty of shopping in the stores that lined the right hand side of the street. Jill saw a gift shop, a grocery, a liquor store and a clothing store.

"It doesn't look like it did four hundred years ago," she said, "but the layout is the same. Just then she saw a church nestled behind the stores. "Oh, Michael, this is it! That's Saint Brigid's." She saw the cemetery behind and to the right of the church. "Somewhere in that cemetery Mary Whalen is buried next to her husband John."

They decided to start there, and Michael parked the car in the small church lot. They walked through the cemetery, and it was obvious that many of the plots were hundreds of years old. Most of the markers were impossible to read anymore. "It's okay," she said as much to herself as to Michael, "I know Mary is here somewhere. I didn't expect to find her after all this time." Suddenly Jill looked up and gasped.

"What is it?" asked Michael, and looked in the direction she was staring at.

Overlooking the town, they saw a house on the edge of the nearby mountain.

"That's it," cried Jill. "That's our house."

They returned to the car. Michael drove as Jill continued to stare at the home. Just down the road was a left turn. Michael took it, and they found themselves on a paved road heading for the side of the cliff. The road turned north, and they began a steep climb. A long hairpin curve sent them south again, and when they reached the top the road suddenly flattened out and the house was right there. A car was parked in the driveway, another in front of the house. Michael pulled in behind it. As he did, two men and a woman came out the front door.

"Hello," said Michael. Jill was staring at everything, almost oblivious to the people.

"Welcome," one of the men said. He stepped forward and put out his hand. "I'm Roderick Brennan. This is my wife Esther," he said as the woman came forward, "and this is our friend Colm."

"Pleased to meet you," said Michael. He introduced Jill and himself and everyone shook hands.

"What a wonderful view you have," said Jill.

"Isn't it marvelous?" said Esther as she stared at Jill. "We love it here."

Michael had a feeling something was up. "It seems you were expecting us," he said to Roderick. "Did you know we were coming?"

Jill turned to look at him. "How could they know that?"

Colm surprised her, saying, "I told them you would be here soon. You made good time."

Thoroughly confused, Jill said, "But how. . .?"

Colm was delighted to have taken her by surprise. "Liam the cook is my brother," he said. "He called me just after you left the restaurant. I don't live far from here, so I came over to tell the Brennan's you were coming."

Synchronicity at work, marveled Jill.

"We have all read the book," said Esther. "We've actually just known Colm a short while. Liam gave the book to him, and he recognized the house you were talking about as ours. He dropped by one day, gave us the book to read, and we have been friends since then."

"You must be looking for verification," said Roderick, "so please, have a look around. Tell us what you remember."

"And no leading her on," Colm added. "Let's see what she can tell us about her house."

Jill was happy to tell them what the house looked like in the 1600s. It had changed completely now, of course, and there was no way for them to verify much of what she told them. The outside of the house was still stone, but it now had a second floor and a modern roof. The inside was completely different, but the fireplace where she used to cook was still in the same corner.

Jill headed back outdoors and everyone followed. She pointed out the home next door where the Whalens had lived. However, there were now ten homes leading to the top of the rise where there used to be just five. She turned to look where the barn had stood. There was nothing there now but grazing sheep. The Brennan's had no knowledge of a barn ever being there.

Finally, Jill turned towards the bay. She walked to the edge of the cliff and stopped. "I used to stand here and just let the wind hit my face. It was my favorite spot. There was a bench here that Niall had made," she continued, pointing to her right.

"There's been no bench since our family owned the property," recalled Roderick. "Sorry."

"To my left there was this huge boulder. It was taller than Niall, at least seven feet high."

"Aye," said Roderick, "that we can confirm."

"Really?" asked Jill, her face brightening.

"My father remembers that rock when he was a boy. The constant rains we have here in Ireland have been eroding the soil for years. I'd guess you used to stand about ten or twelve feet farther out than where you are now. One day the soil beneath that rock just gave way, and it tumbled over the cliff. It just missed a car as it was making the turn down there." Roderick pointed to a spot in the road that Jill and Michael had just driven by. "That was 1932 that the rock went down."

"That rock was here for all these years?" Jill asked.

"Must have been. There wasn't any other rock around like that one. Too big to move, and it really wasn't in the way of anything."

"Did they find anything after the rock fell?"

"Find anything?" repeated Roderick. "Like what?"

Jill saw him give his wife a startled glance. "Not everything made it into the book," she said. "Back when the English threw us off the land and gave it to the Scots, Niall assumed they would not let us take any valuables with us. So a few days before they came, he buried a box with our valuables under that rock."

"Really?" said Esther. "That was a long time ago. What did he bury?"

"My necklace."

Roderick looked astonished, and Michael saw Esther's jaw drop. "Tell us about it," Esther finally said.

Jill closed her eyes and pictured it, as she had done before in Simon's office. "It was a wonderful surprise," she said. "Niall gave it to me shortly before he left for the war. It was a beautiful necklace containing emeralds and rubies on a gold chain."

"I'll be damned," said Roderick.

Jill watched as Esther looked at her husband and gave him a small nod.

"Let's have some liquid refreshments," Roderick said, and invited them all back into the house. Michael, Jill, and Colm gathered around the kitchen table while their host went to fetch the mead. "We only serve mead in the Brennan household on very special occasions. I think this is one of them."

Esther brought glasses for everyone, and then excused herself. Roderick poured five glasses of the sweet, strong drink. "When Esther returns, we will have a toast," he said.

A minute later, Esther came out of her bedroom carrying a long, thin black box. She walked up next to Jill, smiled and opened it. "Did your necklace look something like this?"

Jill felt her knees go weak, and Michael reached out an arm to help support her. "Oh my word," she said, and burst into tears. Through the sobs she managed to say, "That's it. That's the necklace."

Esther took it out of the box and held it up for all to see. It was in excellent condition, considering its age. She asked her husband to tell the story behind it.

"When the rock went over the cliff, during a torrential rainstorm, they say the noise was astounding. My grandfather thought perhaps it had been struck by lightning, although he never found any evidence of that. After the rain ended, he went out to see what had happened, my father right at his heels. It was my father that saw the box. He never understood how it didn't go over the edge too, it was so close, but it was snagged by an underground root. They brought it inside and opened it up. There was actually a box inside a box."

"That's right," said Jill. "I forgot."

"Niall had done a fine job," continued Roderick. "That box was as waterproof as you could get. It had obviously survived for many years, but we never dreamed it went back that far."

Jill was mesmerized by his story.

"They opened the box and dumped the contents out on the table. As I recall, there were some papers which were pretty much decayed, probably deeds of some kind, a few pieces of jewelry, mostly men's, some odds and ends, and this necklace. My grandfather said they could get a nice piece of change by selling the stuff, but my grandma, she had a way with her. She could get feelings off things by touching them. Did it all her life. They call it psychometry. Anyway, she picked up each piece, but didn't get anything until she touched the necklace. My father said a chill came over her like he'd never seen before. She said, 'Not going to sell this. Someday a lady will be coming looking for this. We're going to hold it until she gets here.' And that's what we've been doing ever since."

Jill stared at the necklace for a long time. No one interrupted her thoughts. Finally, Esther reached out to give the necklace to Jill.

"Here," said Esther, "I believe this is yours."

Jill was speechless for a moment, and then said, "I couldn't. That life ended a long time ago. It's your necklace now."

Esther wouldn't hear of it. "We have waited a long time to return this necklace to its rightful owner. That time has come."

Jill finally accepted the box with the necklace in it. Michael took it out and placed it around her neck. Chills went through her body. She looked at each person around the table, and then raised her glass of mead. "To Niall," she said.

"And to Jared," added Colm.

"And to Grey," said Esther.

Jill smiled through her remaining tears as she realized they all had read the book.

Roderick turned to Michael. "And to Michael, I'm guessing."

They all raised their glasses and drank.

Acknowledgements

Hundreds of people have helped me over the years in my study of the metaphysical realm. I would like to thank a few of them here.

Patricia "Trish" Newton is a psychic medium and trance channel, and no single individual has taught me more. An excellent medium, Trish has channeled St. Anthony for well over thirty years, and the information he has provided through her has helped thousands of people. Anthony confirmed a past-life in Ireland for my wife and me.

Steve Wilson is a shaman, healer, and ghost hunter; and his knowledge of the Druids and Native Americans is extensive. His drive and dedication to helping others has always been an inspiration to me, and I hope that someday down the road we can work together.

Ray Paine showed me that the physical body just isn't that important; what matters is how a person thinks and acts on those thoughts. He once gifted me with years of research papers—a blessing I'm still working with today.

Many thanks also to my editor, Mary Ann Marazzi, for the yeoman's work she did on this book. The countless hours she put in have made it a much finer work, and it has been a pleasure to work with her.

Finally, to my wife Karen, the love of my life, who is always there for me and always supportive. I feel confident in saying we have been together for many lifetimes, and I'm sure we have many more to come.

About the Author

Barry Homan has believed in reincarnation ever since he was a young child. A spiritualist for many years, he has experienced, on some level, all of the metaphysical ideas mentioned in the book. He lives in Florida with his wife Karen.